LAURA GRIFFIN

AT CLOSE RANGE

A TRACERS NOVEL

$7.99 U.S.
$10.99 CAN.

Don't miss a single book in the
"superb" (*Single Titles*) and "fiercely
passionate" (*RT Book Reviews*)
Tracers series!

and also

EXPOSED • SCORCHED
TWISTED • SNAPPED
UNFORGIVABLE • UNSPEAKABLE
UNTRACEABLE

ISBN 978-1-4767-6175-6

50799

Praise for *Far Gone*

"Perfectly gritty. . . . Griffin sprinkles on just enough jargon to give the reader the feel of being in the middle of an investigation, easily merging high-stakes action and spicy romance with rhythmic pacing and smartly economic prose."

—*Publishers Weekly* (starred review)

"Crisp storytelling, multifaceted characters, and excellent pacing. . . . A highly entertaining read."

—*RT Book Reviews* (4 stars)

"A first-rate addition to the Laura Griffin canon."

—*The Romance Dish*

"Be prepared for heart palpitations and a racing pulse as you read this fantastic novel. Fans of Lisa Gardner, Lisa Jackson, Nelson DeMille, and Michael Connelly will love [Griffin's] work."

—*The Reading Frenzy*

"A tense, exciting romantic thriller that's not to be missed."

—*New York Times* bestselling author Karen Robards

"Griffin has cooked up a delicious read that will thrill her devoted fans and earn her legions more."

—*New York Times* bestselling author Lisa Unger

Praise for the Tracers series

Exposed

"Laura Griffin at her finest! If you are not a Tracer-a-holic yet . . . you will be after this."

—*A Tasty Read*

"Explodes with action. . . . Laura Griffin escalates the tension with each page, each scene, and intersperses the action with spine-tingling romance in a perfect blend."

—*The Romance Reviews*

Scorched

Winner of the RITA Award for Best Romantic Suspense

"Has it all: dynamite characters, a taut plot, and plenty of sizzle to balance the suspense without overwhelming it."

—*RT Book Reviews* (4½ stars)

"Starts with a bang and never loses its momentum . . . intense and mesmerizing."

—*Night Owl Reviews* (Top Pick)

Twisted

"The pace is wickedly fast and the story is tight and compelling."

—*Publishers Weekly*

"With a taut story line, believable characters, and a strong grasp of current forensic practice, Griffin sucks readers into this drama and doesn't let go."

—*RT Book Reviews* (Top Pick)

Unforgivable

"The perfect mix of suspense and romance."

—*Booklist*

"The science is fascinating, the sex is sizzling, and the story is top-notch, making this clever, breakneck tale hard to put down."

—*Publishers Weekly*

Unspeakable

"Laura Griffin is a master at keeping the reader in complete suspense."

—*Single Titles*

Untraceable

"Taut drama and constant action. . . . Griffin keeps the suspense high and the pace quick."

—*Publishers Weekly* (starred review)

ALSO BY LAURA GRIFFIN

Deep Dark

Shadow Fall

Beyond Limits

Far Gone

Exposed

Scorched

Twisted

Snapped

Unforgivable

Deadly Promises

Unspeakable

Untraceable

Whisper of Warning

Thread of Fear

One Wrong Step

One Last Breath

EBOOKS

Edge of Surrender

At the Edge

Unstoppable

AT CLOSE RANGE

Laura Griffin

Pocket Books

New York London Toronto Sydney New Delhi

Pocket Books
An Imprint of Simon & Schuster, Inc.
1230 Avenue of the Americas
New York, NY 10020

This book is a work of fiction. Any references to historical events, real people, or real places are used fictitiously. Other names, characters, places, and events are products of the author's imagination, and any resemblance to actual events or places or persons, living or dead, is entirely coincidental.

First Pocket Books paperback edition February 2017

POCKET and colophon are registered trademarks of Simon & Schuster, Inc.

For information about special discounts for bulk purchases, please contact Simon & Schuster Special Sales at 1-866-506-1949 or business@simonandschuster.com.

The Simon & Schuster Speakers Bureau can bring authors to your live event. For more information or to book an event, contact the Simon & Schuster Speakers Bureau at 1-866-248-3049 or visit our website at www.simonspeakers.com.

Manufactured in the United States of America

10 9 8 7 6 5 4 3 2 1

ISBN 978-1-4767-6175-6
ISBN 978-1-4767-6176-3 (ebook)

For Cheryl

CHAPTER 1

Everything about this felt wrong, and Tessa couldn't believe she was here as they bumped along the gravel road, their headlights cutting through the tunnel of trees. When they reached the clearing, James rolled to a stop and shoved the car into park.

Tessa gazed straight ahead at the moonlight shimmering off the inky lake.

"This okay?" he asked.

"Fine."

He turned off the music, and she listened to the drone of the cicadas and the guttural croak of bullfrogs outside. An electronic chirp sounded from her purse. Crickets, her sister's ringtone. Tessa silenced the phone and dropped it into the cup holder.

"Who is it?" he asked.

"No one."

The car got quiet again and James reached for her, pulling her across the seat and sliding his warm hand under her shirt.

"Wait. Maybe we should talk first."

"We don't have much time." He squeezed her breast.

"James, I mean it."

He leaned back and sighed. "Talk about what?"

"Us. This."

His face was shadowed, but still she could see the heat in his eyes as his hand glided up her thigh.

"So talk." He kissed her neck, and she inhaled the musky scent of his skin—the scent that drew her to him in the most primal way, in a way she'd never been able to resist no matter what the consequences. She responded to this man on a molecular level, with every cell in her body.

He kissed her mouth, softly at first, then harder. He pulled her close, shifting her until she was almost in his lap.

"I can't stop thinking about you." His breath was warm against her throat, and whatever she'd wanted to talk about was gone now. He slid his hand over her shirt, deftly popping open the buttons one by one. Then the fabric was off her shoulders, and air wafted over her skin. She reached for his belt buckle.

A sudden flash of light made her jump. She squinted over her shoulder at the blinding white as a car pulled up behind them.

James went rigid. "Damn it, a cop."

The car's door opened. She hurriedly pulled her shirt on and darted a look at James.

"Don't talk," he said.

A light beamed into the driver's side, and she shrank back against the door as James buzzed down the window.

"Evening, Officer."

"This your vehicle, sir?"

"Yes, it is."

The flashlight beam moved to Tessa's face, then dipped lower. She tugged the sides of her shirt together and looked away.

"Step out of the car, sir."

James gave her a warning look and pushed open his door.

She sank down in the seat. Perfect. This was just what they needed. Could they be charged with something? Trespassing? Or public lewdness, maybe? Her cheeks burned and she glanced back at the cop.

Pervert. He probably staked out this lakeside park every weekend and waited for couples to pull in. He probably got a sick thrill from embarrassing people.

Pop! Pop!

The noise rocked the car and she lurched against the window, shrieking. Terror seized her as she gaped at the open door.

He's shooting. He's shooting. He's—

The flashlight shifted. Tessa scrambled for the door handle. She shoved open the door and lunged from the car, landing hard on her hands and knees.

Pop!

The sound reverberated through her brain, her universe. She clawed at the grass and stumbled to her feet. Adrenaline spurted through her veins as she raced for the woods.

He was behind her, right behind her. She sprinted for the cover of the trees, screaming so loud her throat burned.

No one can hear you. You're all alone.

An icy wave of panic crashed over her, and her cries became a shrill wail. Her heart pounded as she ran and ran, waiting for the bite of a bullet.

Hide, hide, hide!

She plunged into the woods, choking back her screams as she swiped madly at the branches. Thorns tore at her skin, her clothes, but she surged forward. It was dark. So dark. Maybe he wouldn't see her in the thicket.

He killed James. He killed him killed him killed him. The words flashed through her mind as she swatted at the branches.

She had to get out of here. She had to get help. But she was miles away from anyone, stumbling blindly through the darkness. Branches lashed her cheeks and they were wet with blood or tears or both as she plunged through razor-sharp brush and her breath came in shallow gasps.

She tripped and crashed to her knees. Pain zinged up her legs, but she pushed to her feet and kept going, deeper and deeper into the woods. No one was out here to help her. Her only chance was to hide.

She smacked hard into a tree. She swayed backward, then caught herself and ducked behind the trunk, forcing her feet to still, even though her pulse was racing.

No noise. Nothing.

Only the whisper of wind through the branches and the wild thudding of her heart. She dug her nails into the bark as she strained to listen. She couldn't breathe. It felt like someone was squeezing her lungs in a big fist. She shut her eyes and tried to be utterly still as she fused herself against the tree and waited.

In the distance, a soft rustle. She turned toward the sound and felt a swell of relief. Had she lost him?

Please, God. Please, please, please . . .

A faint *snick* behind her, and Tessa's heart convulsed. She hadn't lost him at all.

• • •

Dani Harper steered her pickup down the narrow road toward the whir of lights. She reached the clearing and pulled up beside a white van, surveying the scene through the mist. A pair of uniforms stood off to the side. Beyond a line of haphazardly parked vehicles, swags of yellow tape cordoned off a silver sedan.

She glanced at the logo on the van and her nerves fluttered. The Delphi Center. Her boss must have called them. The lieutenant didn't like using outside help, but San Marcos PD didn't have the resources to handle a scene like this.

Dani reached for the poncho she kept in back, then thought better of it. It would be hot as a trash bag, and she was already sweaty from her yoga class. She pushed aside the grocery sack containing the frozen dinner she wouldn't be eating anytime soon and grabbed a baseball cap, settling it on her head and pulling her ponytail through the back as she got out. Her cross-trainers sank into the muck.

One of the uniforms trudged over, and Dani recognized him as he passed under the light of a portable scene lamp. Jasper Miller. Six-three, 250. He was a rookie out of Houston, barely six months on the job.

"Hey, Dani." He smiled, catching her off guard again with those boyish dimples that seemed at odds with his huge build.

"Tell me you didn't touch anything." She pulled a pair of gloves from the box she kept in the back of her truck.

"I didn't touch anything."

She tugged the latex over her hands and took out a mini-flashlight. She picked her way across the damp grass, careful not to step on any sort of evidence.

"When did you get here?" She ducked under the scene tape.

"Oh, about"—he checked his watch—"twenty minutes ago? Not long after the first responder. Old lady that lives off the highway thought she heard someone shooting off fireworks here in the park."

"And them?" She nodded at the two crime-scene technicians crouched behind the sedan, examining something. A tire impression, maybe? Whatever it was, they'd erected a little tent over it in case it started to rain again.

"They showed up five minutes ago," Jasper said.

The car was a late-model Honda Accord, squeaky-clean right down to the hubcaps. It must have arrived before the rain. The driver's-side door stood open, and Dani's stomach tightened with dread as she walked around the front, sidestepping a numbered evidence marker. She halted and stared.

The victim lay sprawled in the grass. Khaki pants, button-down shirt, short haircut. He had a bullet hole just below his neck, and flies were already buzzing around it, making themselves right at home. They hovered below his belt, too, where the front of his pants was dark with blood.

Dani felt a wave of dizziness. Then it was gone.

She stepped closer, glancing up at the blue tarp someone had thoughtfully erected over the body. She switched on her flashlight and crouched down for a closer look. On the victim's left hand was a wedding ring, and Dani's heart squeezed.

Some woman's whole world would be shattered tonight. It was shattered already—she just didn't know it yet.

She glanced up at Jasper. He looked nervous and eager for something to do.

"I've got a portable scene lamp in the back of my truck," she said. "You mind?"

He trekked off, and she focused on the victim again. Given the location at this park, she'd expected a teenager, but he looked more like an accountant. She studied his face carefully. His eyes were half-shut and wire-rimmed glasses sat crooked on his nose. A determined line of ants had already formed a trail into his mouth.

Dani aimed her flashlight inside the vehicle.

No wallet, no cell phone, no computer case. The wallet was likely in his pocket, but no one could touch him until the ME's van arrived. She skimmed her flashlight over the car's interior, paying close attention to the floorboards and cup holders.

Jasper returned with the lamp and started setting up.

"Was this other door closed when you got here?" she asked.

"I told you, I didn't touch anything."

She looked back at the CSIs pouring quick-dry plaster into an impression on the ground. Roland Delgado glanced up at her.

"Hey, there, Dani Girl."

"Hey. Who else is here?"

"Another one of your uniforms." Roland nodded at the trees near the lake where flashlights continued to flicker. "He's combing the woods with Travis Cullen."

Travis Cullen. So no Scott tonight. Dani felt a twinge of relief as she stood up.

She leaned into the car and popped open the glove compartment. The insurance card was sitting right on top inside a protective plastic sleeve.

She stepped away from the Accord and turned her back on the victim as she dialed Ric Santos. He answered on the first ring.

"Where are you?" she asked.

"On my way. What do we got?"

"White male, thirty to forty, gunshot wound to the chest and groin, point-blank range."

"Groin?"

"That's right."

"Damn. What else?"

A low grumble had her turning toward the road. Her nerves skittered as a gunmetal-gray Dodge pickup pulled into the clearing and glided to a stop beside the crime-scene van.

"No ID yet," she told Ric. "But there's an insurance card inside the vehicle. James Matthew Ayers, 422 Clear Brook Drive."

"That's near the university."

"There's a hangtag on the mirror. A university parking permit."

Scott Black slid from his pickup and slammed the door. He reached into the truck bed to unlatch the shiny chrome toolbox. He pulled out his evidence kit and glanced up.

Their gazes locked.

"Dani?" Ric asked.

She turned away. "What's that?"

"The permit. Is it A or B?"

"B. Faculty parking."

"Shit."

"What's your ETA?"

"Five minutes," Ric said.

"You'll probably beat the ME."

She ended the call and closed her eyes briefly. Rain-drops dampened her face and water trickled between her breasts. She was in yoga pants and a tank top, and she wished she'd had time to change into something better suited for detective work because it was going to be a long night.

She took a deep breath and made a mental list. She had to interview the first responder. And she had to get a K-9 team out here. She sent her lieutenant a text coded 911 for urgent.

Roland and the female CSI were still crouched behind the car, and the woman was snapping pictures. She had to be the Delphi Center crime-scene photographer, but Dani had never met her.

Scott stood beside the Accord now, his back to the victim as he skimmed his flashlight over the ground. The firearms expert was tall and broad shouldered, with the super-ripped body of a former Navy SEAL. Instead of his usual tactical pants and combat boots, he wore jeans and a leather jacket tonight, so maybe he'd been out when he'd gotten the call. Dani knew from experience that his jacket had nothing to do with the weather and everything to do with the Sig Sauer he carried concealed at his hip.

Something glinted in the grass, and Scott crouched down to tag it with a numbered marker. Two minutes on the scene and already he'd discovered a piece of evidence. He stood and squared his shoulders, and Dani felt a pang deep inside her as he approached.

He stopped and towered over her, and for a moment they just stared at each other.

"Was the passenger door closed when you got here?" he asked.

"That's right."

"Where's the girl?"

"No sign of her." Dani nodded at the woods. "One of our officers is searching near the lake with Travis."

Jasper joined them by the car. "How do you know there's a girl?"

Scott knelt beside the body. "He didn't come all the way out here to jerk off." Scott looked at Dani. "You have an ID yet?"

"Nothing confirmed."

He watched her for a moment with those cool blue eyes. His gaze shifted to the woods. "You need a K-9 team."

She bristled. "I know."

He strode over to his truck and opened the toolbox again. He took out a metal detector, which would help him locate shell casings or bullets, and maybe even the second victim if she was wearing jewelry or a belt.

Then again, the killer might have taken her somewhere else. Dani glanced back at the road and got a queasy feeling in her stomach. Where was she?

She turned her attention to the lake, visible just beyond the trees. It was a scenic spot, usually—a tranquil little oasis for couples. But not tonight.

She glanced at Scott again, and he was watching her closely—so closely it made her wonder what he was thinking.

"You coming?" he asked.

She nodded at the body. "I'll stay with him until the ME shows."

Scott walked off, and Dani let her gaze follow him until he disappeared into the woods.

The medical examiner's van rolled up, followed closely

by Ric, and Dani's stomach tightened as she thought of everything she didn't like about this case. And it wasn't even an hour old yet.

Ric walked over, his expression grim as he took in the scene. "The media has it."

"That didn't take long."

"It was all over the scanner," he told her. "I give us ten minutes, tops, before they roll in here with their cameras. We need to barricade the road."

"Daniele."

She turned toward the sound of Scott's deep voice calling her from the woods. He was a tall silhouette at the edge of the trees, and from his tone Dani knew it was bad.

"What is it?" she yelled back.

"I found her."

CHAPTER 2

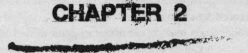

Dani was up before dawn, guzzling coffee. By eleven thirty she'd made it through two autopsies without incident, but her nerves were frayed as she whipped into the parking lot behind the police station.

Ric was leaving the station and crossed the lot toward her as she got out.

"Glad I caught you," he said.

"Where were you? I thought you wanted to observe." She slammed the door and looked him over.

Both of them had worked late, but Ric looked like he'd caught even less sleep than she had. As in, none at all.

He raked his hand through his disheveled hair. "I was at the hospital."

"What happened? Is Mia okay?"

"False alarm again."

"Is she all right?"

"She's fine. The baby's fine. Far as they can tell, anyway." He didn't sound convinced.

Dani was friends with Mia and had known about the pregnancy even before Ric. Mia had had a rough time of it, with severe nausea that continued into the third trimester. She'd had trouble gaining weight, and the doctors had been worried, but supposedly everything was okay now.

"Sorry you were solo this morning." Ric rested his hands on his hips. "How were the autopsies?"

Horrible. Sickening. Dani wished she could scrub down her brain and get rid of the images. "Fine."

"Listen, I just talked to Reynolds and asked him to make you the lead on this. He thinks you're ready."

She stared at him. "You're joking."

"No."

"*Ric.*" Her stomach knotted. "I've worked a grand total of four homicides. You were in charge, and those were open-and-shut cases. This thing's a nightmare."

He watched her with those brown-black eyes that were usually so alert and observant. But right now Ric looked tired. Not just tired—anxious—and she wasn't used to seeing him this way.

"I know what you're thinking," he said, "but you *are* ready, Dani."

Yeah, right. She wasn't ready at all, but that had nothing to do with it. Ric wasn't ready. His wife was due to give birth any day now, and there was no way he could focus on that plus a case of this magnitude.

But making her the lead? She didn't have the experience, not by a long shot. What if she screwed it up? And inexperience was only one of her problems. This case was complicated. And political, given the university connection. And then there was the problem of Scott.

Ric watched her steadily, and Dani felt the heavy weight of his expectations. *Shit.*

"Fine, I'll do it," she said.

As if she had a choice.

He clamped a hand on her shoulder. "Relax, okay? We wouldn't ask you if you couldn't handle it."

Sure they would.

"Don't worry, you're a natural," he added. "It's in your blood."

Dani gave him a long look, trying not to get offended. It was no secret that some people thought she'd made detective through favoritism and not merit. Dani's dad had been a cop, her oldest brother was a cop, and her other brother was a prosecutor with the DA's office.

But Ric knew better than anyone else that she'd worked her ass off to make detective, so his comment probably wasn't a jab. She was just being cranky.

"Where are we on the female victim?" he asked now. "We get an ID?"

She took a deep breath and tried to clear her mind. Holy hell, she was the *lead* investigator. She had to know everything, down to the last detail. Ayers had been positively identified, but the woman was still a mystery.

"At this point, no clue." Dani pictured her on the autopsy table and stifled a shudder. "No ID with the car or the personal effects. No phone. No identifying scars or tattoos. According to the ME's office, her prints aren't in the system, and still no missing person's report. Dr. Froehlich believes she's late twenties, but that's about all he'd venture to say at this point. He might have more in the formal report." Dani paused. "You sure the wife doesn't know who she is?"

Ric and Jasper had gone over there in the middle of the night to notify her.

"She said she doesn't." Ric rubbed the stubble on his chin. "I've got some other ideas, though. Let me keep working on that angle. Meantime, Reynolds wants you at the Delphi Center."

She glanced at the building. "Doesn't he want an update first? That's why I came in."

"I'll update him. He needs you at the lab, lighting a fire under those people. All the evidence from the scene, we need it turned around ASAP."

• • •

The Delphi Center occupied land that had once been a working ranch before it was donated as the building site for the nation's largest private forensics laboratory. The lab was staffed by scientists called Tracers, who specialized in practically every forensic discipline under the sun.

After showing her ID at the security gate, Dani curved her way up the drive. The Greek-style building was surrounded on all sides by junipers and cedars and giant oak trees. Oh, and corpses, too. She couldn't forget that. In addition to a world-class crime lab, the Delphi Center was home to a decomposition research center—also known as a body farm.

Dani spied a group of people in white coveralls clustered beside a pit. They knelt in the dirt, toiling under the relentless July sun. Despite the hot and stinky working conditions, they were lucky to be here, and they knew it. Students from the nearby university sat on waiting lists for years to learn bone excavation from one of the country's top forensic anthropologists.

Dr. Kelsey Quinn glanced up from her work, and Dani waved but didn't slow down. No time to stop and chat, and she'd had more than enough gore for one day.

At the front desk, Dani picked up a visitor's badge and went straight to the back of the building, which housed the garage. The cavernous room could have fit a small plane, but right now it was all cars. Dani was glad to see the silver Accord in the center of everything and Roland standing beside it.

As she walked over, he glanced up. "I was beginning to think you forgot about us."

"I was at the ME's."

Roland made a face and reached for a Slurpee on a nearby table. He took a big sip and offered her some.

"I'm good, thanks."

With his gray coveralls, muscular build, and tattooed forearms, he looked more like a mechanic than a science geek, but Dani happened to know he had a master's degree in criminalistics.

"We've been working since seven," he said.

She glanced across the room at Brooke Porter, another one of Delphi's trace-evidence experts. Brooke was hunched over a worktable with earbuds stuffed in her ears and didn't look up.

"Any good news?" Dani asked Roland.

"Yes and no." He wiped his brow with the back of his arm. "Come have a look."

He crossed the concrete floor, which looked clean enough for heart surgery. All of the Tracers Dani had met were neat freaks. Probably a prerequisite for the job.

Roland led her around the Honda, and she saw that the rear door on the driver's side had been removed. It was sitting nearby on a large plywood table. The window was missing.

"Spent all morning trying to get the embedded slug out without scratching it," he said.

"How'd you do that?"

"Very carefully." He grabbed a clear plastic tray. Using a pair of bamboo tongs, he picked up a small chunk of metal. "Through-and-through bullet. Passed straight through his sternum and lodged in the top of the door."

Dani frowned down at it, noting the dark smudges of blood. It looked more like a glob of chewing gum than a spent bullet. "Will they be able to do anything with that?"

Roland shook his head. "Don't know. Scott's got the Midas touch and all, but this looks like shit to me, so I wouldn't count on it." He glanced up at her. "What about the ME? He get anything at autopsy?"

"Two slugs, one from each victim. Both looked useless, but I'm no expert."

Roland smiled. "That's what we're for. He send them over?"

"This morning."

"Well, lemme show you what else I've got going. Although it isn't finished yet." Roland turned to a counter behind him and opened a cardboard box.

Dani leaned over to look inside. "The tire tread from Woodlake Park."

"A plaster cast of it, yeah. We managed to get it before the rain really started coming down. It's pretty good. I haven't ID'd it yet, but I can tell from the size and wheelbase it's from a sedan."

"Could it be from the Accord?"

"Not this Accord." He nodded at the car. "Different type of tire. I've got to run it through the database to see precisely what it is, and then I can tell you what kind of vehicle you're looking for."

"How do you run this through a database?"

He grinned. "That's the fun part. First, I have to put it in a box that films it from all angles and converts it to a digital image. Then I can submit it to the system, see what pops. I haven't gotten to that yet. We've been busy on the inside of the car."

"*We?*"

They turned around, and Brooke was watching from her stool. No more earbuds.

"You taking credit for my work again?"

"Hey, that hurts, Brooke. Didn't I just buy you a Slurpee?"

Dani walked over to Brooke's table, where she was clipping a slide onto the stage of a microscope. The CSI had dark hair and mesmerizing blue-green eyes. The spark of excitement in them now told Dani she'd found something.

"Three hairs," Brooke said. "All from the same source, all *with* the root and follicular tissue."

"Which means DNA?"

"Exactly. Have a look."

Dani peered into the microscope and saw what looked like a big rope.

"This hair is fourteen inches long. It's naturally light brown, and you can see that it's bleached blond from the tip to about half an inch from the proximal end."

"So, it's probably her hair, not the killer's," Dani said.

"Assuming her killer is a man," Brooke said.

Dani glanced up. "Good point." She looked back at the car. "What about fingerprints? Particularly on the front passenger door?"

Brooke slid from her stool and walked over to the car. "I went over it twice with an alternative light source. The rain doesn't help us. Fingerprints are typically composed of dust and oils, so I was only able to lift two from the door's exterior, both on the underside of the door handle, most likely whoever opened that door last. Could be the killer's, could be the victim's. Depends how everything went down."

"The pathologist printed her at the autopsy," Dani said. "You have the file yet for comparison?"

"Not yet. I just checked my email, too, so maybe he's running behind. You told him we were handling all the evidence, not just ballistics, right?"

"That's right. What about fibers or anything else inside the car?"

"I vacuumed up plenty of stuff from the floor mats and upholstery, but so far nothing jumps out as unusual."

Dani glanced around the lab, feeling deflated. Bullets, tire impressions, fingerprints, and fibers—all amounting to nothing at this point. The car alone should have been a treasure trove of evidence, but she had no new leads. So much for lighting a fire under everyone.

"How long on that tire tread?" she asked Roland.

"Tomorrow afternoon, maybe?"

She scowled.

"What? I spent all morning on your slug and just got slammed with a shit ton of evidence from El Paso. You can't always be front of the line, babe."

"Help me out, Roland."

He sighed. "Lunch tomorrow. That's best I can do. You want something sooner, go hit up Scott."

Dani found her way through a labyrinth of hallways and followed the sound of gunfire to the ballistics wing, Scott's domain. He'd been working there as Delphi's chief firearms examiner ever since a knee injury had forced him out of the SEAL teams. Scott was good at his job and had a knack for explaining ballistics to lay-people, so prosecutors liked to put him on the witness stand. He'd built quite a reputation for himself in his new field, but he was an adrenaline junkie and Dani knew he missed jumping out of airplanes and fighting terrorists.

Dani got a flutter in her stomach as she neared the firearms lab. Seeing Scott last night had been weird. Fifteen years she'd known him, and he'd always treated her like Drew Harper's kid sister. And then for the past six months he hadn't treated her like anything at all. He hadn't said so much as a word to her since New Year's Eve, when they'd shared a drunken kiss in the parking lot of a sports bar. Afterward had been one of those surreal *Did that just happen?* moments. They'd both been wasted, and Dani wouldn't even have thought Scott remembered it except that he'd pointedly ignored her ever since.

Until last night.

Not that he'd said anything. But they'd been in close proximity for hours, and the memory had hovered between them like an electric charge.

Dani reached the firearms lab and peered through the window to see a man in tactical pants and a black golf shirt loading a magazine. She rapped loudly on the window, but he didn't hear her because of his ear protectors. She waved her arms and he glanced up.

Young. Stocky. High and tight haircut. She didn't recognize the guy, and he looked fresh out of the military. He walked over and opened the door.

"Is Scott around?"

"No, ma'am." His gaze darted to the badge clipped beside her gun. "He went home for the day."

"Home? It's barely one."

"He was here all night. Him and Travis. Some big murder case came in."

"Is Travis here?"

"No, ma'am. He left, too."

She gritted her teeth.

"You might try Smoky J's. The barbecue place? They were talking about grabbing something to eat. They left 'bout twenty minutes ago, so if you hurry, you might catch them."

• • •

Scott knew the instant she walked in. He'd had his eye on the door, half expecting her to track him down.

"Hey," she said, dropping into the chair beside him.

"Hey."

"We were just talking about you, Dani," Travis said around a mouthful of food. "How's the case coming?"

"It's coming." She looked at Scott. She wore her usual jeans, along with a lightweight blazer that covered her Glock 23. Her shiny dark hair was loose around her shoulders, and she'd obviously had a chance to clean up since last night. Unlike him.

"Want some lunch?" Travis nodded at his plate. "I've got more than I can eat here."

She glanced at the barbecued ribs and winced, confirming Scott's suspicion that she'd attended the autopsies earlier. "No, thanks. I'm checking in on that evidence." She pinned her gaze on Scott. "You finished with those shell casings yet?"

"Yep."

"And?"

"No hits." He chomped into his brisket sandwich.

"How many casings?"

"Five," Travis answered for him. "Perp didn't pick up after himself."

"What about prints? Or DNA? He could have left something when he loaded the magazine."

"We ran all of it through trace," Scott told her. "They didn't get anything."

Her green eyes dimmed and she looked away. "Well, crap."

Scott reached for his drink and watched her.

"What about the two bullets the ME sent?" she asked. "One from each victim."

"Nothing," Travis said.

"Nothing at all?"

"The slugs are useless," Scott told her. "They're smashed to hell, no rifling marks."

"Roland sent you guys a bullet, too. It was embedded in the car."

"Yeah, I heard," Travis said. "And I haven't seen it yet, but I'm guessing it's in worse shape than the others."

"So, that's it?" Dani asked, a little worry line between her brows. "Five shell casings and three bullets and you can't tell me anything about the murder weapon?"

"You're looking for a Glock nine-mil," Scott said. "That's as much as we know right now. We might know more when we finish the tests."

"And when will that be?"

"Depends."

"Ballpark it."

Scott lifted an eyebrow at her. That bossy tone of hers turned him on, but damned if he'd ever tell her that. "One to three days." He had some more tricks up his sleeve, but he didn't want to get her hopes up until he had a chance to revisit the crime scene.

She looked at Travis, as if he might have better news.

"Sorry, Dani, we're working as fast as we can." Travis checked his watch and pushed his plate away. "I gotta run. I've got a deposition at three." He stood and nodded at Scott. "See you tomorrow, bro."

Dani watched him leave, then her gaze settled back on Scott.

"You look tired," he said.

"Thanks." She grabbed a potato chip off his plate. "You don't look tired at all."

He leaned back in his chair and rubbed his hand over his chin. He needed a shave and a shower and at least five hours of uninterrupted sleep.

"What else?"

She grabbed another chip. "What else what?"

"What else is wrong?"

She watched him a moment, and he waited for her to say something evasive. Dani wasn't normally one to dump her problems out on the table. But something in her expression today told him she wanted to talk.

"Reynolds wants me to be the lead."

"What about Ric?"

"His wife's about to have a baby. This case is going to get complicated."

"It's complicated already. What about Sean?"

Her gaze narrowed. "Thanks for the vote of confidence."

He didn't say anything, just watched her. Scott knew

she could handle it, even if she didn't. But he wouldn't have expected her boss to make her the lead on such a high-profile case less than a year after her promotion. They lived in a college town, so anything involving the university was front-page news. The story of a local professor getting offed while he was busy getting off was sure to keep the rumor mill buzzing for years.

Dani crossed her arms, and Scott tried not to get distracted by her breasts.

"So, what are you going to do?" he asked.

"My job. What choice do I have?"

"You could tell him to pick someone else, that you're not up for it."

She just looked at him. He knew damn well she'd never do that, and so did she. Dani was competitive, not to mention tenacious as hell when she wanted something. And right now she wanted to prove herself.

"Thought I'd find you here."

Scott turned around, and Drew Harper clamped a hand on his shoulder. Dani greeted her brother with a lackluster smile as he dragged a chair back and sat down.

"I heard about your new case." He looked from Scott to Dani. "You working it, too?"

"She's the lead," Scott said.

Drew's brows arched. "*You*?"

"Yes, *me*." She sounded insulted.

"Yeah? Well, congrats, Danno. It's a big case. The DA's all over it."

"Already?"

"You bet your ass. It's an election year."

She shook her head and looked away.

"What?"

"You guys are vultures."

By "you guys" she meant lawyers, and Scott didn't disagree. But at least Drew worked for the prosecution. He'd been with the DA's office since graduating top of his class at UT law.

Drew nudged Dani's elbow. "What are you so touchy about? This is a headline grabber. It could make your career."

"Jesus, Drew."

"What?"

"Show some respect," she said. "These people haven't even been dead twenty-four hours."

Drew shot Scott a *What's with her?* look, no doubt pissing Dani off more.

She slid back from the table and stood. "I've got to get back to work." She gave Scott a pointed look, and his pulse quickened. "I need those test results, ASAP. If you get anything at all, call me."

"*When* I get something, you'll be the first to know."

CHAPTER 3

Dani swung into the driveway and stared at her darkened house. Her front-porch light was out and her hedges needed trimming. Not exactly a shining example of home security, but she'd been going full speed at work and hadn't had time for anything else.

She grabbed her grocery bag and got out, glancing up and down the block at the familiar cars. Pretty quiet, even for a Monday. Only a few dog walkers out and a guy on the steps of his porch drinking a beer and talking on his phone. He lifted his bottle at Dani, and she gave him a wave.

She let herself inside, stepping over the pile of mail under the mail slot—ads, mostly, and a bunch of bills she didn't want to think about. She scooped everything up and dumped it atop the sealed cardboard box beside her door.

Another stack of unopened mail greeted her in the kitchen as she dropped her frozen pizza on the counter and switched on the oven. She stripped off her jacket and holster and checked her phone for anything from Scott on the ballistics tests.

No battery left. She plugged the phone into the charger and debated whether to call him for an update. He'd said he'd let her know as soon as he had anything, but maybe he'd gotten sidetracked.

And maybe she was just looking for an excuse to call him.

She thought back to New Year's Eve. *One* kiss, and her skin still flushed at the memory—which was nothing short of embarrassing. She couldn't stop wondering what it meant to him, if anything.

Scott had been back in Texas four years now, and she'd seen him with plenty of women, but never the same one twice. The only thing that seemed to hold his attention was his job. She'd spotted his truck in the Delphi Center parking lot on weekends and evenings when she'd stopped by to deliver evidence, which probably shouldn't have surprised her. He'd always been a hard worker.

Scott and Drew had started hanging out the summer after Scott's mom died from breast cancer. Scott had a special talent for showing up at mealtimes, and Dani's mother never blinked an eye, just set an extra place at the table and kept the food coming. It was the same summer Scott and Drew got jobs on a house-painting crew, and for three months they'd walked around with sunburned noses and flecks of paint in their hair. Scott would turn up at the breakfast table when Dani hadn't even known he'd spent the night, and he and her brother would wolf down pancakes before heading out to paint houses or blow their hard-earned cash at the movie theater.

Scott had been quiet that summer, but it was a different sort of quiet from now. She'd sensed a change in him since he'd come back from combat. A fundamental shift. He seemed apart from everyone, even when he was in a room filled with people. Something about him was darker and more somber now, and

Dani missed the playful glint in his eyes and the way the corner of his mouth would tick up whenever he teased her.

She shook off the memory as she slid her pizza in the oven. Another gourmet meal in her new kitchen. One of these days she was going to have to unpack and get organized.

The doorbell rang, and she glanced at the clock. She went to check the peephole and was surprised to see Ric. The look on his face had her yanking open the door.

"What's wrong?"

"Why aren't you answering your phone?" he asked as he stepped inside.

"Battery's dead. Is everything okay?"

"Yeah. At least, I think so." He pulled out his phone and checked it. He texted something to someone— probably Mia—then slid the phone in his pocket and turned to look at her. "I came by to update you."

"Come on in. You want a drink?"

"I can't stay."

She led him into the kitchen. "You sure?"

"Yeah, our dinner's melting in my front seat." He glanced around at the cardboard boxes lining the walls of her living room. "You ever think about unpacking anything?"

"I've got a system. One room at a time."

He leaned back against the counter and heaved a sigh. He still looked tired, but his eyes showed a glimmer of excitement.

"You got an ID, didn't you?"

He nodded.

Dani braced herself. She'd been longing for a name

since the moment she'd seen the victim sprawled face-down in the dirt. She'd been shot twice in the back.

"Tessa Lovett, twenty-six. Her white Volkswagen was on University Boulevard collecting parking tickets when I called over there. DMV records matched up."

"She local?"

"She is now. Moved here from New Mexico about three months ago."

"Married? Children?" Dani held her breath.

"No. And no roommate. She's got an apartment over on Cypress Cove." He pulled out his phone and tapped open a DMV record, then showed her the screen.

Dani's breath whooshed out. "That's her."

Tessa Lovett had straight blond hair, brown eyes, and a smattering of freckles across her nose. In her photo she looked pretty. And years younger than she'd looked on that autopsy table, all gray and inert.

Dani grabbed a notepad and jotted down the info. "Cypress Cove. That's not far from James Ayers."

"Yeah, I noticed that, too."

"So, is she a student?"

"Research assistant in the biology department. I'll go by campus tomorrow, find out more about her employment history. They gave me her contact info. She has an older sister in Santa Fe. We sent a uniform over there this evening to notify her. Officer's supposed to get back to me soon."

Dani wrote everything down. "I can check out the apartment tonight."

"Wait until morning."

"Why?" She glanced up.

"Reynolds called Delphi to help us process the scene. They're meeting us over there at seven A.M."

"I bet Minh's pissed."

"Yeah."

Their one and only full-time CSI didn't like it when the department brass called in outside resources. But Minh specialized in fingerprint work, and most of his experience was in burglary and auto theft cases. This case was complicated and would likely undergo a ton of scrutiny when it ended up in court, so there was no room for error.

"Anything back on ballistics?" Ric asked.

"No prints on the shell casings, and so far all the slugs they recovered are worthless in terms of rifling marks. Also, I heard back from Roland. Tire impression behind the Accord traces back to a Goodyear tire. Based on that and some other info, Roland's concluded the vehicle is a Ford Taurus."

Ric scoffed. "That narrows it down."

Tauruses were some of the most common cars around, making up a good chunk of taxi, police, and rental fleets around the country.

"At least we know it's not an SUV or a pickup," she said. "So, the victim's wife. You spoke to her again today?"

"Went back to her house, yeah."

"You happen to notice what she drives?"

"A Jeep Grand Cherokee. And I checked out her alibi. She said she was at Pilates, then came home and made dinner."

Dani tipped her head to the side. "How does she strike you?"

"At the moment? Pissed off. And she's humiliated, too."

"Not so much grieving?"

"Not so much."

Still, people grieved in different ways. And in phases. By tomorrow the woman might be a basket case.

"She seem like she'd be comfortable with a gun?" Dani asked.

"Not really, but you never know. And she could have hired it out."

Dani glanced down at her notes. "Wow. You've accomplished a lot in twenty-four hours."

"So have you."

She forced herself not to argue. She needed to project confidence. Leadership. She might *feel* completely out of her league, but everyone else didn't need to know that.

Ric's phone buzzed with another text. Probably Mia.

"Well, your dinner's melting," Dani reminded him. "Cherry Garcia?"

"Super Fudge Chunk," he said, already moving for the door. He tugged out his phone and checked the message.

"Everything okay?" she called after him.

He waved over his shoulder and walked out the door.

● ● ●

Scott passed Ric Santos as he turned onto Dani's street. He swung into her driveway and parked behind her crappy old Chevy.

What the hell was he doing? He hadn't been here in months, not since the day he and her brothers had helped her move. They'd spent an entire Saturday afternoon loading boxes in and out of a U-Haul in exchange for pizza and beer. Since that day, Scott had had no legitimate reason to come over here, so he'd forced himself to stay away.

He looked at her house now. The white 1930s bungalow was small and quaint. Nothing fancy, but still something about it made him uneasy. A light switched on in the bedroom, and he thought about her walking around inside, maybe getting ready for bed.

Dani was a nice girl. *Woman.* She was from a rock-solid family that had been good to him over the years. She wasn't the kind of woman you fucked around with, and Scott didn't have room in his life for anything else.

He thought about that damn kiss. It had been over before it even started, and still it had been dogging him for months.

It was his fault. He'd kissed *her*, but he'd been half-drunk and it had taken them both off guard. He wondered what she'd do if he showed up at her door right now and did it again. Would she give him the shove, or would she invite him inside to finish what they'd started?

Scott had a feeling he knew. And he couldn't have a one-night stand with his best friend's sister. He figured one night was about how long it would take for him to get this obsession out of his system. One should be plenty. Then he could forget about Daniele Harper and get on with his regularly scheduled life.

Scott walked up her sidewalk and banged on her door. The TV was on inside, and he could hear a newscaster droning on about the weather. He surveyed the weedy lawn and overgrown bushes surrounding her porch. She should know better than to let stuff like that go. He rapped on the door again, and finally it swung open.

"You ever hear of a doorbell?" she asked, stepping

back to let him in. She wore black yoga pants with a loose-fitting T-shirt, and her feet were bare.

"Your TV's too loud."

She closed the door and led him into the kitchen without comment, as though his visiting were a regular thing. The place hadn't changed much since his last trip. The walls were still bare and she still had cardboard boxes stashed everywhere.

"You planning to unpack ever?"

"I'm pacing myself."

He spied a pizza box on the counter alongside a sixteen-ounce bottle of Coke. Dani was a junk food addict, although you wouldn't know it from looking at her. She worked out plenty, but Scott liked to give her crap about it.

"You eaten yet?" She opened the oven and pulled out a giant pizza covered with processed cheese.

"I'm good, thanks."

"Coke? Beer?"

"No." He leaned back against her counter and folded his arms over his chest. "You know, peanut butter on whole wheat takes less time to make and has twice the protein."

She shot him a glare as she slid her dinner onto a cutting board. She hunted up a paring knife and started butchering the pizza.

He smiled slightly. "Hey, you want a Ka-Bar knife for that? Think I've got one in my truck."

Another glare. "To what do I owe the pleasure of your company this evening?"

"I finished testing the embedded slug. The one from the car door."

"And?"

She sounded so hopeful. She probably thought his coming all the way over here meant good news, when what it really meant was that he liked to torture himself by hanging out with a woman he wanted but couldn't have.

"And nothing."

Her face fell.

"No rifling marks whatsoever. So, that takes care of all the recovered bullets. Also, we concluded all the tests and nothing on the shell casings."

She leaned back against the counter, her dinner forgotten. "That's disappointing."

He watched her eyes. The little worry line was back between her brows again.

"Brooke came up empty, too," she said, "with all the prints on the car."

"I know."

"I'm still waiting on the results of the hair and fibers she vacuumed from the floorboards, but realistically? I'm not expecting much. That seems like a long shot. We were really pinning our hopes on fingerprint evidence or DNA."

"And no sexual assault?"

"No. Basically, we've got a huge crime scene and a mountain of physical evidence." She sighed. "But nothing that points to a suspect."

"Hey, don't get discouraged. You'll catch a break."

"How do you know?"

"Because you're good."

Her gaze settled on his, and silence stretched out. She had that look again, that one she got sometimes when she was trying to read his thoughts.

Which was his cue to leave. "I need to head out."

He moved for the door, and she trailed him into the living room.

"Well, I appreciate the update."

"Right."

"Really. I know you've been working round the clock on this."

He opened the door and stepped onto the porch, and suddenly he had the urge to keep her talking. "I passed Ric on my way over. Anything new on his end?"

"We got an ID on the woman."

He arched his brows in question.

"Tessa Lovett, twenty-six. She was a research assistant at the university. Delphi's going to help us process her apartment in the morning, see if we turn up any leads."

"And what's your theory?"

She leaned against the doorframe as though she had nothing better to do than talk to him while her dinner got cold. "Well, the phones and wallets are missing, but no jewelry stolen, and the car wasn't taken, obviously. So a robbery motive doesn't add up. We're leaning toward a love triangle. Maybe the perp had been in communication with one of them."

"Hence, taking the phones."

"Maybe." She shrugged. "It's early days yet."

"Those are the most important ones."

She sighed. "Are you *trying* to stress me out right now? Because I've got more than enough to keep me up all night worrying."

He tugged out his keys. "Get some sleep, Daniele."

"Yeah, you, too."

• • •

The man peered through the long-range lens and tapped his phone.

The call connected. "Go."

"White female. Five-two, one-ten, brown and green. Drives a white Chevy pickup. Alpha Zulu Charlie three-two-six-niner." Pause. "You copy?"

"Got it."

He hung up. He adjusted the lens again. No alarm system, no dog, only a Glock.

He watched the windows as a light went on at the west side, the one bathroom. The window was five feet off the ground, and the original pane had been replaced by glass bricks. The other twelve windows were old, and they'd probably been painted shut a few dozen times. Back door was a thumb-turn dead bolt, nothing serious.

The phone vibrated in the cup holder. He checked his watch. Fifty-two seconds, even faster than he'd thought. He swiped the screen a few times and then tapped open the file.

Daniele Louise Harper.

"Hello, Daniele." He stared down at the phone and smiled.

CHAPTER 4

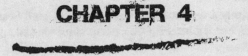

Dani's boss spotted her in the bull pen and charged straight toward her. She swallowed a curse. She'd meant to just dash into the office to grab a file, but that never worked.

"How'd it go at the apartment?" Reynolds asked, stopping beside her cubicle. The lieutenant was short and bulky, with a bristly gray buzz cut that reminded Dani of a wild boar.

"I'm heading over there now."

"I thought you'd be finished."

"The crime-scene techs had to bump us to nine. They got sidetracked this morning with a carjacking over in Blanco County."

"You have a visitor first," he informed her.

"Who?"

"Audrey Ayers. She's in the interview room, and she wants to talk to you."

"To me specifically or—"

"Asked for you by name. You haven't met her?"

"Not yet. I was going to stop by there today."

"This is better," Reynolds said. "She came in on her own, wants an update. So, maybe she won't notice if you turn it into an interview." He crossed his arms and regarded her skeptically. "You want me to sit in?"

"I can handle it." She hoped. "How long has she been here?"

"Only a few minutes. I was about to send Sean in there, but it's better if you do it, since she asked for you."

Dani deposited her keys on her desk and took a deep breath. Sean was good with female witnesses. Women tended to let their guard down with him without even realizing they were doing it. But if Audrey Ayers had asked for her specifically, then she should handle it. Plus Dani wanted to get a read on her.

She grabbed a notepad—mainly as a prop, because the interrogation room was equipped with a camera. She thought of stopping by the coffeepot, but her nerves didn't need the caffeine. Interviewing bereaved family members topped Dani's list of things she dreaded about her job, second only to watching Y-incisions.

She stopped to glance through the small window at the young widow seated at the interview table. She wore designer workout clothes and had her hair pulled back in a smooth blond ponytail. Judging from the mutilated Styrofoam cup in front of her, someone had already offered her coffee.

Dani entered the room, and the woman jumped to her feet. Her eyes were pink and swollen.

"Detective Harper?"

"Thanks for coming in. I'm sorry for your loss." Dani took the seat across from her, eyeing the little mound of Styrofoam chips beside the cup.

"They said you're in charge of everything." Audrey folded her arms over her middle and leaned forward in the chair. "Have you made an arrest yet?"

"At this point, no."

At this point. Dani sounded stuffy as hell, and she tried to relax.

Audrey buried her face in her hand. "It's been a day and a half. I thought you'd know by now."

"We're still developing leads. And processing evidence, conducting interviews."

Audrey glanced up and hope flared in her watery-blue eyes. "Are there any witnesses? I mean, it's a public park, right? There has to be someone—"

"We're looking into that."

Audrey bit her lip and gazed down again, and Dani watched her closely. She wasn't at all like Ric had described, and her initial anger at hearing about her husband's death seemed to have given way to genuine grief.

Or at least, that's how it looked.

Audrey Ayers was twenty-nine, a full decade younger than her husband. And the driver's-license photo Dani had seen didn't do her justice. Even with red-rimmed eyes she was beautiful.

"Would you mind taking me through Sunday night again?" Dani asked. "I understand you were at your health club . . . ?"

She let the question dangle, waiting for Audrey to pick up the story. Dani had memorized every detail of Audrey's statement to Ric, and Dani wanted to see if anything changed in the retelling.

Audrey pressed a fist to her mouth, as if trying to contain her emotions. "I left the house at six for my class."

"Pilates?"

"That's right." Audrey sniffed and gave her nose a dainty rub.

"And that's over on Sycamore?"

"Yes."

Dani flipped open her notepad and jotted it down. She had all this already, but she wanted to underscore the idea that detectives bought into her story—which might well turn out to be true. Audrey's alibi had checked out, but they still hadn't eliminated the possibility that she had hired someone to kill her husband.

"James was working." She squeezed her eyes shut. "Or so he *said*. He spent so much time at that damn lab." She plucked a tissue from the sleeve of her zipper top and dabbed her nose. "I can't believe I didn't know. How could I not *know*? It's such a cliché."

Dani watched her but didn't say anything, hoping she'd fill the silence.

"I swung by the grocery store after to pick up a bottle of wine and some steaks. By the time I got home it was eight, and he still wasn't back, so I called to check in . . ."

She trailed off. Investigators still hadn't located the cell phones of either of the victims, but Audrey had shown her phone to Ric during his initial interview, and he'd seen two unanswered calls and a half dozen text messages from Audrey to her husband.

Dani decided to switch gears. She cleared her throat. "So, Mrs. Ayers . . ."

Something flickered in her eyes at the "Mrs."

"The woman with your husband has been identified as Tessa Lovett."

Audrey's mouth tightened into a thin line. "Yes, I heard."

"You heard from . . . ?"

"They mentioned it on the news this morning."

"Did you know her?"

"No."

"And do you know the nature of her relationship with your husband?" Dani felt cruel for asking, but she needed to see Audrey's reaction.

"You're asking if I knew he was having an affair? No."

"Had you had any recent suspicions that something was going on?"

Audrey glanced down and began shredding the tissue in her hands. "There were some things that seemed . . . off." She looked up. "He told me he was stressed at work. The new job, the move." She shook her head. "I thought we were okay, though. We were trying—unsuccessfully—to have a baby for the last three years. That's been part of the stress."

Dani couldn't help but feel sympathy as she looked at Audrey. She'd been hoping to start a family, and meanwhile her husband had been running around on her.

"So, had you ever met Miss Lovett?"

Audrey's eyes sparked. "No. I told you. I didn't know any of this until a detective showed up at my door to tell me James was *dead*." She pressed her fist to her mouth again as if trying to keep her words in.

Dani looked at her notebook. "What time did you say it was when you got home from your class and your errands?"

"Around eight."

"And what time did you call your husband?"

"Right after that. I'd expected him home by that point, so I called, but he didn't answer. It wasn't anything unusual."

"What wasn't?"

"James ignoring his phone."

Dani just looked at her, trying to keep her face blank.

"Look, I know what you're thinking," Audrey said in a wobbly voice. "But I really didn't know. James covered his tracks well. He's smart. Was." She closed her eyes. "*Was* smart. God."

Dani flipped through her notebook, giving Audrey a few moments to compose herself before she sprung the next question on her.

"Mrs. Ayers, you and your husband moved here last fall from New Mexico, a town north of Albuquerque. Is that correct?"

"Yes," she said, ripping the tissue into little white flakes. "He was offered a full professorship in the biology department."

"Are you aware that Tessa Lovett recently moved from there?"

Audrey's hands stilled. "She . . . what?" She shook her head as though trying to clear it.

"Tessa Lovett lived in New Mexico until three months ago. She just moved here."

Audrey glanced down. Her cheeks flushed, and Dani couldn't tell if it was from anger or embarrassment.

Audrey looked up and her eyes were brimming with tears again. "Wow." She gave a weak smile. "You must think I'm pretty dense, huh?"

Dani didn't say anything, just watched her closely. She was pretty sure this woman hated her now. But it couldn't be helped—Dani needed her reaction.

Audrey shook her head again. Then she stood up, checking her watch. "I have to go."

Dani stood, too.

"I've got to pick up James's mom at the airport." The

widow took a deep breath and seemed to steady herself. "Would you please call me if anything happens?"

"Absolutely." Dani tugged a business card from her pocket and jotted her cell number on the back. "And feel free to call me if you think of anything that might help us."

Audrey stared down at the card, then met Dani's gaze. "Are you married, Detective?"

"No."

She gave her a long look and then reached for the door. "Good for you."

• • •

The lake shimmered emerald green in the light of day, and it was hard to believe two people had been murdered here just hours before.

Dani rolled her unmarked police unit to a stop beside Scott's pickup. The CSIs at Tessa Lovett's apartment had been talking about a team from Delphi returning to Woodlake Park, and Dani knew that team would include Scott. Five shell casings recovered but only three bullets? He wouldn't be able to live with that math.

Christine Metz was leaning against her patrol car and talking on her phone. She finished her call as Dani got out.

"Where are they?" Dani asked, glancing around.

Christine nodded toward the lake. "Over there. They brought some kind of special metal detector."

Dani set off for the shore, and Christine fell into step beside her.

"How'd the canvass go?" Dani asked.

"Jasper and I have been out here five hours. There

are definitely some park regulars—mostly dog owners and mostly this morning. But no one recalls any suspicious people around here recently."

"Any Ford Tauruses?"

"No one remembers any."

Dani had hoped they'd be able to locate a witness who had seen something and shrugged it off at the time, such as an unusual person or vehicle scoping out the park.

Dani stopped where James's silver Accord had been parked. New tire tracks crisscrossed the area, which seemed disrespectful somehow. The place felt like hallowed ground.

Christine was watching her with interest. "So, it happened right here?"

"About three paces over, yeah." Dani walked to the spot and crouched down. Traces of the plaster used to create the tire impression were still visible despite the rain. "From what we can tell, the couple parked here facing the lake and someone pulled up behind them. James got out and confronted the attacker, was shot twice. We think the attacker either dragged Tessa from the car or she went out the passenger side and fled into the woods."

Dani was leaning toward the second scenario. If the attacker had dragged her from the car, he would have had tight control over her, especially given that he was armed. Dani believed she'd fled during or immediately after the shots that killed James.

"What about the door?" Christine asked. "I saw the crime-scene photos on the wall in the conference room. It looked like the passenger door was closed."

"It was." That detail had been bothering Dani, too.

"You think she took the time to close the door behind her?"

"I think the shooter closed it. We never recovered a purse or cell phone from the car, so I'm thinking the perp went back to grab a few things and possibly he shut it then."

Dani stood and looked around, trying to think of something they'd missed.

"And he was shot in the groin?" Christine asked. "Sounds like a crime of passion."

"Sounds like." But Dani still wasn't convinced.

She trekked the short distance to the lake, where Jasper stood beside a wooden pier. Travis was crouched at the end of the pier, rummaging through the tackle box he used as an evidence kit.

"We struck out on those interviews," Jasper told her.

"I heard. You pass out your card?"

"Yeah. Maybe someone might remember something down the road, call it in." He looked at Dani. "How'd it go at the apartment?"

"Okay."

"Just okay?"

"So far, yeah."

Tessa's one-bedroom apartment was a typical single woman's place. Mismatched furniture, cheap decorative touches, baskets of laundry and piles of mail sitting around. It looked a lot like Dani's place, but at least Tessa had managed to unpack most of her stuff.

Dani glanced around. Where was Scott? She skimmed her gaze over the lake and noticed some bubbles on the surface. Following the hike-and-bike trail along the shoreline, she watched the bubbles give way to ripples.

Scott emerged from the water wearing a black dive suit and scuba tank. He pulled a regulator from his mouth and waded to shore, and she noticed the device in his hand—probably the waterproof metal detector. He shrugged out of the tank, then unzipped the wet suit and peeled it off his shoulders.

Dani halted. The last time she'd seen Scott without a shirt on he'd been sixteen and he'd come over to help Drew mow the lawn. Dani had stepped outside as Scott was walking up the driveway, and for the first time in her life she'd felt that warm *pull*. He was strong and lean, and she remembered the metallic scent of sweat on his skin and the smell of fresh-cut grass. He'd pinned her with those cool blue eyes, and she'd been completely unable to move.

It was the same as now, only now he had a man's body, a warrior's body, all hardened and scarred, and something dangerous glinted in his eyes as he approached her.

"I found it."

She cleared her throat. "You found . . . ?"

He held out his hand, and she stared at the bullet in his big palm. A chill moved through her. So very small, and yet the chunk of metal had pierced straight through a woman's body and ended her life.

"Looks like she was standing in the woods near the water when she got shot," he said. "First shot was a through-and-through bullet that ended up in the lake."

Travis stepped over. "Wow. She's a beauty."

Christine and Jasper walked over to check out the slug.

"How's it a 'beauty' exactly?" Christine looked at Travis.

"Good marks," he said. "The rifling inside the barrel puts a spin on the bullet to stabilize it in flight as it leaves the gun. Every gun leaves unique marks, so we can enter them in the database, see if they match up with any other weapons or bullets we know of from other crime scenes."

"The silt in the lake's perfect for this," Scott said. "It's almost like the ballistic gel we use at the lab." He unzipped a pocket on his dive suit and took out a drawstring pouch, then dropped the bullet into it.

"Can you run it today?" Dani asked.

"That's the plan." Scott grabbed his scuba tank as if it weighed nothing and hitched it onto his shoulder.

"Call me as soon as you're done. I need those results."

He lifted an eyebrow. "Yes, ma'am."

He and Travis walked back to the pickup, and Christine stared after them as they heaved their gear into the truck bed.

"Dear Lord." She looked at Dani. "Did you see that six-pack? I think it was an eight-pack."

Jasper scowled. "Jeez, Christine."

"What? I'm married but I'm not dead."

Dani's phone vibrated in her pocket and she pulled it out to check the screen.

"Reynolds," she told Jasper before she answered.

"Have you wrapped up at the apartment yet?" the lieutenant wanted to know.

"I left there half an hour ago. Why?"

"I need you to go to the parks and rec headquarters on Cotton Mill Road."

"I'm near there now," she said, sensing the urgency in his voice. "I'm at Woodlake Park."

"What's happening at the park?"

"The CSIs just recovered the through-and-through bullet from the female victim. They think the marks look good, so it could be a lead."

"Well, I've got a better one. I think we've got the murder weapon."

• • •

Back at the Delphi Center, Scott changed out of his dive suit and into his work uniform—tactical pants and a black shirt with the Delphi logo on the front. He liked that he could dress down for work and didn't have to wear a noose around his neck unless he was testifying in court.

Travis was already in the lab test-firing a nickel-plated pistol into a water tank.

"Where'd we get that?" Scott asked.

Travis pulled off his ear protectors. "Drug raid down in Webb County." He shook his head. "Cops recovered it from under the mattress in a baby crib, if you can believe that."

Scott could definitely believe it. Some people were criminally stupid.

"I bet you a round of beers that this gun's in the system already," Travis added.

"No way. Not touching that bet."

Scott pulled on some latex gloves and unpacked the bullet he'd retrieved from the lake. He looked at it again before stepping up to the microscope and using some putty to secure it to the stage. He examined it at five times magnification and whistled with approval.

"Looks good?" Travis asked.

"Yep."

The bullet was pristine, thanks to the soft silt of the lake. Plus Scott had handled it carefully. He'd seen way too many perfectly good slugs ruined because some ham-handed investigator dug them out of a wall or a fence post using a pocketknife. Scott never handled evidence with metal tools.

The markings on a spent bullet were like a fingerprint. The lands and grooves were unique to each gun, which enabled investigators to link previously unrelated crimes and crime scenes. Theoretically, Scott could scan this bullet into a database maintained by the feds and hope for a match.

But would he get one? Hard to say. If the bullet was from a drug-related homicide, he'd be willing to bet yes. But this case was different. Originally, it had seemed like a crime of passion, maybe a jealous boyfriend taking revenge. But the more Scott investigated, the more it seemed like something else entirely. Something cold and calculated that wasn't going to be as simple as scanning a slug into the system and getting a hit.

Scott was determined to try anyway. He would love to be able to deliver Dani some good news right now, something that might take that worried look off her face. She was under a lot of pressure, and he wanted to help her.

Travis's phone buzzed on the counter, and he grabbed it. "Cullen here." His gaze darted to Scott. "No shit? Okay, we'll be ready for it."

"What is it?" Scott could tell by Travis's tone that it was something big.

"That was Jasper with SMPD. Sounds like they found the gun."

CHAPTER 5

Dani waited for Ric in front of the admissions office, and it wasn't hard to spot him among the backpack-toting summer school students in shorts and sandals.

"Science building's over here," Dani said, leading the way. "The professor said four o'clock, so we're running late. Think he just finished a class."

Ric glanced at his watch, then at her. "Any more word on the gun?"

"No. It's not even at the Delphi Center yet."

"Why not?"

"Minh wanted to run it for prints first." She rolled her eyes. "More turf wars, I'm guessing. He said he'd make it quick and then send it over there for ballistics tests. It's a Glock nine-mil, so we're pretty much expecting a match."

"And it was found in a trash can?"

"West side of the lake at the base of the hike-and-bike trail. Maintenance worker was collecting garbage this morning, said the bag felt unusually heavy." She glanced at Ric. "You look skeptical."

"Jasper told me he was going to look through all the trash bins when we worked the scene."

"He says he must have missed this one. You think it was dumped later, not right after the murders?"

"I don't know."

They reached the science building. Ric pulled open the door and held it for a trio of female students. One of them glanced back at him with a coy look.

Dani smiled.

"What?" Ric asked.

"Nothing."

They crossed a crowded lobby that wasn't much cooler than the air outside. It was an older building, with dingy linoleum floors and chipping paint, and it felt like the air-conditioning system could use an upgrade.

"I've been thinking about our game plan," Dani said as they neared the elevators. A pair of students stepped off, and she and Ric took their places.

"You're the boss. How do you want to do it?"

Dani jabbed the button for the third floor. "You interview the supervisor and I'll try to find some of their coworkers."

"How do you know their coworkers overlap?"

"They were on the same research project. Tessa was his assistant. Something about chromatids and gene splicing? The professor went into it on the phone, but it was over my head."

"I'm sure Mia could translate it." As one of the Delphi Center's top DNA experts, Ric's wife kept up with developments in the field.

"Or maybe one of James's colleagues here could put it into English for us," Dani said.

The elevator grumbled to a stop, and after a long pause the doors slid open. They stepped into a dimly lit hallway that smelled like formaldehyde.

"Damn, this place is a dump," Ric muttered.

"Yeah, not exactly the Delphi Center." Dani checked

a sign on the wall and motioned for them to turn left. "He's in three sixteen."

"Detective Harper?"

They turned around to see a tall man in a white lab coat striding toward them. Bald as a cue ball, he had a pair of wire-rimmed glasses perched atop his head.

He thrust out a hand at Dani. "Mike Kreznik. And you must be Detective Santos?" He shook hands with Ric, too. "You want to meet in my office? Or perhaps the conference room?"

"Your office sounds good," Ric said.

"Actually, does James Ayers have an office?" Dani asked. "If so, I'd like to see it. Tessa's, too."

Kreznik frowned. "Tessa didn't have an office. Not as a research assistant." He scratched the back of his neck. "James is just down the hall. *Was.*"

"Mind if I take a look? Ric can handle the interview, if you're short on time."

"Uh, sure." Kreznik checked his watch. "Let me just—hey, Ollie." He waved to a man at the end of the hallway. "I'd like you to meet some people."

The man walked over with a wary look, and Kreznik made introductions. Dr. Oliver Junger was short and paunchy, with only slightly more hair than his boss. He wore a white lab coat over jeans and a T-shirt.

"These are the detectives investigating . . . what happened." Kreznik cleared his throat. "They need to see James's office."

Dani smiled at Junger, hoping to put him at ease. "I'd like to take a quick look around."

"Sure, this way."

She traded looks with Ric before following Junger down the hall. "Were you and James friends?"

Junger glanced over his shoulder. "No."

Okay. "And did you know Tessa?"

"I did not."

He stopped at a closed door where a pile of flowers and teddy bears and handwritten notes had accumulated. Junger opened the door and stepped over everything without so much as a glance. Dani followed him into the small, windowless room.

"This is what we refer to as our junior executive suite," Junger said drily. "I've got one just like it down the hall."

"Nice," she said, glancing around.

A desk, bookshelves, and a file cabinet crowded the space, hardly leaving room for anyone to stand. The bookshelves were crammed with thick volumes. Several stacks of binders sat on the end of the desk alongside a putty-colored computer. In lieu of windows, James had a pair of framed prints on the wall. Dani recognized the creation scene by Michelangelo.

"He considered himself a Renaissance man," Junger commented.

She glanced back at him, detecting a bite in his tone.

"The *Creation of Adam*." He nodded at the prints. "And, of course, the *Expulsion from the Garden*."

"From the Sistine Chapel," Dani said, and Junger's eyebrows arched with surprise. *I went to college, too, thank you very little.*

Dani turned her attention to the file cabinet. She pulled a pair of latex gloves from her pocket and tugged them on, ignoring Junger's frown of disapproval as she opened the top file drawer, then the bottom. Both were empty.

"He hadn't exactly settled in yet," Junger said.

"And James moved down here when?" Dani knew the answer already, but wanted to see if the victim's co-worker did.

"Last September."

"And Tessa?"

"She came later. About three months ago, I think."

Dani waited for more.

"She was his research assistant at some little college in New Mexico, where he used to work. He considered her indispensable." Junger rolled his eyes. "Or so I'm told." He pulled a phone from his pocket and checked the screen. "Listen, Miss Harper, I teach a lab in ten minutes, so if there's nothing else—"

"There is. I'm wondering if you can describe their relationship."

He leaned against the doorframe. "Their relationship?"

"Yes."

"Well, let's see. They were having an affair, correct?"

"Were they open about it?"

He shrugged. "It was pretty obvious. To me, anyway. They sometimes left work together, took breaks together."

"And do you think his wife knew?"

"No."

Dani tipped her head to the side. "You don't think so?"

"If she knew he was having an affair, I don't think she knew it was with Tessa."

"Why do you say that?"

"She came by here once, and I saw her and Tessa talking. I didn't get the impression there was any animosity there."

Dani pulled open the top desk drawer and poked

through the usual collection of pens and paper clips. No notes or scraps of paper. No loose keys or business cards or receipts that might offer a lead.

"What about anyone else?" She glanced up. "Was James romantically involved with anyone else in the department, that you're aware of?"

"No."

"What about a student?"

"I highly doubt it."

"Why?"

Junger smiled slightly. "He was a middle-aged lab geek. Not exactly Channing Tatum." Another glance at his phone, but he didn't move to leave. He seemed annoyed to be here, and yet happy to bad-mouth his dead colleague.

"Do you know if Tessa was seeing anyone else?"

The smile faded. "No."

"No, she wasn't seeing anyone else, or, no, you don't know?"

"I can't be sure, but . . . no. She was all about James." He looked away.

Dani opened the remaining desk drawers. Notepads, a stapler, a box of pens. She gave each drawer a thorough check, but saw nothing personal stashed inside, not even the useless detritus that normally builds up in people's desks.

She glanced up at the professor, who was still watching her with interest.

She definitely wanted this guy's contact info. He had some sort of issue with the victims—or at least with James—and she had a feeling she'd be talking to him again.

Dani's phone vibrated with an incoming text and

she pulled it from her pocket. Reynolds. He wanted her back at the station house.

She smiled at Junger. "Thanks for showing me around. Please call us if you think of anything helpful." She gave him a business card and then jotted down his contact information before heading back down the hall. Ric stood beside the elevator with his cell phone pressed to his ear.

"Yeah, we're on our way." He gave Dani a tense look as the elevator doors opened, then ended his call as they stepped inside.

"Lemme guess. Reynolds?"

"Yeah. He put a rush on those prints that Minh lifted off the gun recovered from the park."

"He got prints? Really?" Fingerprints were worlds better than a ballistics match, second only to DNA in terms of kick-ass leads.

"We got a hit."

"*Yes.*" She did a fist pump. "Finally, a break."

"The fingerprints belong to Scott Black."

CHAPTER 6

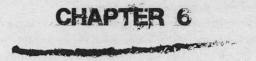

Dani stepped into the observation room, which was already filled to capacity. Jasper, Sean, Ric, and Rachel Patterson, the local DA, were crowded around a video screen.

"They just started," Ric said as Dani pulled the door shut behind her.

She took a spot near the wall, as far away as she could get from Rachel, whose presence here was just the latest in today's string of unpleasant surprises.

Ric leaned close. "He waived his right to an attorney."

Dani clenched her teeth and didn't say anything as she stared at the video feed of the interview happening only a few footsteps away. Lieutenant Reynolds had his back to the camera, but Dani didn't need to see his face to read the tension in his body language.

"Do you know why you're here, Mr. Black?"

Scott didn't answer. In contrast to Reynolds, he leaned back in his chair, his long legs stretched in front of him and his thumbs tucked casually into his belt loops. He looked like he was in a friend's kitchen, not a police interrogation room.

"Mr. Black?"

"No, but I figure you'll tell me."

Reynolds shifted a manila file folder in front of him. "A nine-millimeter semiautomatic pistol was recently recovered from a crime scene." He paused. "Our CSI lifted your fingerprints from the gun."

Scott didn't respond. His blue eyes didn't show even a flicker of interest as he gazed at the lieutenant.

"Mr. Black? You sure you don't want to rethink that attorney?"

"Nah, I'm good."

Dani's chest tightened as Reynolds shifted in his chair, clearly winding up for another question.

"Do you own a nine-millimeter semiautomatic pistol?"

"I own a lot of pistols."

"This one's a Glock."

"A Glock, huh? 'Fraid I can't help you there." Scott folded his arms over his big chest. "Never had one, never will."

"You have something against Glocks?" Reynolds sounded defensive. Every cop in Dani's department carried a Glock.

"Not really my style."

"The most widely used firearm in law enforcement isn't good enough for you?"

"I carry a Sig. For accuracy and stopping power, you can't beat it."

"And how long have you carried that weapon?"

"Since BUD/S training."

Rachel huffed out a breath and looked at Ric. "This is a disaster."

"It's a joke, is what it is," Ric said. "The guy used to be a SEAL. He's trained to withstand waterboarding. You think Dunkin' Donuts in there is gonna rattle his cage?"

Rachel glared at him. "Is this *funny* to you? Do you

know how many times I've put him on the witness stand? He's testified in seven trials in this year alone."

Reynolds was shuffling through his folder now. "Could you tell me exactly where you were at nine fifteen P.M. this past Sunday night?"

"Nine fifteen P.M."

"That's right."

"An hour before I showed up at Woodlake Park to help you people out with a crime scene."

"That's right."

"No."

Reynolds leaned forward. "What's that?"

"No, I can't tell you exactly where I was at that time."

The lieutenant shifted in his chair, and Scott watched him with a trace of amusement in his eyes, as if he might actually be enjoying this.

"Can you tell me *generally* where you were?" Reynolds sounded annoyed.

"Let's see." Scott rubbed his jaw. "Generally, I was on I-35 headed to Austin to meet some friends at a bar on Sixth Street."

"Male friends? Female?"

"Both."

Rachel made a hissing sound and shook her head. Dani watched her, wondering if there was something more to her reaction than the fact that one of her favorite expert witnesses was being questioned in a double homicide.

"And did you?" Reynolds eased back in his chair. "Meet up with them, that is. Can they verify your whereabouts?"

"No."

"Why not?"

"Because before I got there I received a call from work directing me to a crime scene. So I turned around."

"And what time was this?"

"About nine forty-five."

"I see. And what time did you arrive at the crime scene?"

"I couldn't say for sure. Probably ten ten."

"So, between nine fifteen and ten minutes after ten, did you see anyone who can corroborate where you were?"

"Nope."

Dani flinched at his glib tone. Rachel shook her head.

"Did you know James Ayers?" Reynolds asked, changing gears.

"No."

"What about Tessa Lovett?"

"No."

"Never went out with her?"

"Nope."

The lieutenant took a photo from his file and slid it in front of Scott, who didn't even glance at it. "Any chance you bumped into her somewhere, maybe bought her a drink?"

"No."

"Are you sure?"

"I'm sure."

Was Scott telling the truth? Dani had no idea. Women flirted with him all the time, and he probably didn't remember all of them.

Reynolds opened his file again. "Did you say you've *never* owned a Glock nine?"

The lieutenant was circling back now, looking for

holes in the story, or details that had changed. Dani had used the same technique on a suspect in the same damn interview room just a few hours ago. But instead of being flustered and weepy, this suspect was calm and defiant.

And his attitude was pissing off not only the lieutenant and the DA but no doubt the chief of police, who was probably watching this interview from the comfort of his office down the hall.

Dani cast a look at Ric, but he was focused intently on the screen.

"Mr. Black? You say you've never owned a Glock?"

Scott sighed. "That is what I said."

"You ever borrow a Glock from anybody?"

"No."

"Ever purchased one from a friend and had it in your possession temporarily?"

"No."

"Ever kept one for a friend?"

"No." Scott glanced at his watch again and stood. "We finished here? I've got work to do, so unless you plan to arrest me for something, I'd just as soon wrap this up."

Scott knew that if they had enough to arrest him, they would have done it by now. He also knew he had every right to walk straight out that unlocked door.

The lieutenant got to his feet. "Stay available," he ordered.

Scott looked straight at the camera, and Dani felt it like an arrow through her heart. He yanked open the door and walked out.

• • •

As soon as she stepped into the bar, Scott felt her. He always felt her. He tried to lock it out of his mind as he checked the baseball score one last time and finished his drink.

The bartender sauntered over and smiled. "Another round for you guys?"

Travis lifted his beer. "Not yet."

"I'm good," Scott said as Dani strode over to their end of the bar.

"Where the hell have you been?" she demanded.

Scott glanced at her as he pulled out his wallet. She looked the same as she had earlier, right down to the detective's shield clipped to the waist of those snug-fitting jeans.

He slid a couple twenties across the counter and nodded at Travis. "I'm out."

"You need a ride?"

"No."

Travis cast a chilly look at Dani, but she was too worked up to notice it as she followed Scott toward the exit.

"Scott?"

"What?" He pushed through the door into the muggy July night.

"What the hell?"

He stopped and stared down at her. Her green eyes flashed with frustration—slightly different from the lust he'd seen in them this morning at the lake.

A Harley roared to life in the parking lot, drowning out conversation as he walked toward his truck with Dani hurrying to keep up with his long strides. The noise faded as he neared his pickup and took out his keys.

"*Hey.*"

He stopped and turned.

"Could you wait a goddamn minute? I've been looking for you for hours."

"Why?"

Her eyebrows shot up. "*Why?* Um . . . because you're suddenly a *suspect* in a double homicide. Jesus Christ. Are you planning to explain to me what's going on?"

"You're the detective. You figure it out." He turned toward his truck and caught a blur of movement as she swooped in and snatched the keys from his hand.

Anger rippled through him and he turned around. "Gimme my keys, Dani."

"You can't drive."

"Wanna bet?" He stepped closer and glowered down at her, and she held his keys behind her back. "Now, Dani."

"No."

She glared up at him, and that was it. He'd had it. He yanked her against him and kissed that mouth that had been making him fucking crazy. He felt her startled gasp.

He'd surprised her. Completely. And that should have been his signal to stop, but he couldn't have if he'd wanted to. And he *didn't* want to, not when she arched against him and kissed him like she'd been thinking about it maybe even half as much as he had.

She was hot and sexy, and the way she squirmed against him sent a lightning bolt of lust straight to his groin. She tasted so good, even better than he remembered. She moaned and pushed at his chest, and only then did he realize what her squirming was really about. Her fist thudded against his shoulder as she jerked out of his arms.

• • •

Dani stumbled back and stared up at him. He was breathing hard just like she was. Something dangerous flickered in his eyes and he dragged her against him again.

"Stop." She pulled away. "You can't just . . ."

"What?" He gave her a rough shake. "What can't I do, Daniele?"

Before she could answer, he dropped her arms and stepped back, leaving her suddenly adrift in a sea of cars and pickups. She glanced around and realized it was the same as the last time, the same sloppy, drunken mistake in the same damn parking lot, and she flushed with embarrassment as she looked up at him.

"You can't *kiss* me! You're a suspect in my investigation!"

He scowled and looked away.

"Why aren't you taking this seriously?" she yelled, so angry she actually stomped her foot. "You've been implicated in a double homicide."

His jaw tensed. "I wasn't there, Daniele."

"Your gun was there!"

"It's not mine."

"Your prints are all over it." She got up in his face. "You have to explain that. And you have to get yourself a lawyer. What the hell's wrong with you? You know how the system works."

"I don't have to do jack shit."

She gaped at him. "*Yes*, you do. You look totally guilty."

"I'm not."

"It doesn't matter! You *look* guilty. And I can't believe I'm even standing here having this conversation with you in a stupid parking lot."

She glanced around, flustered as she noticed people turning to stare as they walked out to their cars. How did he do this to her? How did he make her completely batshit crazy while he somehow remained completely cool? It had to be the alcohol.

She shoved his keys in the pocket of her blazer and squared her shoulders. "Get in. I'll take you home." She stared up at him, daring him to challenge her, and as the moment stretched out, her heart started to pound. Whose home? And then what?

Heat simmered in his eyes, and she felt a warm shudder from the top of her head to the soles of her feet. Her skin was tight suddenly, and she wanted to kiss him again even though her lips were still numb and tingly from the fierceness of his mouth and the whiskey she'd tasted on his tongue.

He eased closer, and she tried not to flinch under his gaze. His kiss did something to her, made it impossible for her to think straight.

Boots crunching on the gravel nearby had her turning around. Travis paused beside his black 4Runner, watching them warily. Scott looked at him, then back at Dani.

"I'll get a ride with Travis."

Her heart squeezed. "Fine." She tossed his keys at him and he caught them against his chest. "Do whatever the hell you want."

CHAPTER 7

Scott's house was dark, and he didn't bother with lights as he let himself in and stood in the kitchen for a moment, just listening to the quality of the silence. Then he took off his jacket and grabbed a bottle of Jim Beam from the cabinet. He poured a drink and went into the living room to sink onto the sofa.

His head pounded. Still. It had been pounding all day, and it would be worse tomorrow because of all the booze. He squeezed his eyes shut and rubbed the bridge of his nose, but he couldn't get the image out of his brain. For two full days it had been stuck there—Tessa Lovett sprawled in the mud by that lake, a pair of nice, neat bullet holes in her back.

He tipped back his glass, and the bourbon washed away the taste of Dani. He couldn't believe he'd kissed her again. What the hell was he thinking?

Headlights swung into the driveway. Scott's pulse kicked up until he saw that it wasn't a Chevy pickup but a BMW. Scott reached for the remote and found the Astros game he'd been watching at Schmitt's.

The back door opened and closed and Drew stepped into the kitchen. "Hi."

"Hi."

Drew stood beside the breakfast table, his tie loose around his neck. He hadn't even been home yet. He walked into the living room and sat down on a leather ottoman.

"Why didn't you call me?"

Scott flicked a glance at him. "About what?"

"Hiring a fucking lawyer, that's what. You're a prime suspect in a homicide."

Scott stared at the game.

"I put in a call to a law school buddy of mine." Drew took out his cell phone and swiped at the screen. "Name's Joe Billingsly. He's a defense attorney in Austin. I'll text you his contact info."

"No, thanks."

Drew leaned forward. "What do you mean 'no, thanks'?"

"What I said. I don't want an attorney."

Silence settled over the room.

Drew stood up and rested his hands on his hips. His eyes were filled with frustration and disappointment. It was such a Dani-like expression that Scott had to look away.

"You know, this renegade thing you got going doesn't work out here in the real world. This shit's serious." Drew paused for effect—one of his courtroom techniques. "You could end up in jail. Or worse. This is a death-penalty case."

"Drew . . ." Scott sighed.

"What?"

Scott looked up at his best friend. They'd played football together, mown lawns together. They'd gotten drunk together and high together and even gotten laid together on a few lucky occasions. But all that was years ago, before Drew had gone off to law school and Scott had gone off to war. Things were different now.

Scott was different. And if Drew stood in his living room for one more minute telling him about the "real world," Scott was going to have to hurt him.

Scott tossed back the rest of his drink.

"Unbelievable," Drew muttered. "Nice talking to you, man."

He stalked out of the room, and Scott didn't look up. The windows rattled as Drew slammed the door.

• • •

Brooke Porter knelt down and beamed her flashlight over the sodden carpet. She could have used more light, but that was the problem with crime scenes—sucky working conditions were the rule and not the exception.

"Hey, Roland," she called. "Turn that lamp this way, would you?"

Roland was in an intense discussion with a firefighter. A *female* firefighter who had captivated his attention the second they rolled up to the scene in the Delphi Center van.

"*Roland.*"

He looked up.

"The lamp?"

He shifted the scene lamp to face her direction, then resumed his discussion.

Brooke shook her head and took out her utility knife. After deciding on precisely which area she wanted, she used the blade to cut a four-by-four-inch square. She held the knife in her teeth as she deposited the carpet sample in a metal can.

Someone stepped into her light, and she glanced up.

"Brooke Porter?" a male voice asked.

She tried to make out the silhouette, and her heart gave a little lurch when she recognized him. Ric Santos, the sexy homicide detective from San Marcos PD. She set down her blade. "May I help you?"

"I hope so."

She secured the lid over the metal can and tapped the edges with the hilt of her knife to give it an airtight seal. If her hunch was right, this patch of carpet had been doused with an accelerant. Brooke wouldn't know for sure until she took the sample to the lab and ran tests.

She stood up and tucked her tool into the pocket of her white Tyvek suit. The detective stepped out of the glare and she could see him better.

"I'm Ric Santos with SMPD."

"Mia's husband." She tipped her head to the side. "Aren't you a little out of your jurisdiction?"

"Just a little." The detective glanced around the small room, which was a giant mess. What had once been a quaint lakefront cabin was now a fire scene swarming with emergency vehicles. Ric shifted his gaze back to her. "Curtis said I'd find you here."

"*Dr.* Curtis?"

He nodded.

That got her attention. Why on earth had a San Marcos cop asked her boss's boss—the number two man at the Delphi Center—about her?

Brooke gathered up her cans of evidence. She attempted to grab her evidence kit, too, but her hands were overloaded. Ric grabbed it for her.

"I'm just wrapping up here," she said, squishing her way across the carpet and passing through what was left of the cabin's front door. The entire place had been reduced to a charred black skeleton now crawling with crime-scene techs. Ric walked her down the sidewalk.

"My department just sent some evidence to your lab and we need a rush on it," Ric said.

"Define 'rush.'"

He lifted a swag of crime-scene tape, and she ducked under it. He followed.

"We need results by tomorrow."

Of course he did.

Brooke crossed a narrow gravel road to the crime-scene van. She set down her cans and opened the cargo doors.

That a homicide cop wanted a rush on his evidence was nothing new. That he'd called her boss's boss and then hauled his butt out to a crime scene at 11:00 P.M. to personally put in the request was a little unusual.

Brooke loaded the cans into a plastic tub, where they wouldn't rattle around during transport.

Ric had a curious look on his face. "Paint cans?"

"Yes, but they've never been used. We get them straight from the manufacturer." She pulled her gloves off and stuffed them into her pocket. "We use them for transporting evidence that might contain accelerants so the chemicals don't evaporate before we get a chance to run tests."

"I see."

She turned to face him. "What's this evidence and why is it so important?"

"It's a pistol. A Glock nine, and we think it was used in a double homicide."

"The professor thing."

He nodded.

"So you want me to fingerprint it?"

"Our guy already did that."

She felt a stab of irritation as she loaded her evidence kit and shut the cargo doors. "If you already ran it—"

"We need someone to corroborate his findings. Or disprove them."

She folded her arms over her chest. "You don't trust your own guy?"

"We also need you to run the weapon for anything else," he said, ignoring her question. "Biological evidence, trace chemicals, whatever."

Brooke gazed up at him, trying to get a read. She didn't like this at all. He was basically asking her to redo something that had already been done because he believed his police evidence tech was incompetent or had botched the job or both. And this was a high-profile case, which meant the stakes were through the roof. Whatever the test results were, they were going to be scrutinized by an army of prosecutors, defense attorneys, and jurors down the road.

"Look, Detective—"

"Ric." He smiled, and Brooke felt a little flutter. She had to remind herself he was married to a colleague. A very pregnant colleague.

"Look, Ric, I'd love to help you, but I've really got my hands full right now, as you can see. There must be someone over at the state lab who could do this. Did you try over there?"

"No."

"Why not?"

"Because you're the best."

She drew back, startled by such a bold statement, even though it was true.

"We want you. It's important. This is a death investigation."

"Yeah? Well, so is this." She nodded at the medical examiner's van, which was pulling out of the driveway at that very moment. "So are *many* of my cases. Why should your case jump to the front of the line?"

"I can't tell you."

She rolled her eyes.

"I wish I could. Just trust me that it's urgent."

• • •

Dani felt antsy on the drive home. She'd felt that way all week—jumpy, anxious, even paranoid. For days now she kept getting this weird sensation as though someone were tickling the back of her neck with a feather.

She glanced in the rearview mirror for anything suspicious. Nothing, of course. No one was following her or watching her. She was simply going crazy. She was totally off her game this week, and she blamed Scott.

He'd pulled the same crap again, and again she'd reacted like a stunned teenager who'd never been kissed. Warmth flooded her cheeks and she tried to shake off the memory. But she couldn't. Because she didn't really want to. His scent, the feel of his body—all of it was seared into her mind. Why did he keep doing this to her? If he wasn't interested, why did he keep stirring her up this way?

She needed to focus. On the case, not Scott. She had to figure out what the hell was going on with her investigation.

She passed through an intersection and glanced

down a tree-lined street. It was Ric's neighborhood. On impulse, she hung a right at the next corner and navigated her way to his house.

No cars in the driveway, but the garage was closed and a TV flickered in the living room, so someone was home. He was probably cuddled up on the couch with his wife, picking out baby names. Dani should leave them to it.

She was about to pull away when she noticed a shadowy figure waddling down the sidewalk. Dani slid from her pickup.

"Mia?"

The figure stepped from the shadows into the light of a streetlamp. It was Mia, all right. She wore shorts and tennis shoes and a fitted pink T-shirt that looked like it had a beach ball stuffed under it. Mia's strawberry-blond hair was pulled back in a ponytail and her skin shimmered with sweat.

Dani grabbed a water bottle from her cup holder and walked over. "What are you doing out here? It's got to be ninety degrees."

"Ninety-two." She stopped beside Dani and took the bottle. "Thank you." She tipped it back for a long sip, and Dani tried not to stare at her huge bump. "Thanks," she gasped, handing back the bottle. "I feel like I'm about to burst. I wish I would."

Dani bit her lip. Pregnancy was a mystery to her. She wasn't in the club, and based on what she'd seen, she didn't know if she ever wanted to join.

"So . . . you're just out for a walk or . . . ?" Dani didn't finish the question because she couldn't think of a plausible reason why anyone would be power walking in this heat while nine months pregnant.

"Trying to get the baby to drop." Mia pressed her hands against her lower back and sighed. "One of the nurses told me walking helps. That and sex." She smiled. "But Ric's not home yet, so . . ." She tugged a phone from the depths of her cleavage and checked it. "You know where he is? I thought he was with you."

"No idea. But you should definitely text him. He'll be home in a flash."

"I should."

Dani cast a look down the block. She got that nervous feeling again, and she knew Ric wouldn't like Mia out walking around in the dark.

Dani started up the sidewalk toward their house, and Mia fell into step beside her.

"I guess you need to talk to him about work?" Mia asked.

"It can wait till morning. I just wanted to bounce some ideas off him."

"I hear it's a tough case."

"Yeah."

Mia shook her head. "I feel for his wife. She's got to be torn between heart-wrenching grief and wishing she could string him up by his wandering little penis."

"Yep."

Dani surveyed the house as they neared the porch. Pots brimming with marigolds flanked the steps, and a porch swing swayed gently in the breeze. The place positively glowed with homeyness, as though it somehow knew there was a baby on the way. Dani's house seemed like a hovel by comparison. She needed to drag out her lawn mower and do a quick pass, but the weekends always seemed to get away from her.

Mia's phone dinged as they reached the door. A

smile spread over her face as she read the screen. "He's on his way home and offering to pick up ice cream. I'll tell him to skip it."

"No way. You two chow down. I'll catch him tomorrow."

"You sure?"

"Absolutely."

Mia opened the door and a waft of chilly air drifted out. She tipped her head back and sighed.

"Lock your doors. Tell Ric I'll see him tomorrow." Dani smiled. "And good luck with that other thing."

CHAPTER 8

Dani was late to her own meeting and bypassed the coffeepot on the way to the conference room as Ric walked into the bull pen.

"Late night?" Dani asked.

"Yeah."

"How's Mia?"

"Climbing the walls."

"Listen, I'm glad I caught you." Dani checked her watch. "You're taking that gun to Delphi, right? I think we need to put a rush on it. Reynolds will probably approve the expense—"

"It's done."

She stared at him. "You took it in already?"

"Last night."

"We need to put a rush—"

"I did."

"Really?"

"Really."

"How fast can they turn it around? We can offer to pay an expedite fee."

He rested a hand on her shoulder. "Dani. *Breathe.*"

"Sorry." She took a deep breath, blew it out. "I get bossy when I'm nervous."

"I know."

Of course he knew. They'd been working together

since she was a rookie. Which made it all the more un-real that she was now leading *him*, giving him orders instead of taking them.

She studied his face, amazed that he seemed so calm. He looked tired, and she doubted he was getting much sleep these days. But he didn't look frantic, as she did. She'd glanced in the bathroom mirror this morn-ing and been totally caught off guard by the deer-in-the-headlights look reflected back at her.

"Sorry," she repeated, then wanted to kick herself. "I just keep thinking . . . there has to be some mistake. That weapon's not in the firearms database. It hasn't been through the system. But why else would Scott have handled it?"

Ric didn't answer, but his silence was answer enough. The simplest explanation was also the most impossible for Dani to accept.

Ric knew Scott, but not like *she* knew Scott. It wasn't like Ric and Scott went way back. It wasn't like Ric knew, as she did, that no matter what the evidence said, there was absolutely no way Scott had committed this crime.

She could feel the advice coming. "What is it?"

"I know this is your first time leading up a case like this, but you've got to be objective, Dani."

"I know."

"Do you really?"

"Yes."

Ric studied her. All along, he'd sensed her loyalty to Scott. She'd never said anything about her feelings, but Ric had known them anyway because he was a good detective.

"Come on, let's go," he said, pushing open the door of the conference room.

Dani stepped into the room and tried to step into her confident persona. She could do this. She *was* doing this. She was heading up her first major investigation, and they were making progress. They actually had a suspect list neatly printed on the large whiteboard.

She averted her gaze from Scott's name at the top of the list as she took the seat at the head of the table and looked over her team. "Where's Jasper? He's supposed to be with us full-time."

"Reynolds sent him to cover a motor vehicle accident on Route 12," Sean said.

"Since when does a motor vehicle accident trump a homicide investigation?"

"The driver is Yvonne Greene," Sean told her.

"Who?"

"Some rich doctor's wife. She's a loose cannon. We've had her in twice on DUIs. She swerved around a work crew this morning and crashed her Mercedes into a tree, and now she's threatening to sue everyone out there."

Dani flipped open her notepad. "Okay, well, someone update Jasper when he gets in. Meanwhile, I assume everyone read the ME's report? No sign of sexual assault, no foreign DNA under the fingernails—of either victim. And, based on the bullet wounds, the pathologist concluded James was shot first in the chest at point-blank range, then in the groin."

The men winced.

"Sean, let's start with you." Dani made direct eye contact with the detective as he folded his arms over his chest and watched her. Sean was strong and athletically built. He was a nice-looking man and could be charming when he wanted to. He could also be a pain in the ass. Like now, for example. Sean was older than Dani, and she knew he resented that she'd been tapped for this job instead of him.

"Where are we on the purse and the phones?" she asked.

"Still no sign. We did a thorough canvass of the area, and I even checked with pawnshops. Those two iPhones haven't turned up anywhere. Ditto the victim's purse and the two wallets. I checked with the banks and credit card companies, and no movement on any of the accounts."

"And the phone carrier?"

"No outgoing calls since the night of the murder." He opened a file. "Last one from James was a call to his wife's cell phone about five o'clock. Last one from Tessa was a call to James about eight fifteen."

"Probably when they made plans to meet," Ric said.

The door opened, and Reynolds walked into the room.

Dani bit the inside of her mouth and tried not to lose focus. "Okay, so . . . although the phones and wallets are missing, it doesn't look like a robbery. It has the hallmarks of a crime of passion, especially when you consider the nature of the attacks. James Ayers had been shot in the chest, so the shot to the groin is just malicious."

"I'd say being shot in the chest is pretty malicious, too," Sean commented.

"You know what I mean. It's unnecessary." Dani opened her file to the ME's report on Tessa. "And the female victim shot twice in the back? The pathologist said the first shot was fatal and the second shot was someone standing directly over her, point-blank range. So, again, that seems like overkill."

"Where are we on the wife?" Sean asked. "Maybe she hired Black."

Dani tried not to flinch.

Silence settled over the room, and Sean glanced around. "What, we're not investigating just because we know the guy?" He shook his head. "This is a small town. We know everybody."

"We *are* investigating." Ric gave him a sharp look as he flipped open his notepad. "I looked at the money. The widow, Audrey McCabe Ayers, has two checking accounts—a joint and a separate—and two savings accounts, one with close to a million dollars in it. No large withdrawals, and I went back two years."

"A *million* dollars?" Sean leaned forward. "Where'd she get that kind of money? Her husband's a bio teacher, right?"

"Professor of microbiology," Dani confirmed. "He makes eighty-five grand a year, which is slightly less than he was making at his last job."

"Think she has family money," Ric said. "She mentioned her dad owns a Ford dealership in Corpus."

"*McCabe* Ford?" Sean looked at Dani. "Damn, you better believe she's loaded. They've got, like, three or four dealerships down there. Jeeps, Fords, Chevys."

"Let's get back to Scott Black," Reynolds said. "Who checked out his alibi?"

"He doesn't have one," Sean said. "The phone dump shows a call placed from his phone at seven sixteen to a friend in Austin, and it pinged off a cell phone tower here in town. Next call was to his cell phone about nine forty-five, which was the Delphi Center calling him to the crime scene. That call pinged off a tower on the outskirts of Austin."

"He could have committed the murders, then rushed up there," Reynolds said. "He had, what, half an hour?"

"Plenty of time," Sean said.

"And he was alone," Reynolds continued. "And he never made it to the bar to meet his friends, so no one can vouch for his whereabouts."

"Let's go back to the crimes, though." Ric looked at Dani. "You're right—this does look like a crime of emotion. Not exactly what you'd expect from a special ops badass hired to do a hit."

"Unless he and Tessa were having an affair," Sean put in. "Then maybe he'd be emotional."

Dani clenched her teeth and tried not to react. She looked at Reynolds, who was staring pensively at the whiteboard.

Damn it, she needed to take control of this meeting. She wanted everyone out working the case, tracking down new leads that were actually going somewhere, not sitting around, speculating.

"Let's get back to the facts," Dani said. "Fact one: James Ayers and his wife moved down here last fall from New Mexico, and his new job came with a pay cut. Fact two: three months ago, his former research assistant made the same move, also taking a pay cut. Fact three: Tessa Lovett and the professor left their workplace Sunday evening and were shot and killed during what looks like a lakeside tryst."

"We need to figure out why they left their old jobs and came here for less money," Ric said. "I'll check into it."

"Right. And we need to figure out what else might be going on in that workplace," Dani said. "The colleague of theirs I interviewed—Oliver Junger—said people seemed aware of their affair, with the exception of James's wife. And she lied to me, by the way. She said she'd never met Tessa, but Junger said he once saw them talking together. Maybe there was some other love triangle going on." She looked at Ric. "You interviewed their supervisor, Kreznik, right? We should look at him."

"Not a bad idea," Ric said. "He told me he was the one who originally hired both of them."

"I'll run background on the guy," Sean said. "See what I can come up with."

"And the other thing—maybe James was having multiple affairs," Dani said. "Based on the mementos piled up outside his office, looks like he was a popular professor."

"I can go by there again," Ric said. "We can gather up the notes and cards and see if there's anything that raises a red flag."

Dani nodded. "I'll call up Tessa's sister in Santa Fe, see if she can shed any light on Tessa's personal life. If the romance was going south for some reason, the victim might have confided in her sister." Dani glanced at her watch. "Let's get going."

Everyone started to file out.

"Hey, Sean, hold up a sec."

He stopped to look at her, and she waited until everyone was out of earshot.

"I know you're ticked off they made me the lead."

He held her gaze, not denying it. "It wasn't your decision."

"I need to know that any hard feelings you have won't get in the way here. Are you committed to the case?"

His face tightened. "That's insulting."

"It's important. This case is a mess, and I don't need any added problems to deal with. I can't afford to screw this up."

"Then don't." He walked out, leaving her alone in the empty conference room.

She took another look at the whiteboard, where the timeline of the murders had been neatly mapped out and Scott's name topped the suspect list.

"Dani?"

She turned around to see Christine standing in the doorway with flushed cheeks, as though she'd just run up a flight of stairs.

"I got that report you wanted from the bank. Scott Black's credit card activity?" She held out some stapled paperwork. "There's an ATM withdrawal."

Dani skimmed the list until she spotted it. She glanced up. "Did you check with the bank?"

"Went by there personally. They've got it on tape."

Dani stared down at the report. "That son of a *bitch*."

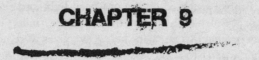

CHAPTER 9

Brooke studied the smooth black pieces under the ultraviolet flashlight, looking for anything she'd missed. Granules of fingerprint dust shimmered pink under her beam.

The door swung open and a wedge of light fell over her table.

"Hey, close the door, would you?"

"We have a visitor," Roland said.

Brooke shoved her goggles to the top of her head and looked over her shoulder. She'd expected Ric Santos to show up this morning, but the man who followed Roland into the lab wasn't someone she knew. Brooke plucked the earbuds from her ears as he neared her table.

Wide shoulders, strong build. He had a look of confidence, and she didn't need to see the badge clipped at his waist to know he was a cop.

"You must be Sean Byrne," she said.

"That's me." He smiled. "Guess you got my message earlier?"

"I told Ric I'd call him when I was finished."

"Thought I'd drop by to see if we could get an update." He stopped beside her and gazed down at the dismantled gun scattered across the parchment paper.

"I've made some preliminary findings, but I still need to go through it all again."

"What have you got so far?"

Brooke switched on the overhead light and shot a look at Roland, giving him the unspoken *Thanks a lot* for bringing this guy back here. Detectives were notoriously persistent—at least the good ones were—and they always tried to rush her.

She looked at Sean Byrne and slid off her stool, putting a bit of space between them as she swiftly reassembled the weapon. "Six good prints," she told him, placing the Glock on the center of the paper. "Three on the grip, three on the slide."

The corner of his mouth curved up with a smile. "You're quick at that. You shoot?"

"God, no."

He leaned a hand on her table. "Why not?"

Why didn't she shoot? Because she spent a huge chunk of her time dealing with the aftermath of people who did. But that was getting a little personal with a man she'd met ten seconds ago.

"Not really my thing," she said.

She pivoted to her computer and pulled up a digital image of the full fingerprint card for Scott Black. His prints, like those of all Delphi Center employees, as well as police officers and others involved in the criminal justice system, were in the database. Brooke tugged off her gloves and maneuvered the mouse, overlaying the digitized images of the prints she'd recovered from the gun with the prints from the database.

"The friction ridge details on all six prints are consistent. In other words, my findings corroborate those of your CSI. The prints belong to Scott Black."

Sean stared at the screen. Besides a slight tightening of his jaw, his face gave nothing away.

Was he buddies with Scott or not? Law enforcement was a tight community, but the people at Delphi
weren't LEOs in the traditional sense. They were scientists. And the lab was enormous. Brooke had worked
here for years and still hadn't met everyone—*including*
the ballistics tracer whose fingerprints were on her
computer screen right now.

Of course, she knew his name and she'd caught a
glimpse of him in the coffee shop a time or two. There
wasn't a woman at Delphi who hadn't noticed Scott
Black.

"We sure this is the gun?" Sean looked at her.

"From a ballistics perspective, no. The tests haven't
been run yet. And I hear you have a spent bullet from
the crime scene? But since that bullet was recovered by
someone who now happens to be a suspect—"

"It's worthless as evidence," Sean finished for her.

Brooke leaned against the table and looked at him,
and she saw that his eyes were a warm hazel. Superlong
eyelashes, too, which she didn't really want to think
about, because this guy was everything she didn't like
about detectives—pushy, arrogant, and overconfident.
But he was undeniably attractive, which was just her
luck, because she was taking a break from men.

"You're right about that. But I can tell you with cer-
tainty that this is your gun." She adjusted the overhead
lamp. "See the muzzle here?" She picked up a pencil
and pointed to a tiny speck of brown, almost invisible
to the naked eye.

"What's that, blood?" Sean eased closer to look.

"Yes, due to blowback. When the bullet leaves the
barrel, air races to fill the space, creating a vacuum that
can pull tiny bits of material, such as blood, back to the

gun. One of our DNA tracers swabbed this and ran it against a sample we have from the ME. It belongs to the male victim."

"He was shot at close range."

"I heard."

She gazed up at the detective, frustrated that she still couldn't read his expression. Was he happy about this news or not? On the good side, he had a suspect whose prints were all over what was clearly the murder weapon.

On the bad side, that suspect was a law enforcement insider who had actually *worked* the crime scene. From a legal perspective, it was nothing short of a nightmare. If this case ever went to trial, a defense attorney would have no trouble calling the ballistics evidence into question. And if the ballistics evidence was in question, what about all the other evidence that had been handled by the Delphi Center? A skilled attorney could tear apart the entire case.

"Damn." Sean rubbed his jaw. "I'm thinking Rachel's going to have a shit fit when she hears this." He glanced at Brooke. "'Scuse my language."

"I'm sure you're right."

"Hope she doesn't shoot the messenger."

"Is that you?"

"Yep."

"Well, I still have some things to finish. I haven't had a chance to empty the magazine yet to see if there's anything of interest on the remaining bullets."

"Any chance you can finish up this afternoon and send over your report?"

"That depends. Any chance you guys can stop pestering me for updates?"

He smiled. "Message received. I'll get out of your way."

• • •

Scott knew right away when Dani arrived, but this time he was cheating. He'd told her to meet him here.

He stared through the scope at the target downrange. He was prone in the dirt with the sun overhead, which was just how he liked it—except for the wind, which had picked up to a brisk fifteen miles per hour. Scott got to his feet and dusted off his hands.

Dani strode down the row of men sprawled on the ground with their rifles. The steady pop of gunfire all but ceased as guys paused what they were doing to watch her. It wasn't just because she was the only woman out here. It was the confident way she carried herself, like she didn't give a shit what people thought.

Her eyes sparked with temper as she reached Scott's station. "You're unbelievable, you know that?"

He reached down and picked up his rifle. "You sound like your brother."

Her cheeks flushed at the mention of Drew. "I should arrest your ass right now."

Scott lifted an eyebrow. "For what, exactly?"

"Lying to investigators. Wasting my valuable time in the middle of a murder case."

"I didn't lie."

"By omission, *yes*, you did." She folded her arms over her breasts. "Why didn't you tell us you had an alibi?"

"The ATM footage."

"Yes, damn it."

He smiled. "You're a good detective. I figured you'd find it."

Her cheeks flushed even pinker. She stepped closer and glared up at him. "Two people are *dead*, Scott. And my team and I are spending time on *you*."

A few stations down, Travis lay on the ground adjusting his scope. His hands stilled and he looked at Dani. Travis didn't like that the police had put Scott on their suspect list.

"I know you enjoy jerking people around," she was saying, "but this isn't funny."

"You know what else isn't funny?" Scott eased closer and lowered his voice. "You believing I shot an unarmed *woman* in the back."

She gazed up at him. "I never believed that."

"No?"

"No."

For a long moment they just stood there, locked in a staring contest. She blinked first and turned away.

Scott grabbed his binoculars and hooked them around his neck. She swept her gaze over the rifle range, where several dozen men were taking aim at distant metal plates. She looked back at Scott and her attention settled on the rifle in his hand.

Her brow furrowed. "What is that?"

The scope, she meant, not the gun. It was the same .300 Win Mag he always used.

"A Leupold scope. It's new." Which was an understatement. It wasn't even on the market yet, but Scott did some freelance work for various manufacturers, testing out products.

Dani stared at his gun, and he recognized the look in her eyes.

"Want to try it?"

She glanced up, and he could see the debate going on inside her head. Should she maintain her pissed-offedness or cave in to temptation?

Temptation won out, which for some crazy reason turned him on.

Dani pulled off her jacket and tossed it on a wooden cabinet that served as a table for car keys and boxes of ammo. Scott gave her his gun, and she examined the scope for a moment before setting the weapon carefully on the ground. He handed her some ear protectors. She arranged them on her head, then stretched out prone next to his rifle.

Scott stretched out beside her as she loaded a cartridge and gazed out at the target. She snugged the stock into her shoulder and peered through the scope. "Damn."

"I know."

Scott gazed out at the range as Dani settled in. The brisk northerly wind was tinged with sagebrush, reminding him of sniper school in the deserts of California. His training had been hot as hell, triple digits most days. But even with the scorching temperatures, it was worlds better than Afghanistan, where he'd go for hours at a time on a rooftop or an outcropping of rock, completely motionless and soaked with sweat. He wouldn't move an inch to eat or sleep or even take a piss as he looked out over a road or a valley, the invisible guardian angel to dozens of young troops. Protection was a waiting game, and even some highly skilled marksmen weren't cut out for it.

Beside him Dani took a deep breath.

"Wind's about fifteen miles per hour," he murmured. She pulled up and glanced at the range flag, then settled back with the gun. She didn't look at him, and all that emotion from earlier was gone now. She'd turned it off like a switch. It was a talent she had. Her nostrils flared slightly as she inhaled a breath. Exhaled.

And then she was serene.

Scott watched her for a moment, then lifted the binocs and waited. A full minute ticked by.

She pulled the trigger and a puff of dirt kicked up in front of the target six football fields away. Dani muttered a curse.

"Low and to the left." He eased the binoculars down and looked at her. "Relax."

She huffed out a breath of frustration. The distance was nothing special, not for her. But the wind made it harder. In sniper school he'd been trained to make intricate calculations in his head to adjust for wind and elevation. Dani used the Kentucky windage method, which she'd learned years ago at her family's deer lease, which basically meant she did it by instinct. Of course, she practiced, too. Shooting wasn't a skill you could let slide.

Dani chambered another round. She closed her eyes briefly and adjusted the stock against her shoulder. She took a deep breath.

Scott loved to watch her get in the zone. He loved her utter concentration, her intense focus. In some of his darker, needier moments he fantasized about her looking at him that way.

He lifted the binocs and waited.

Another small breath, barely perceptible.

Crack.

"Nailed it," Scott said.

"Really?"

The pride in her voice gave him a warm buzz.

Shooting-wise, there weren't a lot of SEALs who could touch him. Dani was the only civilian who even came close.

"Man," Travis said. "Sweet shot, Dani. It's windy as hell today, too."

She cleared the gun and sat up. "It's a nice scope." She looked at Scott as he stood up. "Will you keep it?"

"That's the plan."

He pulled her to her feet, then picked up his rifle.

"I've got to get going," Travis said, picking up his gun case and looking at Scott. "You want to come with me or—"

"I'll get a ride with Dani." Scott looked at her and caught her startled expression.

"Suit yourself." Travis nodded at her. "Nice shooting."

They watched him leave. Then they were standing alone together, surrounded by the popcornlike sound of gunfire.

She was thinking about the case again. Scott could see it in her eyes. He'd never seen her so worried about a case before, and he knew his involvement was making it harder for her.

"You know, you should have told me," she said. "I wasted half a day looking for an alibi for you."

He didn't say anything as he slung his gun over his shoulder and grabbed his phone off the wooden cabinet. He checked the screen. No messages, which shouldn't have surprised him, given what had happened this morning.

"You're not out of the woods yet. That Glock isn't in the database, but your prints are all over it." Dani paused and waited expectantly. "Well?"

"Well, what?"

"You have an alibi, so we know you didn't pull the trigger. But my lieutenant thinks you bought the gun for whoever did."

"Oh, yeah? What about you?"

She looked away. "I don't know what the hell to think anymore."

Scott stepped closer, and the confusion on her face put a knot in his chest. He didn't like that she didn't fully trust him.

"So, what is this, anyway?" She crossed her arms. "Why'd you call me out here on a workday?"

"Not a workday for me."

Her gaze narrowed, and he watched her figure it out. "You mean—"

"I'm on leave. Curtis informed me this morning."

"Until when?"

"Until we sort this mess out."

"But . . . your alibi. The ATM footage—"

"Doesn't mean shit if I knowingly provided the murder weapon. It's like you said—I'm not out of the woods yet." He looked away and tried to swallow down his bitterness.

"What are you going to do?"

He looked down at her. The genuine concern in her voice got to him, but he tried not to let it show.

"Come here," he said, stepping away from her.

"What?"

"I want to show you something."

• • •

Scott led her into the building, which had corrugated-metal walls and a concrete floor. Dani stood just inside the doorway for a moment to let her eyes adjust to the dim lighting. A muted *pop-pop* came from the back, and Dani looked past the reception counter to the indoor pistol range. The soundproof glass didn't quite block out the noise.

The guy behind the counter looked bulked up on steroids and was covered with tattoos. His gaze was on Dani as they approached the counter.

"We're here to see Joe," Scott said.

A man poked his head out of an office behind the counter. "Come on back."

Scott led Dani into the office. The walls were lined with deer and elk heads that stared sightlessly at one another across the room.

"Joe Camden," Scott said, "Detective Daniele Harper with SMPD."

Dani shook the man's hand. She pegged him for military, probably navy, judging from the faded anchor on his forearm.

"Dax Harper's sister," Camden said.

She forced a smile. "That's me."

He looked her over skeptically, obviously failing to see the resemblance between Dani and her six-foot-four, 250-pound brother.

"How is he?" Camden asked. "Haven't seen him around lately."

"He's with Austin PD now."

Camden nodded and turned to Scott. "I pulled up everything for the weekend in question. It's all yours. I'm headed out for lunch, so make yourselves at home."

Dani watched in disbelief as he walked out of his office, leaving them alone with his desk and his file cabinets and his laptop, for crying out loud.

She shot a look at Scott, who had already taken over the guy's chair. "He's just going to leave us alone with his computer? What the hell?"

"Sit down."

Dani glanced around. A couple of metal folding chairs were against the wall, and she dragged one of them behind the desk beside Scott. He was scrolling through video footage on Camden's laptop.

"Scott, what is this about?"

He ignored her, intent on the screen as he fast-forwarded through the footage. Dani recognized a bird's-eye view of the reception counter just outside the door.

A steady stream of customers flowed through the doors with dizzying speed. The vast majority were men. Most wore baseball caps. They zipped up to the counter, showed ID, paid the attendant, then zipped out the door or back to the pistol range.

Scott tapped the mouse and the footage froze. "Here."

Dani leaned closer. The picture was blurry, but she'd recognize the wide shoulders and military-straight posture anywhere. Scott's face was hidden beneath the brim of a navy-blue Astros cap.

"Ten twenty-seven A.M.," Scott said. "I'm usually here Saturdays by ten thirty."

"What—"

"Just watch." He tapped the mouse, and the video started moving again.

Dani scooted her chair closer, so close she could see the side of Scott's jaw twitching. She focused on the computer screen as several more people zipped up to the counter.

Suddenly the film halted. "There," he said.

A large man stood at the counter. He wore a camo jacket and tan gloves. The brim of a hunting cap obscured his face.

"That's him."

Dani looked at Scott, and the intensity in his gaze sent a chill down her spine.

"Who?"

"I was in here one Saturday using the outdoor pistol range. This guy was shooting right beside me. There was a man on the other side of him—retired army, I think—and this guy was chatting him up, trying to get his opinion about a pistol he wanted to buy from his brother-in-law."

Dani's breath whooshed out. "A Glock nine."

Scott tapped at the man's image on the screen. "He asked me to weigh in, tell him what I thought of the gun."

"So you handled it."

"I looked it over, burned through a mag. Gave him my professional opinion."

"Which was?"

"It was fine for a Glock, if that's what you're into."

Dani stared at the screen, a tight knot of dread forming in her gut. She looked at the date stamp.

"February fourth." She leaned her elbows on her knees and buried her head in her hands.

"It was pretty cold that day," Scott said. "He was wearing gloves, and I didn't think much about it at the time. He was clumsy with the gun, not much of a shot. But I'm thinking now that was an act."

She didn't look up. *February fourth.* Five and a half months before the murders. Two and a half months before Tessa Lovett moved here.

She felt dizzy, sick. A dull ache was forming in the back of her head and seemed to be oozing up her skull.

"Dani, look at me."

She lifted her gaze. "Do you realize what this means? This isn't some . . . some . . . crime of passion. This is . . ." She looked helplessly at the screen. "I don't know *what* this is!"

"I do. This is me being framed for murder."

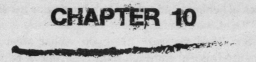

CHAPTER 10

"What is Black's connection to the victims?" Sean asked, leaning back in his chair. He laced his hands behind his head and stared at the whiteboard where everything they knew so far had been mapped out.

"He doesn't have one," Dani replied.

"How do you know?"

"He swears he doesn't know either of them," she said. "Never laid eyes on them until he saw their bodies at the crime scene."

Sean looked at Ric, and Dani felt a stab of annoyance. "Are you suggesting he's lying?" she asked.

Sean shrugged. "People lie to us all the time. Why would Scott Black be any different?"

She took a deep breath and tried to tamp down her temper. Sean was needling her, had been since the beginning of the case. He'd picked up on her personal connection to their prime suspect, and he wasn't going to let it go. And he shouldn't. Sean could be a pain sometimes, but he was a good detective, and he was right that they had to look at every suspect without bias.

"Ric, what do you think?" she asked.

He was standing beside the whiteboard, arms folded over his chest as he studied the crime-scene photos.

"Ric?"

"Why would they try to frame him?" He looked at Dani. "Assuming your theory's right and this is a setup."

Her theory *was* right, but she didn't want to argue that point right now.

"Question is, why Scott Black?" Ric asked.

"I don't know." She hated that she understood so little about this case, and she was the lead investigator. It made her feel incompetent. "Maybe it's as simple as his job."

"How do you mean?" Sean asked.

"I mean he's a ballistics expert, very well-known in his field. Plus he's ex-military."

Sean's gaze narrowed. "So?"

"So, he's a regular at this firing range, goes there every Saturday morning at ten thirty. He owns plenty of guns and handles them frequently. People hit him up for advice all the time about shooting and weapons. Even the equipment manufacturers ask him to test their products for them."

"Your point is?"

"My point is he handles firearms constantly, on the job and off. Some five-minute interaction with a random stranger who wanted advice on buying a gun wasn't going to stand out." She waited for them to digest that idea. "Also, he works at the Delphi Center, where we routinely send our evidence in major cases, cases we're not equipped to handle here. If someone can undermine the integrity of the lab's chief firearms expert, that undermines the integrity of the whole lab. Basically, all our physical evidence becomes worthless if Scott is a suspect."

Silence stretched out as Dani's words sank in.

Ric turned to the whiteboard. "The timing's unusual."

Unusual? That was putting it mildly. More than any other element of the case, the timing was eating away at Dani like battery acid. Her stomach roiled as she looked at the timeline drawn on the board. As of today, their timeline of relevant events had been extended from four days to more than five months.

February fourth. Someone had been plotting this crime since February fourth, months before Tessa Lovett even moved to town.

"Are we ready to say the professor's the true target now?" Ric asked. "Way back in February, the killer or killers couldn't even know this girl would be living here."

"Yeah, I'm thinking James Ayers is the true target," Dani said. "But, again, why? What's the motive? Even if we assume he was having an affair with this woman back when they worked together in New Mexico, it seems a little late for revenge, don't you think?" She looked at Ric, who was staring at the board as if some new clue would magically appear. "You still think it's reasonable the wife is behind all this?"

"I liked that theory at first, but . . ." Ric looked at her. "I'm liking it less now."

"Especially given the money situation," Sean added. "The wife's loaded and he's not. Guy doesn't even have a life insurance policy. What does she stand to gain from killing him?"

"Besides getting rid of a cheating husband?" Dani asked.

"Yeah, but she *claims* she didn't know he was having an affair."

"I don't buy that," Dani said. "I mean, the night of the murder, she was asleep at home when you showed up to notify her of her husband's death, right?" She looked at Ric.

"Yeah, so what?"

"So, if her husband was due home for dinner, but he still wasn't home by one in the morning, you'd think she'd be out looking for him or at least calling around," Dani said. "I know I would."

"Unless she'd already figured out he was with his girlfriend," Sean said.

"That's right." Dani nodded. "Plus, she lied to me when I interviewed her. She said she never met Tessa Lovett, but Oliver Junger says he saw them talking together at the university."

"So you think she did know about the affair," Ric stated.

"Hell, yes. Women know." Dani looked at the board. "What she might *not* have known was that this woman followed her husband here all the way from New Mexico. She seemed genuinely surprised about that."

"Okay, then, where are we?" Sean asked. "Who else besides the wife is pissed off enough to want this guy's dick shot off?"

"Maybe no one," Dani said.

Sean and Ric turned to look at her.

"I mean, maybe no one's pissed off at him. Maybe it's just supposed to look that way. Yes, this man was shot in the groin while he was with his mistress. And, yes, the woman was chased down and shot in the back. We've been reading those facts as signs this was a crime of passion, but maybe that's a ruse."

"Like the gun thing," Ric said.

"Exactly." Dani eased closer to the board and studied the timeline. "The killer didn't do this in the heat of anger. He's cold and calculating."

"He secured the murder weapon months in advance," Ric said.

"And he secured a fall guy, Scott Black," she added. "And then he waited, probably observing and tracking James's routines until he found just the right moment for the kill."

Sean shook his head.

"What?" Dani asked.

"A lot of assumptions."

"Like what?"

"Like this phantom shooter at the firing range, for one."

Dani laughed. "How is he a phantom? We have him on videotape."

"No, you have some guy walking up to a counter on videotape. And you have Scott Black *claiming* he was asked to fire that guy's gun that day. So, what? We can't even be sure that gun is the actual murder weapon."

"Scott said—"

"That's exactly my point!" Sean stood up. "Christ, Dani. Be objective for once. He *said* it's the same gun, but so what? What do you expect him to say? He's being looked at for murder."

Dani clenched her teeth and stared at the crime-scene photos, trying not to get defensive. She *knew* Scott hadn't done this. So she'd taken everything he'd told her at face value. But that wasn't her job. Her job was to be skeptical.

Her job was to be a cop.

"I mean, how can Black even remember all this in such detail?" Sean asked. "We're talking about some guy he had a conversation with five months ago. I hardly remember the guy who took my coffee order this morning."

Scott remembered because he had amazing snap-shot memory. It was a survival skill he'd developed during sniper training. He'd told Dani about memory drills in which his instructor would spread random objects out on a table covered by a tarp. The tarp would come off, and Scott would have thirty seconds to memorize every detail before the objects disappeared again and he'd have to draw a picture. Scott's observation skills were honed razor sharp, so it wasn't surprising to Dani that he could recall a long-ago encounter so vividly. But she couldn't say that here. She had to be objective.

Sean was watching her defiantly, waiting for her to leap to Scott's defense.

"Okay, you're right." She took a deep breath. "We need to nail down this theory before we eliminate Scott Black as a suspect."

"Which means nailing down who the hell this guy is in the video," Ric said.

"Right." She pulled a notepad from the pocket of her jacket. "We have a physical description but not a name. The range doesn't keep a customer database or even a sign-in log."

"Unbelievable," Sean said. "I have a harder time getting into my nephew's birthday party at Chuck E. Cheese's."

"It's totally believable," Ric said. "These are Second Amendment people. You can bet your ass they're not fans of databases and registries for gun owners."

"Okay, whatever." Dani was getting impatient. "We

have a physical description based on Scott's account and we have the security footage. No footage of the parking lot, unfortunately, so we don't have a vehicle."

Ric's phone buzzed and he quickly pulled it from his pocket. By his calm reaction, Dani could tell it wasn't Mia.

"I need to take this," he said, and stepped outside the room.

Dani looked at Sean. "We have a date and time, though. We could try gas stations in the area, see if maybe he stopped to fuel up or get a snack on the way to or from the range that morning. Those places definitely record vehicles coming and going."

"Sounds like a long shot."

"Try it anyway."

"What about you?" Sean asked.

"I'm still stuck on motive. If the professor is the true target, we need to find out who had a reason to want him dead. I keep coming back to his workplace. If this isn't a love triangle, then maybe the motive has to do with whatever they're doing there. We need to find out more about what they're working on."

"Wasn't Ric going to talk to someone there?" Sean asked. "That guy who hired him down from New Mexico?"

"Mike Kreznik. And he hired both victims, not just James."

Ric walked back into the room. The expression on his face made Dani's stomach tighten.

"What's wrong?"

"That was the university. I've been leaving messages for Kreznik, and he hasn't gotten back to me. Turns out he's dead."

"He . . . what?" Dani gaped at Ric.

"Killed in a house fire. I was at the crime scene, too. I watched them cart him out of there on a damn gurney. Had no idea it was him." Ric sank into a chair and ran a hand through his hair.

"A house fire," she stated, still not believing it.

"Damn, what are the odds?" Sean looked from Dani to Ric. "Arson or accidental?"

"They're still investigating." Ric gave Dani a dark look. "But my money's on arson."

• • •

Dani pulled into the Delphi Center parking lot and scanned the vehicles. No gunmetal-gray Dodge pickup, but she hadn't expected one. Scott was on leave, possibly *unpaid* leave, until this case could be sorted out, and who knew when that would happen? With each passing hour, her investigation seemed to be getting more complicated.

Dani pulled into a space at the edge of the lot and spotted the person she'd come to see tromping through the woods, trailed by a bedraggled group of students. Dani met them at the lab's back door, where they piled their shovels and spades into a long, flat tray.

Kelsey didn't look surprised to see her, so she'd obviously listened to Dani's phone message. The auburn-haired anthropologist turned to her students, who were swilling water from bottles and canteens.

"Group A, you're on cleanup," Kelsey said. "Hose down the equipment and spread everything out to dry. Group B, get the bone bins into Lab Three. We'll be examining them next class."

The students swung into motion, sorting through gear and pulling out hoses.

"Hi," Kelsey greeted Dani. Her cheeks were pink, and clearly she'd spent most of the day in the sun. "You're here about Mike Kreznik."

"Sorry to interrupt your class."

"We're finished. Come on." She motioned for Dani to follow her, then took out an ID badge and swiped her way into the building.

Dani walked alongside her down a cold, dim corridor past a row of windows. Beyond the glass she saw rows of stainless steel tables—empty, thank goodness—and long black counters topped with microscopes and other high-tech equipment she couldn't identify.

Kelsey ushered her into an office and nodded at a chair. "Have a seat. I just need to wash up."

Dani took a plastic chair opposite Kelsey's desk. Dani had been in here once before. It was just as messy as Dani remembered, but Kelsey had added to her collection of bone-themed memorabilia, including a skull-shaped coffee mug.

Kelsey whisked back into the room with a pair of water bottles. "Drink?"

"Thanks, I'm fine."

"Hot out there." Kelsey pulled off her baseball cap and tossed it aside as she sat down. "So, the remains have already been released to the family, I'm afraid. I can't actually show you the body."

"Not a problem," Dani said with relief. She was still squeamish from the autopsies. "I'm mostly interested in your conclusions."

Kelsey tapped at her computer keyboard and pulled up a report. "Well, as you know, they don't call me in to do a postmortem unless it's bad."

"I'm aware."

"Skeletons, floaters, fire vics—those are my typical cases." She turned to the computer screen and brought up an X-ray image of a skull. "The body was burned beyond recognition and no jewelry was recovered. I used dental records to make a positive ID. Did you talk to Clarke County Fire and Rescue?"

"That's why I'm here. Based on their preliminary findings, they don't think it's arson. They're leaning toward an accidental fire, with the point of origin being a hot-water heater with a faulty pilot. At least, they *were* thinking that until I told them about the connection to the other two murder victims."

Kelsey's brow furrowed. "What connection?"

"Kreznik worked at the university in the same department as the two people who were recently murdered at Woodlake Park."

"The biology professor and his girlfriend."

"That's right."

"Wow." Kelsey looked at her screen. "I wasn't aware of that." She sighed. "But it doesn't change my findings. I discovered no indication of premortem injury. That includes bone trauma, lead wipe—"

"Lead wipe?"

"Tiny metallic deposits left behind when a bullet passes through bone. Furthermore, fire investigators recovered no bullets or shell casings at the scene."

"But can you always tell if there was foul play?" Dani asked. "I mean, what if he was strangled or smothered before the fire, for example? You might not necessarily be able to tell from the bones, right?"

"Depends. In about a third of manual strangulation cases, we see a broken hyoid bone. That was actually one of the bones that remained intact with this victim.

However, if someone put a pillow over his face? Or poisoned him to death and then set his house on fire? You're right, we wouldn't see evidence of that from the bones. And the remaining soft tissue was severely damaged in this case."

"The fire chief said it looked like he died in his bed."

"Correct. The lack of bone trauma, coupled with a lack of suspicious evidence at the scene, such as accelerants, et cetera, led them to believe this was an accidental fire, not arson. Your investigation will prompt them to reconsider that, I'm guessing."

Dani's phone buzzed and she checked the number. Ric. "Sorry. You mind?"

"Not at all." Kelsey gestured to the nearby door. "Take it in the lab, if you like."

Dani got up and stepped into the adjacent laboratory. She glanced around nervously, but the steel tables were empty, free of any decaying bones or rotting corpses.

Dani answered the call. "Hey, what's up?"

"Where are you?" Ric asked, his tone urgent.

"At the Delphi Center interviewing Kelsey Quinn, who autopsied Kreznik. She's got nothing to indicate anything other than accidental death. Fire investigators are saying there's no sign of foul play."

"Yeah, don't be so sure. I'm at the university. Just finished talking to Dr. Oliver Junger."

"The man I interviewed yesterday."

"Hell of a nice guy," Ric quipped.

"Yeah, I know."

"Listen, I got a link between Ayers and Kreznik, beyond the fact that they work in the same department. Junger tells me his boss Kreznik has been a biology professor here for three years. Before that he worked at a place called Trinity University."

"There's an original name."

"No kidding. But guess where this Trinity University is located."

A chill went down Dani's spine. "Don't tell me it's in New Mexico."

"Just outside Albuquerque, same school where Tessa and James used to work. And that's not all. We've got something interesting on the cell phone records. Both Tessa and James placed multiple calls to the same phone number at Trinity the week before they were murdered."

Dani stared at the shiny metal table in front of her, her thoughts racing a mile a minute.

"Dani? You there?"

"Yeah. What are you thinking?"

"I'm thinking this case is getting weirder by the minute. All three of them come from the same place and turn up dead in the same week." Ric paused. "Why? What are you thinking?"

"I'm thinking it may be time for a field trip."

CHAPTER 11

Scott pulled up to Dani's house and parked. He shouldn't be here. He was still a suspect, and just the sight of his truck outside her place might get her in trouble. He wanted to talk to her, even though what he needed to do was leave her alone.

But he couldn't. He'd never been able to.

Scott walked up to her door and knocked. She didn't answer and he knocked again, harder this time. She was definitely home. Her truck was in the driveway and he could hear the TV going inside—news, from the sound of it.

Finally the door swung open. Once again, she was in yoga pants with her feet bare. Instead of a loose-fitting T-shirt, tonight she had on a skimpy black top that clung to her body.

"You shouldn't be here."

"Give me a minute."

She stepped back to let him in, then cast a cautious look up and down the street before closing the door. He thought she was worried about someone seeing him, but then she flipped the bolt.

His gaze narrowed. "What's wrong?"

"Nothing." She led him into the kitchen and went to the fridge to pull out a frozen lasagna. "You eaten yet?"

"I'm good." He leaned back against her counter and

looked around. Piles of mail were stacked on one end of the breakfast table. On the other end sat a purse, a phone charger, and Dani's favorite leather jacket. A small roll-on suitcase stood beside the back door.

"You going somewhere?"

"What? No."

She was lying again, but he didn't know why. She slid her dinner into the oven and set the timer.

"That'd be faster in the microwave."

"Yeah, but it's better in the oven." She grabbed a bottle of water from the counter and took a swig, watching him with a wary look in her eyes. "What brings you here?"

"Bryce Maxwell."

"Who's that?"

"Retired army guy I told you about. He was at the range with me that day your suspect showed up."

At the word "suspect" her brow furrowed.

"I tracked him down and talked to him, and he remembers the interaction." Scott pulled a slip of paper from his pocket and slid it across the counter toward her. "Here's his contact info so you can follow up."

She didn't even glance at the paper. "Follow up? On *your* interview?"

"That's right."

She stepped closer, and Scott tried not to look at her breasts in that shirt. "You're not investigating this case. The police are."

"You sure?"

Her cheeks flushed. "I can't talk to you about this. You should know that. You shouldn't be dropping by my house in the middle of the investigation."

For a moment they stared at each other. She

looked frustrated, and he took some sort of perverse pleasure in that. He was frustrated, too. About a lot of things.

"And anyway, you can't just go around interviewing people."

"Oh, yeah? Last I checked it's a free country."

"Don't give me that crap, Scott! You're interfering with a homicide investigation and I won't stand for it!"

He stared down at her. He was almost a foot taller and probably outweighed her by a hundred pounds. It was ridiculous the way she glared up at him with that challenge in her eyes. Did she think she could arrest him? Take him down? He'd have her disarmed and underneath him in about two seconds. Just the thought of it sent a shot of lust through him.

He eased closer, but she stood her ground.

"Stay away from my case," she said.

"I can't."

"Try."

"How about you guys try figuring out who murdered two people so I can clear my name and get back to work?"

"We *are* trying. We've been working round the clock since the call came in. We've got three detectives and a uniform working full-time on this thing."

Her phone buzzed on the counter, and she ducked around him to answer it.

Scott tipped his head back and tried to rein in his temper. Sparring with her wasn't going to help. But he wasn't going to just sit around and wait for detectives to stumble onto leads he already had. Dani was a good investigator, but her department was overwhelmed, and Scott knew better than most how things could slip through the cracks.

She had her back to him now, talking quietly into her phone, and from her tone it sounded work related. His gaze fell on the suitcase again. Where the hell was she going? And why wouldn't she tell him?

Didn't matter. He'd find out.

She hung up and turned around. For a moment she just looked at him. Then she walked across the kitchen and switched off the oven.

"So much for dinner. I have to go in."

"Anything serious?"

She shrugged. "The usual." She glanced at the piece of paper he'd left on the counter. "Look, I appreciate the name."

"And you'll go interview him?"

She gave him an impatient look. "I can't discuss this with you."

"In other words, I'm still a suspect."

She just looked at him, not confirming or denying anything, which told him what he needed to know.

He shook his head and walked to the front door. She followed him and reached around him to flip the bolt, and he stepped outside as she glanced nervously up and down the street.

"Hey."

Her gaze snapped to his.

"What's wrong, Daniele?"

"Nothing."

Another lie for the triple.

"Thank you for the lead," she said.

"Anytime."

• • •

Brooke waved at the security guard and stepped through the glass door into sweltering night. Working in a windowless laboratory, she tended to lose track of time, and she was surprised to see that the sun had already dipped below the trees. The mosquitoes were out in full force, and she swatted them away from her face as she made her way to the parking lot.

Nine o'clock, and there were still plenty of cars. Would she ever work at a place where everyone wasn't a workaholic?

Doubtful.

Her profession tended to attract people who were a little bit geeky and a whole lot passionate about what they did—people who paid attention to details, but not necessarily those of a personal nature. She herself was a prime example. She'd been working seven days straight and had no break in sight. She was taking work home with her tonight and planned to be right back here early in the morning.

Her phone chimed as she neared the parking lot. She didn't recognize the number, so she stuffed it back into the pocket of her jeans. As she reached her car, it chimed again.

She pulled it out and stared down at the screen. It could be her ex-boyfriend calling from a friend's phone. She wouldn't put it past him to spoof his number, either. But maybe it was a coworker.

"Porter," she answered.

"Brooke?" The voice was low and masculine, and she recognized Sean's Southern accent in that one syllable. "You working late?"

She looked around, instantly on guard. "How did you know that?"

"Just a guess."

"How did you get this number?"

"I'm a detective."

She checked the area around her car before sliding behind the wheel and locking the doors. Sean Byrne had tracked down her number. Her *unlisted* number. She should definitely be pissed, but she wasn't and she didn't know why.

"You there?"

"What is it you want, Detective?"

"First off, it's Sean. And I wanted to see if we could catch up on some things about the case."

"I just left work for the evening, so—"

"Same here. Want to meet for dinner?"

She stared through her windshield at the darkening woods. She hardly knew him, and he wanted to have dinner with her? The mere mention of food had her stomach rumbling.

"I assume you're hungry," he said. "I know I am. How about Smoky J's?"

"Actually, I'm not hungry. I was going to go home and get some work done."

"How about a drink, then? What about Schmitt's Beer Garden?"

She started up her car, and her heart was racing. Was this a date, or did he really just want to talk about the case? She highly doubted that was all he wanted.

She pictured him in her lab earlier, all tall and confident and peering over her shoulder while she worked. He'd smelled good. It was a silly thing to notice, but she definitely had.

She should say no. If he really wanted to know about the case, he should call her in the morning at work, where she'd have her notes and everything in front of her.

"Brooke?"

"Yeah."

"You know Schmitt's?"

"What time?"

"I'm leaving the station house now. I can meet you in ten minutes."

"Give me fifteen. But I can't stay long."

"It won't take long, I promise."

She highly doubted that, too.

• • •

Sean watched her walk into the bar. Short and slim, she didn't attract much notice as she slipped through the crowd of beer-swilling frat boys near the counter. Sean caught her eye and waved her toward the back, where he'd snagged them an empty picnic table on the patio.

She didn't look happy to be here, and he doubted it was just because of the frat boys and the country music.

Usually, Sean didn't have trouble getting a woman to meet him for drinks or anything else. But Brooke Porter wasn't usual, not in any way. Was that why he was here? Maybe. He had never been one to back down from a challenge, especially where a woman was concerned.

She stopped beside the picnic table and gazed down at him for a moment before swinging her leg over the bench and sitting directly across from him.

"Hey," he said.

"Hi."

A waitress stopped by and saved them from more small talk. Brooke ordered a Guinness. It seemed like a heavy beer for her, but he kept his comments to himself and asked for a Shiner bock.

When they were alone again, Sean looked her over. "You know what I want to talk about?"

"No, but I can guess." She glanced around the bar, and he could tell Schmitt's wasn't her scene. "You don't like my findings."

Not what he'd expected her to say. "Like doesn't figure into it. Findings are findings. I'm an investigator, so it's my job to be objective."

She arched an eyebrow at him, and he noticed her eyes were an unusual shade of . . . something. Not really blue or green, but somewhere in between.

"So you're *not* buddies with the suspect whose prints are all over the murder weapon?" she asked.

"Nope."

She didn't say anything.

Sean smiled. "What, you don't believe me?"

She shrugged. "Law enforcement's a tight community. He's testified in a lot of cases involving your department."

"True. But I barely know the guy. And even if I did, it wouldn't matter. Fact, I'd think you'd be the one with the problem, seeing as how you two work for the same forensics lab."

Another shrug. "Delphi's a big place. I don't know him."

The waitress dropped off their beers. Sean watched her sip the foam off the top of hers.

"I've been thinking about your results and I wanted to ask you a question."

She waited.

"You said you recovered prints from the grip and the slide. Not the trigger?"

"Trigger pulls are narrow. We don't always get prints there."

"I understand. What about the rest of the weapon?"

"Are you suggesting I'm not thorough?"

"I'm sure you're very thorough. But you said yourself you're not a gun person." He waited for her to say something, but she didn't. "Scott Black is, though."

"And?"

"And a guy like him, he doesn't just own a gun, he uses it. He handles it. Practices with it. Fieldstrips it and cleans it between uses, too. You see where I'm going here?"

"His prints would be on the inside."

"All over the inside. So the fact that you *didn't* find his prints there, when you found them all over the rest of the weapon? That raises some questions in my mind."

She sipped her beer and watched him. "You're right."

"I'm right about . . . ?"

"Well, as I said when you stopped by my lab un-invited, I wasn't finished with my examination yet. I make it a habit to go through everything twice, and on my second pass I *did*, in fact, recover a print from the back of the recoil-spring assembly. Unfortunately, it's only a partial."

"Why didn't you tell me?"

"I did. It's in the report I sent over. I emailed it to Ric"—she pulled out her phone and tapped the screen—"exactly three hours ago. You didn't read it?"

"Not yet." He watched her for a moment. "A partial, huh?"

"Yes, and it's not consistent with anything we have on Scott Black."

"Is that right."

"That's right. You know much about fingerprint identification?"

"Not near as much as you."

She ignored the compliment and leaned forward. "Well, you're basically looking at various ridge characteristics and analyzing points of comparison. You're looking for three basic patterns: loops, arches, and whorls. The more of a print or prints you have to look at, the more places you have to make a comparison. The standard varies as to how many matching points you need in order to draw a conclusion, with eight points being on the low end and twenty points being on the high end."

"And this partial print?"

"I found zero points of similarity. However, the print is small. There aren't a whole lot of ridge details for individualization."

"But you can rule out Black?"

She nodded. "I can rule out Black. That print was left by someone else."

He noticed the spark in her eyes. She was excited about this finding, and her excitement was contagious.

"You may be interested to know that the print is comprised of oil," she continued. "Do you know Mia, our microbiologist up in the DNA lab?"

"I know her."

"After microscopic examination, she believes the substance is CLP oil. Which is consistent with what you're talking about."

"Gun oil. He left the print when he was cleaning it."

"That would be my guess."

Sean looked across the crowded courtyard, running through scenarios. "And then he wiped the gun down—almost completely—sometime before Scott Black got his hands on it." Sean shook his head, not liking the scenario at all. If it was true, then Dani was right and they were dealing with someone extremely cold and calculating. And this crime had been premeditated not just days or weeks but *months* in advance.

He looked at Brooke for a long moment. "That's a good lead."

"How? I told you, it's a *partial* fingerprint. A small one. With so little ridge detail to go on, you may never be able to use it at trial."

Yes, but its existence on an otherwise squeaky-clean part of the murder weapon told him a lot. "I'll let the lawyers worry about that." Sean nodded at her almost-empty glass. "You want another round?"

"No."

He flagged down the waitress and pulled out his wallet.

Brooke's gaze narrowed. "Where are you going?"

"Back to work." He smiled. "It's a damn good lead, and I've got to follow it up."

•   •   •

Dani tossed and turned in her bed. She had way too many images tumbling through her mind.

She thought of Tessa Lovett sprawled facedown in the dirt.

She thought of Scott's steely gaze as he'd sat through that interview with Reynolds.

She thought of Scott at the bar, of the fierce look in his eyes when he'd grabbed her and kissed her. She'd been just as shocked as the first time, and heat spread through her system as she remembered the way he'd smelled, the way he'd tasted, the way his strong, hard body had felt pressed against hers.

She'd shooed him out of her house tonight, but she hadn't wanted to. What would have happened if he'd stayed?

Dani flipped onto her back and stared at the ceiling. She hated insomnia. She hated that Scott had the power to get her worked up like this. He'd always had that power, and he could do it with only a look. God help her if he ever really touched her. Really, *really* touched her. Not just a kiss.

She closed her eyes. She tried to focus on work and block out everything else. Crime didn't stop just because she was in lust with her brother's best friend. Or because she had a big homicide case. Tonight's callout had been a simple holdup at a fast-food place off the interstate. No injuries, thank goodness, but plenty of legwork all the same. After three hours at the scene, she'd left Minh there fingerprinting the glass door the perp had touched. With any luck it might lead to something because the perp had been either too stupid or too tweaked out on drugs to think about wearing gloves while committing an armed robbery.

Even if the prints didn't yield anything, a side view of his face had been captured on the restaurant's security cam. The footage would be running on local news stations tomorrow as part of the department's Crime Stoppers program. Ric was sure they'd get an arrest.

If only all her cases were so easy.

She blew out a sigh. Sleep wasn't happening tonight, at least not right now. Maybe after some TV. She tossed back the covers and reached for the lamp.

Creak.

Dani froze. She listened. Was that—?

Creak.

Her heart skittered. The sound came from the kitchen, near the back door. Quietly, she reached over and slid her Glock from the holster on the nightstand. Her phone was there, too—a rectangular shadow in the darkness. She eyed it anxiously. She could call 911, but they'd send a patrol car, and if it turned out to be a raccoon on her back porch, she'd never hear the end of it.

Sliding out of bed, she picked up her cell and muted it. Clutching her phone in one hand and her Glock in the other, she crept to the door of her bedroom, her pulse thrumming as she strained to listen. She held her pistol pointed upward, her index finger on the trigger. It was loaded and ready—thirteen in the magazine, one in the chamber. The habit had been ingrained by her father, but even if it hadn't been, she would have known anyway from the weight of it. Thirty-two ounces had a familiar feel to it.

Slowly and silently, she crept through her doorway and into the darkened hall. She hadn't heard any more sounds. The more she thought about the noises, the more certain she was they'd come from near the back door. The utility room was an add-on, an old one, and the slats on the porch back there were weathered and creaky. Maybe she had a possum.

She stayed in the darkest shadows, hugging the wall, her gaze trained on the opening at the end of the hallway where the shadows were paler. As she neared the opening, she slowly eased her head around the door-frame to peek into her darkened kitchen.

Nothing. No shadowy intruder inside her house, no silhouette at the back door. The porch looked empty, and moths and gnats flitted around the light.

Creak.

Dani blinked into the darkness. She held her breath.

A black figure lurched across the utility room and yanked open the door.

"Freeze!" she yelled, leaping around the corner and aiming her weapon at the empty doorway.

She sprinted through the kitchen and into the utility room. She tripped over a laundry basket and tumbled forward, hitting her chin on the dryer. The teeth-rattling smack was followed by a yelp of pain as her temple connected with something hard.

"Shit!" Her phone clattered to the floor and she lunged for it, tapping the emergency call button as she scrambled to her feet. Miraculously, she'd held on to her Glock when she tripped, but it had cost her, and now pain was shooting up her elbow.

"Nine-one-one. Please state your emergency."

Dani raced outside and ducked low behind the deck railing. Where had he gone? She saw no person, no movement, not so much as a shadow.

"Hello?" The dispatcher's voice sounded far away, and Dani rattled off her address and the words "potentially armed intruder."

Movement near her driveway.

Dani sprinted after the shadow, but it darted behind her neighbor's hedge. Dani raced to the cover of her truck and peered over the hood.

Where had he gone?

A dog started barking, pulling her attention across the street in time to see a black-clad figure two houses down, pulling himself over a fence.

"Police! Stop!"

She ran toward him, arms and legs pumping. She dodged around a fire hydrant and then hurdled a scooter that had been abandoned at the end of a driveway. Lights went on in the house where the dog was barking its head off now. Another dog started up, and another, and pretty soon there was a chorus of hysterical barks.

Dani tossed her phone to the ground and used her free hand to haul herself to the top of the fence, scraping the wood for purchase with her bare feet. She hauled herself over and landed in the dirt, clutching her weapon. She was in a backyard with a pool. She looked around frantically.

She glimpsed a shadow near the garage and raced after it. A gate opened with a squeak, slammed shut. Dani dashed across the yard in pursuit. He'd thrown a trash can in her path. She shoved it aside, then yanked open the gate and rushed through. She sprinted down the driveway and took cover behind a car as she glanced up and down the street.

An engine roared to life at the end of the block. Brakes squealed. She took off after the dark pickup, but her heart sank as she did because she knew it was hopeless. It was too far away to catch, too far away to even read a plate. Another squeal of brakes as it careened around the corner.

Dani cursed and ran after it. Her run slowed to a jog as the engine noise faded away.

CHAPTER 12

"He used a glass cutter."

Dani turned her attention away from the chaos in her driveway to see what Ric was talking about.

"See?" He pointed at the small rectangular pane sitting atop her dryer.

"I'll be damned," Jasper muttered. "Never seen that before."

The three of them were crowded into Dani's laundry room beside the point of entry. The small, bump-out addition had a shorter clearance than the rest of the house, and Jasper had to keep his head ducked low just to stand inside.

Dani hadn't even noticed the pane of glass. The little suction cup attached to the pane explained why she hadn't heard a shattering noise when the perp entered her house.

"So . . . it looks like he took out that piece of glass, then reached in and flipped the bolt," she said.

"That would be my guess." Ric gave her a dark look. It was a little more sophisticated than a typical break-in.

Dani adjusted the paper towel she was holding at her elbow. She'd fallen on a metal dustpan when she tripped, and the cut had bled profusely. It was deep, but not enough to warrant stitches.

In addition to the T-shirt she'd worn to bed, Dani now had on a pair of jeans she'd grabbed off the floor of her bedroom when the first patrol car showed up. There were streaks of blood on the leg, and people kept staring at her.

"I can run you in for that," Ric said, nodding at her cut.

"I'm fine. Looks worse than it is."

"You sure?"

"Yeah."

She squeezed past him and tromped down her back porch to survey the traffic jam in front of her house. It looked like a cop convention. Three patrol units, including Jasper's. Two unmarked vehicles. Ric's pickup truck.

"You sure you don't want me to call a bus?" Jasper asked now, and she shot him a glare.

"I'm *sure*."

When he'd first suggested an ambulance, she'd refused, and he'd started to call one anyway until Dani threatened to have his badge. Not that she had that kind of rank, but the phrase had a nice ring to it, plus the added benefit of making him back down.

Ric joined them on the driveway, looking at the uniformed officers milling around in her front yard. Now that the hubbub had died down, it was social hour. Some of Dani's new neighbors stood on their porches in sweatpants and bathrobes, obviously wondering what all the fuss was about. Dani had given a few people the nutshell version and received suspicious looks in return, as though she'd brought some kind of bad luck with her when she moved into the neighborhood.

She turned away from the spectacle to look at Ric. He didn't seem happy, and she wondered if he was thinking the same thing she was—that her break-in might be linked to the homicide case. She hadn't told him about the weird feelings she'd been having lately, like someone was watching her or casing her house. But Ric had definitely picked up on the vibe she was giving off tonight.

"You know, there have been some burglaries here in your neighborhood," Jasper said. "Two on Apple Tree back in June. Another over on Briarcliff last week."

"Those were smash-and-grab jobs," she said. "Cars, toolsheds. Nothing like this."

"So he got a laptop computer bag and a wallet," Ric said, "but he left the purse. Anything else missing?"

She shook her head and glanced back at her door. "I haven't noticed anything else, but—*damn it!*"

"What?"

"I have to get on a plane to Albuquerque tomorrow. My driver's license was stolen."

Ric watched her for a moment. "I can go."

"No."

"It's only twenty-four hours, right? I should be able to swing it."

"No way," she said.

Mia would kill her. And anyway, Dani was *not* going to let this incident throw off her game plan. She finally had a decent lead to follow, and she intended to follow it.

"I'll take my passport," she told Ric. She'd worry about getting her license replaced later. At least she had her badge, which she always kept on her night-stand beside her holster.

Dani dabbed her arm again. The bleeding had completely stopped, so she stuffed the paper towel into her pocket as a familiar white pickup rolled to a stop in front of her house. Dax hopped out. He looked around at all the cars, and his gaze homed in on her as he strode up the driveway.

"Good news travels fast." Dani shot a look at Ric, who shook his head.

"I didn't call him."

"I heard it on the scanner." Her brother rested his hand on her shoulder, which was the closest they got to hugging. "You okay?"

The number of questions loaded into those two little words made Dani's throat feel tight. She knew what he was really asking.

"I'm fine. No injuries." *Sexual or otherwise.*

"Except for your arm," Ric countered, looking at Dax. "She might need stitches."

"I do *not* need stitches. It's just a cut."

Dax rested his hands on his hips and frowned down at her. He was in street clothes. His favorite snakeskin boots, too, which meant he'd been out tonight. And he'd heard about this over the scanner at three in the morning? He must have been coming home from a hot date.

Dax gave her a long, searching look, then glanced at her back door, which stood ajar. Without a word, he walked inside to check things out.

Dani sighed, trying not to get annoyed. In fact, she appreciated the department-wide response more than she could say. She felt deeply touched. She took a lot of crap for being a woman and a cop's kid, but the guys had her back, there was no question of that.

"We need to interview your neighbors," Ric said. "See if anyone got a look at the truck."

"Yeah, just let me grab a jacket." And she had to put a bra on, too.

"I meant us, not you. This isn't your report, Dani."

"But—"

"We'll handle it," Ric said firmly. "Christine's already over there talking to the residents where the truck was parked, seeing if anyone saw anything. You're sure you didn't see a plate? Even a single digit?"

"I barely saw that it was a truck. It was out of there so fast."

"It's better than nothing."

Dax rejoined them on the driveway. He looked her up and down, obviously noticing her bare feet and her blood-streaked jeans with the Glock tucked in the waistband. He nodded his head toward her porch, signaling that he wanted a private conversation. Dani followed him.

"You didn't discharge your weapon?" he asked when they were alone.

"No, thank God. Can you imagine the paperwork? It was a simple burglary."

She tried to keep it light, but her brother wasn't buying it. He had a radar for stuff, and he rested his hand on her shoulder again.

"Are you really okay, Dani?"

"Yes." She forced a smile. "Really, I'm fine."

• • •

Nine hours later she still wasn't fine, but she was closer. She had on fresh clothes and a fresh bandage on her elbow, and she'd managed to pick out most of the splinters she'd gotten embedded in her feet while scaling her neighbor's fence.

She'd had exactly zero minutes of sleep, but the

supersize coffee she'd bought in the airport was keeping her eyes open. And her headache was mostly gone now, thanks to the aspirin she'd been popping like Tic Tacs.

Dani peered out the airplane window at the mountains below. The land looked dry. Thirsty. As they circled the city, she gazed down at the sun-drenched terrain and wondered if the key to her investigation was somewhere below.

Everything was an enigma. Most of all, Scott's involvement. It didn't make sense. His prints were all over the murder weapon. Six good prints.

And then one partial print that belonged to someone else.

Whose was it? The man at the gun range? Was he the killer? But who was he and why had he framed Scott?

If, in fact, he *had* framed Scott. As much as Dani hated to admit it, Sean had a point. No matter what Scott told them, they had no concrete evidence that the gun Scott had handled at the shooting range was actually the murder weapon. It was all speculation, not fact.

The facts they did have were pretty damning. A Glock nine had been used to kill two people. The gun had been recovered near the crime scene. It had one victim's blood on it, along with Scott's fingerprints.

As those facts percolated in Dani's head, her feeling of dread increased. Those facts alone could be enough for an arrest. Those facts, plus some skillful courtroom maneuvering, might be enough for a conviction. Scott could be looking at life in prison, or even the death penalty.

Dani shuddered. She couldn't get sucked into worst-case scenarios. She wouldn't. What she *would* do was uncover a different version of events that explained the facts. Three people were dead. They shared a common field of expertise and two common places of employment. It was up to Dani to figure out what that meant.

She leaned her head back against the seat and her thoughts drifted to her break-in.

Don't think about it.

She tried to force it out of her mind. No point in fretting over it until and unless Ric called with a lead. Which might not happen.

After finishing the canvass of two entire blocks in her neighborhood, police hadn't found a single person who'd noticed the pickup truck used by Dani's intruder. No one had noticed anyone loitering around in recent days, or even any suspicious-looking strangers passing through.

Maybe it was just some kid looking for drug money. It was possible. As Jasper had pointed out, there *had* been a string of burglaries in her area recently.

But she sensed this was different. Several elements of the crime made her think this wasn't just some teen looking for a few bucks to support his habit. The glass cutter, for one. And the vehicle, for another. And then there was the exit route. He'd taken the back way out of her neighborhood, avoiding the multiple traffic cams on Main Street that might have caught him on tape. Plan or coincidence? Dani didn't know.

But she had a feeling.

Stop thinking about it.

Her thoughts drifted to Scott. She closed her eyes and imagined she was with him again, pressed against his body as he kissed her with so much pent-up frustration she'd been dizzy from it. Where had all that come from? And what the hell did it mean?

The first kiss had caught her totally off guard, and she'd chalked it up to New Year's Eve insanity.

The other night seemed different, though. Was he trying to start something?

Not likely. They'd been friends for years and he'd never shown that kind of interest in her. Her brothers would definitely freak. They loved Scott, but as a buddy, not a boyfriend for their sister.

Scott's exploits were legendary. As a teenager he'd been a daredevil, always drumming up crazy things to do—cliff jumping, free-climbing, drag racing. Posted speed limits and NO TRESPASSING signs meant nothing to him.

His exploits with women were just as notorious, especially after he'd become a SEAL. He'd come back from BUD/S with an air of confidence that was like catnip for females, who noticed him wherever he went. Of course, his body didn't hurt. And those intense blue eyes.

That was about the time Dani had started to steer clear of him. She never wanted to be lumped in with those fawning women. She never wanted Scott to think of her like that. She had her pride.

But she didn't want him to think of her as Drew's baby sister, either, which was how he'd always treated her . . . with the notable exception of New Year's Eve.

And the other night.

She couldn't figure it out. She wasn't his type. She knew what kind of woman drew his attention because she'd seen it happen with her own eyes. He went for women who had blond hair and big boobs and flirty smiles that seemed to say, *Bring it on.*

Dani had none of those things. She had average looks and wore no-nonsense clothes, and she didn't flirt with men, she argued. It was just what she did. She'd grown up in a house full of males, and the only way to get anything was to be pushy about it. Her mother often suggested Dani would have more of a social life if she'd tone it down around men, but that wasn't Dani's style, and she didn't intend to change now.

She gripped the armrests as they came in for a bumpy landing. Dani didn't like flying and wasn't looking forward to the return trip tomorrow. But with any luck this whole thing would be over soon. She planned to get in and out of Albuquerque within twenty-four hours. Dani's boss had approved the quick trip when he heard about the connection of all three victims to Trinity University. It was too big an overlap to ignore, and everyone agreed that someone had to follow up on the lead.

She needed a change, however brief. She needed to get away, clear her head, and find a fresh angle on the case. She also needed a break from home. Dax had offered to have her window repaired while she was out of town, and she'd taken him up on it, ridiculously grateful to be able to come home to a fixed door. She didn't like that she felt so paranoid. She was a cop. She was trained in self-defense and she slept with her service weapon within reach.

But in spite of all that, she was still a woman living alone, and every time she looked at her back door now she felt violated. Some nameless, faceless man had broken into her home *while she'd been there*, tucked into bed with the illusion of safety draped over her like a blanket. It made her feel weak and vulnerable and severely pissed off.

So this little business trip her department was fund-

ing couldn't have come at a better time. She needed a
break from a lot of things, including Scott.

When they reached the gate, Dani pulled her carry-
on from the overhead bin and filed past the cockpit,
giving the pilot a nod. She'd introduced herself to him
before takeoff, and he'd welcomed her aboard with her
sidearm and badge, happy to have a potential air mar-
shal on the flight. Dani navigated her way through the
terminal, which was teeming with summer travelers in
cutoff shorts and flip-flops. The crowd seemed unusually thick today, but maybe she was imagining it. Still,
she felt a prickle of unease as she made her way through
the masses.

When she finally reached the car rental area, the
prickle of unease turned to full-blown worry. People
crowded the waiting area, lounging against backpacks
and duffel bags and guitar cases. It was definitely a
young group, with plenty of tattoos and piercings on
display. Everyone was either manically texting or looking stoned out of their minds.

Dani maneuvered her way into the shortest line
and eavesdropped on the conversation at the counter,
where a rental agent was arguing with a young woman
over a reservation.

Damn it, she should have booked something ahead.
Not that she'd had much lead time.

"You'll never get a car."

She whirled around, and Scott's blue eyes stared
down at her. Panic zinged through her.

"*What* are you doing here?"

"Same thing you are." His mouth curved into a smirk.
"I'm headed for Trinity University. It's sixty miles north
of town. Or so I'm told."

"But—"

"There's a music fest in Santa Fe. Everything's over-booked."

Dani stared up at him with disbelief. Had he been on her flight? Impossible. She definitely would have noticed him.

"I was on the nine-fifteen," he said, reading her mind.

"Then why are you still here?"

It was after one o'clock, so he had to have landed hours ago.

"Had to wait on my bag. And my rental car."

She watched him, letting that sink in. Of course he'd checked a bag. Scott didn't go anywhere without his gun, and he couldn't bring it aboard the flight without a badge.

"Wait. Just . . . stop." She held up her hand. "Trinity? So you know about the Kreznik connection. How?"

"How do you think? I've been investigating."

Frustration flooded her. "You're *not* a cop, Scott."

"Yeah, no kidding. I had to check my Sig."

"You can't just go around investigating a homicide. You shouldn't even be here!"

He eased closer, and she felt the tension in his body.

"Listen to me, Daniele." His voice was low and tinged with warning. "In the past week I've been set up for murder, interrogated like a criminal, and suspended from my job. You'd better believe I'm investigating. I need to clear my name or my reputation is history. Do you understand what that means?"

She stared up at him, shocked by the raw anger in his eyes.

"Every case I've ever touched, every trial I've ever testified in during the last four years, will be called into question. So, whether you like it or not, I don't give a damn. I'm not letting loose of this thing until I figure out exactly what the fuck is going on."

She stood there, speechless, as his blue eyes bored into her.

She glanced back at the reservation desk, where tensions were escalating between harried rental agents and their carless customers. Dani bit her lip and mulled her options. Without transportation, this was a wasted trip.

"Fine." She looked up at him. "Where's your car?"

CHAPTER 13

Sean pulled over behind a red SUV and surveyed Kreznik's fishing cabin. Or what was left of it. The whole front of the cabin had been reduced to a blackened shell. Sean noted the crime-scene van with the Delphi Center logo on its side as he got out. He flashed his badge at the county firefighters hanging out in front of the damaged house, and the yellow Labrador sitting at their feet got up and wagged his tail.

"Is Putnam here?" Sean asked. The sheriff's deputy in charge of this case had said he'd be here this morning.

"You just missed him," one of the firefighters told Sean. "The CSI's still here, though. She can update you."

"She inside?"

"Around the back." The guy nodded toward a row of cottonwood trees that shaded what was left of the structure. Beyond the trees, the lot sloped down to the water and a wooden boathouse.

Sean tromped back, looking for the "she" in question, and he was happy to find Brooke crouched in the grass.

"Hey."

She glanced up and looked surprised, then wary. She stood up, and Sean smiled as he approached her. She wore gray coveralls with a Delphi Center logo on the breast pocket, and black leather work boots. Sean had seen Roland Delgado in identical coveralls the day before, but they looked a hell of a lot better on Brooke. Her knees were black with mud and she'd managed to get dirt on her cheek.

"What are you doing here?" she asked.

Was she glad to see him? Hard to tell, because she was tough to read. But he could hope.

"Oh, you know"—he stepped closer—"working."

"This is your case?"

"Depends. I hear it might be arson?"

"Looking like it." She gazed up at him for a moment, maybe waiting for him to explain. When he didn't, she nodded toward the crawl space under the house. The back of the structure was built on stilts because the lot sloped down to the lake.

"I was just checking out that wooden piling. You saw the fire dog up there?"

"Marley," Sean said. "We've met before."

"Yeah, well, Marley sniffed out some hydrocarbons down under the house near this piling. Which also happens to be near the fire's point of origin, so that's a red flag."

"Show me."

She hesitated a moment, then ducked under the structure and led him to a piling in the center. It was dim and moldy smelling under the house, and the ground was still damp from the water used to douse the blaze. Sean looked up at the charred wood above his head, hoping the thing wasn't going to collapse on them.

"Originally the fire was thought to be caused by a faulty hot-water heater in a closet above us." She crouched in the mud, and Sean knelt beside her. "With no sign of accelerants in the home, investigators concluded the fire was accidental. But then they got hold of some other information that made them want to come back out for another look, so they called me out again, along with the canine unit." She glanced at him. "What's this have to do with your case, exactly?"

"I don't know yet. But the dead guy here has links to my other two murder vics."

Her eyebrows arched. "Really?"

"Really. So, what did you find this time around?"

"It's unconfirmed."

"What do you *think* you found?"

She hesitated a moment, as if deciding whether to trust him with an unproven theory.

"Anything you can tell me could really help me out here, Brooke."

"Okay, first thing is, this is a very unusual arson."

"How?"

"Well, there are all kinds of ways to intentionally set a fire, but most arsonists use accelerants, and they're almost always poured on the floor."

"And you looked for that?"

"I took samples of the carpet in the hallway near the hot-water heater closet, and also in the nearby bedroom where the victim was found. No accelerants."

"But Marley disagrees."

"He zeroed in on this piling." With a glove-covered hand, she pulled a penlight from the pocket of her coveralls and pointed it up at the charred wooden slats supporting the floor. Light pierced through gaps in the burned-out patches of subfloor. "See this here?"

"No."

"Here. You hold the flashlight." She handed it to him, and he aimed it at the wooden slat as she took out a pair of tweezers. She reached for something snagged on the wood. Slowly, carefully, she tugged loose a scrap of fabric.

"What is that?"

"I don't know yet, but it shouldn't be here. If I had to guess? It's the remnants of a rag that's been soaked in some kind of flammable liquid, maybe gasoline or kerosene. I found more of these a couple boards over."

"What'd he do, tack them underneath the house and then light 'em up?"

"Possibly." She deposited the scrap into a small metal container and carefully tapped shut the lid.

Sean pulled out his phone and took a picture of the burned wooden slats, then tucked his phone away and ducked low as he followed Brooke out from under the house.

She crouched down beside her evidence kit and stowed her tools. "Whoever did this? He's not your typical firebug." She stood up.

"Yeah, I'm not sure he's a firebug at all. I don't think pyromania is the motive here." Sean's gaze landed on the boathouse near the water. "You been down there yet?"

"No."

Sean walked down the grassy slope and stepped onto the wooden decking that led to the boathouse. A small motorboat covered in a dusty tarp was suspended about four feet out of the water. Sean stared at the hoisting mechanism for a moment. He flipped the switch to activate it, but nothing moved.

"The electrical's out to the house," Brooke said.

Sean looked at the power line connecting the boathouse to the main house. Once again he took out his phone and snapped a picture, this time of Kreznik's boat.

"What is it?" Brooke asked.

"I don't know yet."

"You really think it's related to your murder case?"

"Maybe. How long will it take you to run that evidence?"

She glanced up the hill at the blackened remains of Kreznik's fishing cabin. Then she looked back at him, and he had to resist the urge to reach out and wipe the smudge of dirt from her face.

"Well, I've got some other things on my plate. When do you need this? And don't you dare say today."

He smiled.

"You detectives are all alike." She sighed. "Okay, I'll bump you to the front of the line, but don't call and bug me."

"Who, me?"

"Interruptions slow me down."

"I got it."

"If I come up with anything, I'll call you."

"Call me even if you don't."

● ● ●

Sixty-three miles. Sixty minutes. But it may as well have been sixty hours, as far as Dani was concerned.

She sat in the passenger seat, her nerves jumping as she stared out the window and tried to quell her emotions.

Meanwhile, Scott seemed perfectly calm. And why shouldn't he be? He wasn't the one who stood to get fired for riding in a car with her.

Although *car* was being generous. It was more like a soda can. A bright yellow one. Scott had slid the seat back as far as it would go after climbing behind the wheel, and even then his knees were bent at a ridiculous angle. But there hadn't been much selection. None at all, in fact. All the rental car desks were overrun with festivalgoers, and Scott had been lucky to get anything. Dani would bet money he'd flirted his sexy ass off just to get the keys to this crappy little subcompact.

"So, what's the game plan?" Scott glanced at her. "Does Nathan Collins know you're coming?"

She turned to look at him.

"You have an appointment or you plan to just show up?"

She didn't answer. How did he know about Nathan Collins, specifically?

Collins was the science professor both James and Tessa had been in touch with just days before they were murdered. Dani had tracked down the name through the victims' cell phone records, but there was no way Scott had that kind of access. Was there a leak in her department? Had Ric or Sean talked to him?

Ric wouldn't do that. And neither would Sean, who'd made it clear he didn't even *like* Scott. No way would he leak sensitive information to him. But someone else might have.

Rachel.

Scott and the prosecutor were friends, possibly more. They definitely had a past together. Why did that bother her? Because it did. No point in pretending. She was jealous, which was absurd, because she had absolutely no claim on this man. None.

Scott took his eyes off the road to look at her. "What is this, the silent treatment?"

"How do you know about Nathan Collins? And don't you dare lie to me."

The corner of his mouth ticked up. "Or what?"

"Cut the crap, Scott. Who's feeding you information?"

"No one."

"Where'd you get that name?"

"Google."

"Excuse me?"

"Simple Internet search. Ayers and Kreznik co-authored a paper together when they were at Trinity. Something about nuclear plasmids. The third author on the paper was Nathan Collins, PhD." He glanced at her. "What, you didn't know?"

She looked out the window.

"Dani?"

"No, I didn't."

"Where'd *you* get his name?"

She shook her head. "I shouldn't be telling you any of this."

"You're not telling me jack. I'm telling *you*. These two guys worked with Collins on some project at Trinity. Tessa did, too. She didn't author the paper, but her name is in the acknowledgments. So you've got all three victims linked to the man."

Dani looked at him, and he seemed pretty pleased with himself to have given her something she didn't already have. She gritted her teeth and turned away.

"You're pissed I came out here."

"You're perceptive."

"And yet here you are with me." He gave her that cocky half smile that never failed to make her pulse race.

"You shouldn't be here, Scott. You should have stayed home and let the investigators handle this."

"I'm not about to sit back and let other people determine my fate. That's not how I operate." He glanced at her. "You're welcome, by the way."

"For what?"

"For chauffeuring you around all day. Now, get the chip off your shoulder and tell me how you want to do this."

She sighed. "He has a class that lets out at four thirty, according to the summer school course schedule. Then he has office hours. I plan to catch him there."

"You didn't tell him you were coming, then?"

"Why would I? If he's guilty of something criminal, that gives him time to run. Even if he's not, he might have something to hide, and that gives him time to concoct a story. It's best if I catch him off guard."

"You think he's a suspect?"

"I think he at least knows something. He has a connection to three people who were killed within three days, and all three of them called him shortly before they died. I mean, what are the odds that's a coincidence?"

She looked at Scott, but he didn't answer. He'd gone quiet again, like he had been for most of the drive. He could do that, just tune people out as though they didn't exist.

She shifted her attention to the scenery. They were well out of the city now, and the landscape was sparsely populated, dotted with livestock and scrub trees and the occasional house. She'd never been to New Mexico before, and it was prettier than she'd expected.

She looked at Scott, with his strong profile and his wide shoulders and his big hand resting on the steering wheel. Even in their ridiculous car, he looked utterly relaxed. There was a certain confidence about everything he did, and she envied it. It had been there all along, but his special ops training had magnified it.

He glanced at her. "What?"

"Nothing." She looked at the navigation system. "Your exit's coming up soon. Mission Hill."

"I got it."

She spotted the sign for Mission Hill, population thirty-two hundred. The college was nestled near the banks of a creek on the west side of town.

They exited the freeway, and a sign came into view along the feeder road.

"'Trinity University, three miles,'" Scott recited.

Dani took out her phone and pulled up the map of the campus as Scott navigated his way through town. Dani noted exactly four stoplights along Main Street. Besides a few restaurants and gas stations, it wasn't much of a town.

Another sign pointed to campus. Scott hung a left.

"Okay, according to the college website," Dani said, "there's visitor parking in front of the admissions office, and the biology building is just across the quad."

He silently followed her directions, slowing for the turn. The campus was small and compact. The buildings were white adobe with red-tile roofs, and many were surrounded by walled courtyards dripping with scarlet bougainvillea. The tallest building on campus was a Spanish-style church with a bell tower.

Scott was suspiciously quiet as he turned into the admissions office parking lot and slipped into a space. Dani undid her seat belt and grabbed her bag off the floor.

"I'll text you when I'm done."

He clamped a hand over her arm. "Hold on."

"What?"

"You're about to ambush a guy who may or may not have murdered three people."

"Most likely, he didn't murder anybody. I'm hoping he has a lead for me."

"Whatever. You're not going in there alone."

She shook off his grip. "You *cannot*, under any circumstances, be part of this interview. Get real, Scott."

He pulled out his Sig and checked the magazine.

"Hello? Are you listening?"

He pushed open the door. "Interview's all yours, babe, but I plan to be around."

"Scott—"

"Relax." He smiled. "You won't even know I'm there."

• • •

Scott was right.

She didn't even see him as she stood in the biology office questioning the clerk behind the counter about the whereabouts of Nathan Collins, who had failed to show up for his scheduled office hours.

"I'm afraid Dr. Collins is unavailable," the woman said cheerfully. She was short, midfifties, and had a friendly smile that was completely at odds with the bulldog look in her eyes. This woman was a gatekeeper, and Dani had found the best way to deal with gatekeepers was to get straight to the point. She pulled out her badge and slid it across the counter.

"I need to see the professor immediately. Where can I find him?"

The woman's brow furrowed as she stared down at

the shield, and Dani hoped she wouldn't make a fuss about jurisdiction. "Uh . . ." She glanced up. "Is this a university matter or—"

"I'm not at liberty to say. Where can I find him?"

Another glance at the badge, and she seemed to come to a decision. "Just a moment." She pivoted to her computer and did some clicking around, presumably bringing up the professor's contact info.

"Dr. Collins is on sabbatical right now. Would you like to leave a message for him on his department voice mail or—"

"Sabbatical?" Dani leaned over and peered down at the computer screen. "The course catalog has him teaching Introductory Biochem Tuesday/Thursday at three."

"That information is out-of-date, I'm afraid." The woman jotted some notes on a yellow sticky pad, then peeled it off and handed it over the counter. "Here is his contact information."

"Do you know if he's traveling or—"

"That I can't tell you."

"Can't or won't?"

She gave a saccharine smile. "All I have is his address."

Dani returned to the car, where Scott was already waiting in the driver's seat with the air-conditioning blasting. Her only proof that he'd been shadowing her was the mist of sweat on his forehead.

She tried not to get distracted by his large, muscular build as she leaned over and tapped the professor's address into the navigation system.

"You buy it?" Scott asked her.

"Buy what?"

"The sabbatical thing. Sounds like he changed his plans at the last minute."

"I don't know." Dani glanced at the biology building as Scott backed from the space. Where had he been lurking to overhear all that? She didn't know. He had the ability to drift in and out of places like smoke when he wanted to, which should have been impossible given his size.

"Looks like about a twenty-minute drive," Scott said, surveying the map that popped up on the navigation system.

"Appears to be a rural area."

"Lot of ranches around here."

Scott hung a left onto the road they'd used before as Dani checked her phone for any messages. She had a text from Ric.

Kreznik now a homicide. Case reopened by CCSO.

So the Clarke County Sheriff's Office had reclassified the case. Kelsey or the fire investigators must have turned up something new. Or maybe a witness had come forward with new information.

"There's something weird going on here," Scott said.

"I agree with you." Dani glanced around at the idyllic-looking campus. What did this place have to do with three recent homicides?

Scott pulled back onto Main Street, and Dani surveyed the town. Like the campus, it was small. The Spanish architecture gave it an old-fashioned look, although the school itself was younger than Dani.

"I assume you ran a background check on this guy Collins?" Scott asked.

"No arrests, no outstanding warrants, nothing much of interest. He has a six-month-old speeding ticket in

Roswell, New Mexico, and that's it. Guy's clean." She shook her head. "So it's probably not likely he suddenly decided to fly down to Texas and murder three people. But still . . ."

Scott looked at her. "Yeah?"

"I agree with you. Something's weird here." She glanced down at her phone again. "I'll get a better feel for it when I talk to Collins."

"You're good at reading people."

She glanced up at him, surprised by the compliment.

He looked at her. "Don't look so shocked. You're a skilled detective."

She turned away. Compliments made her uneasy, especially coming from Scott.

Silence settled over the car. Her nerves were back. She had misgivings about being here with him. Even aside from the thought of Reynolds finding out, she was worried Scott would distract her. He did that. Always. And she couldn't afford distractions right now because this investigation was getting increasingly complex and demanded her undivided attention.

"So, are you going to tell me about that?" He gave her a sidelong look.

"What?"

"That bruise on your chin."

She stared straight ahead through the windshield. She was wearing a linen blazer to conceal her sidearm today, so he hadn't seen her elbow yet. But she should have figured he'd notice the bruise that she'd mysteriously acquired after he'd left her house last night. Scott was observant.

"You get in a bar fight? Chase down a suspect?

What?" His tone was light, but the look on his face was serious. Maybe Drew had told him something.

"Someone broke into my house."

"You're serious?"

"Stole my wallet and my laptop off the kitchen table."

"And *assaulted* you?"

"No." She shot Scott a look. "I tripped over a laundry basket and hit my chin on the dryer."

"You fucking went after him?"

"He was in my house. What would you have done?"

Scott didn't answer. The muscles in his jaw tightened. She expected him to tell her she should have waited for the police to show up and help her, but if he thought that, he was smart enough to keep it to himself.

He cut a glance at her, and she could see the worry in his eyes. "Your personal laptop or your laptop from work?"

She scoffed. "We hardly have desktops at work. It was my Mac."

"Was there anything about the case on it?"

"You're thinking the break-in is related?"

"Aren't you?"

She didn't answer.

"Come on. You've been paranoid for days. I've seen it. Has someone been following you?"

She glanced at him.

"Tell me."

"I don't know. I thought . . ." She trailed off, not sure how much to say.

"Tell me, God·damn it."

"I thought maybe someone was tailing me. I never saw a car or anything. It was just a feeling I had over the past couple days."

He shook his head.

"What?"

"Don't discount your instincts, Daniele. You know better than that."

She took a deep breath and tried not to get defensive because he was right. Those feelings of suspicion—however fleeting—were her brain's way of warning her. Even if she didn't know where the feelings came from, they came from somewhere. That was what her dad always told her. *Trust your gut, Dani. Your gut knows things your mind hasn't put into words yet.* Some people called it cop instincts, but it applied to anyone.

She glanced at Scott, and he was still waiting for an answer.

"I don't know. It could be related, but I don't see how. My computer's password protected. And even if someone gets past the password, what is there to see? It's not like I have top secret files on it or anything. The only thing work related is my email."

"That could be important. Have you emailed any reports about the case?"

She'd gone through the same logic. "Not much. The ME's findings are on my computer at work. Kelsey emailed me an autopsy report yesterday, but that's about it."

Scott didn't say anything.

"Maybe someone's fishing around, trying to connect the dots."

"Trying to find out what *you know.* You were at the press conference the other day. Your face has been on TV."

"I realize that. But the whole incident could just as easily be some kid looking for drug money. My wallet had a fair amount of cash in it. I'd hit the ATM on the way home from work because I was traveling today . . . so maybe someone followed me home from the bank? And there have been some break-ins in my neighborhood lately."

"Same pattern?"

"Not really. Mostly cars."

"How'd he get in?"

"Took out one of the glass windowpanes on my back door, then reached in and flipped the bolt."

He gave her a skeptical look. "You didn't hear the noise?"

"He used a glass cutter."

"Damn it, Dani."

"He didn't want a confrontation. He took off as soon as he heard me. I didn't get a good look at him."

"What about his vehicle?"

That was the part she didn't like, the part that had kept her awake all night.

"He was in a pickup truck. He parked a couple blocks over and sped away before I could see the plate."

"Did you get a look at him when he got inside?"

"No."

"Hair color? Skin color? Anything at all?"

Leave it to Scott to zero in on the one detail that had kept her up all night tossing and turning.

"It was too dark. When he jumped in the truck and sped off, the interior light didn't come on. Neither did the headlights, so I really didn't see a thing. He basically disappeared."

Scott pulled into a gas station and swung into a parking space near the convenience store. He cut the engine and turned to face her, and she saw all her innermost worries reflected in his steely gaze.

She didn't believe her intruder was some kid looking for drug money. He had a pickup truck. And he'd
used a glass cutter. And he'd had the forethought to
disable the lights on his vehicle so he could get away
unseen. This wasn't some drugged-out teenager. This
was someone smart.

"Daniele—"

"Don't say it. I don't like it, either, okay?"

"Tell me you called your CSI."

"He fingerprinted my door, my purse, all of it, so
you can stop freaking out."

"Don't make light of this. He was in your goddamn
house."

"You think I don't know that?"

He sighed and rubbed his hand over his chin, which
was dark with stubble now. It had been a long, tedious
day, and it wasn't over yet.

Dani looked around the gas station. It was busy with
cars and trucks and SUVs. A red Ferrari was parked
beside a gas pump, and she did a double take as she
noticed the vanity license plate: AMISH.

She looked at Scott, who seemed oblivious of everything as he stared at her with that grim look. His
tone was protective. He was seriously concerned about
her—which did funny things to her heart.

"Why are we here?" she asked, changing the subject.
"We don't need gas."

"*I* need fuel." He shoved open his door. "Want anything?"

She didn't, but she welcomed the distraction. "I'll
have a Coke. The real deal, with sugar and caffeine."

He went into the store and Dani scrolled through
her phone, but didn't have any more updates. Scott

returned a few minutes later with a plastic bag that he handed to her. Two water bottles, a Coke, and a banana.

"You on a health kick?" she asked suspiciously.

He ignored her and pulled back onto the highway. Dani guzzled her soft drink, and the sugar rush was instantaneous. She returned her attention to the navigation system.

"You're taking a right on the highway up here. It should be a couple more miles."

The two-lane route curved through some rugged canyons that looked rosy pink in the late-day sun. Across an arid valley were foothills covered with spruce trees. Beyond the hills, some low mountains.

"It's prettier than I expected." She glanced at Scott, but he didn't comment. "You ever been here before?"

"No."

More silence. She got fed up and stuffed her drink in the cup holder.

"Reminds me of Afghanistan."

She looked at him, startled. He'd never said a word about his tours of duty. He'd made it clear the topic was off-limits.

"You ever miss it?"

"Afghanistan? No. Place was a hellhole."

"No, I mean the job."

He kept his eyes on the road, and she could tell he didn't want to talk about it. Well, tough toenails. She didn't want to talk about her case with him, and yet he'd been hounding her about it for days. She needed a new subject.

"I've been wondering since you got back."

"Wondering what?" He sounded guarded now.

"How you feel about it. Being home. Not being a SEAL anymore."

He adjusted the rearview mirror, and she waited for him to say something evasive.

"Yes, I miss it."

Wow, an answer. A brief one, but it sounded genuine.

"I miss it every day." He looked at her. "I'd go back there in a heartbeat if I could."

She felt a pinch in her chest and turned to look out the window as the landscape whisked by.

"Do you miss the job or—"

"The people. It's not like anywhere else. Those guys are like . . ."

She looked at him. "What?"

He shook his head.

Like family? Like brothers?

Scott wasn't close to his family—never had been, even before his mother died. His father was a retired marine and a recovering alcoholic. He was known to be a hard-ass, too, and Dani figured their rocky relationship was one reason Scott had joined the navy soon after graduation.

She studied his expression. She didn't know what he'd been about to say, and he'd clammed up. He didn't talk about combat, and he'd never spoken to her about the incident that knocked him out of the teams. Drew had told her that one of Scott's friends had died that same day, but that was all she knew about it.

He looked tense now, and she felt guilty for bringing it up.

But then again . . . she didn't. This was an opportunity to talk to him alone, and she wanted to milk it. So often when she saw him, they were at a bar or a restaurant or at work. They were always surrounded by people—her brothers, his coworkers, other cops—and now, in this rare time alone together, she wanted to talk about all those things she'd been wondering about for years. Did he miss his teammates? Did he miss combat? Was he relieved as hell, like she was, that he'd gotten out of there in one piece?

Had he thought about her at all while he was gone?

The car was silent except for the low-pitched hum of the engine as the road wended its way into the hills. Maybe she didn't want answers to those questions.

"So . . . are you sorry you're home?"

He didn't look at her. "Yes and no."

She waited, hoping he'd expand on his reasons.

"Over there"—he glanced at her—"the littlest things have life-and-death consequences. Here at home, nothing does. For the longest time that bothered me. And then I started at Delphi. What I do there, it's totally different, but it has consequences. Same as what you do."

She watched him, surprised by his words again.

"I'm looking for a turnoff on the right," he said.

And that was it. Personal discussion over.

She returned her attention to the map. "Spruce Canyon Road. Looks like about half a mile."

The hillsides were steeper now and covered with fir trees. Since leaving the college they seemed to be gaining altitude.

She spotted the sign. "Here you go."

He slowed and took the corner, and it was a two-lane road again, but this one was narrower and poorly maintained. The incline increased and the car's engine started to choke.

Scott muttered a curse and tapped the brake.

He slowed but kept going up and up until the road leveled out and the canyon opened up into a wide valley. It was dry and covered with scrub brush. To Dani's right a black wooden fence stretched far into the distance. She looked for a gate or a ranch house, but didn't see one.

Dani checked the navigation system and glanced around. "Slow down," she said as they neared a bank of mailboxes on the opposite side of the road. She leaned forward and read the numbers, comparing them to the address the clerk had given her for Collins.

"This it?" he asked.

"No, but we're getting close."

Scott drove on, and Dani took in the picturesque valley in the evening sun. She stared at the endless wooden fence, all straight and true and freshly painted. Beyond it were undulating hills dotted with oak trees. A pair of chestnut-colored horses stood in the shade, flicking their tails in the breeze.

"Should be coming up here," Dani said. "And this isn't what I expected for a university professor. That fence alone must cost a fortune."

"Forget the fence. Look at those purebreds."

She glanced at him. "Since when are you an equestrian?"

"I'm not, but those are some nice horses."

Another bank of mailboxes came into view, this time on Dani's side of the road. Scott slowed down.

"Five-six-nine," she said. "This is it."

He turned onto a one-lane road, and the tempo changed as the tires hit gravel. The route curved along a dried-up creek bed, and Scott navigated ruts and holes as Dani searched the area for any sign of a house.

They rounded a bend and the road dead-ended at an open metal gate.

Scott halted the car.

Dani got out before he could start telling her what to do. She tromped over to the gate, which stood open over a cattle guard. She didn't see any cattle, though. And instead of a freshly painted wooden fence, this property was cordoned off with rusted barbed wire. A weathered A-frame cabin perched at the top of a steep dirt driveway.

"Think he lives up there?" she asked Scott.

"Somebody does." He stood beside the gate now, examining the heavy-duty chain draped around the fence post. He lifted the shiny combination lock attached to it.

"This lock is new. That satellite dish looks new, too." He nodded at the house. "Don't see a car, but it could be parked behind the house."

"Guess I'll find out. I won't be long." She stepped over the cattle guard and he followed her. "*Scott.*"

"I'm coming."

"You can't just—"

"I can and I will, Dani." He gave her a look that left no room for argument.

"Fine, but I need you to stay out of sight. If I see so much as your shadow . . ." She tried to come up with something threatening.

He smiled down at her. "You'll what?"

"I'll be extremely pissed at you."

"Damn. Wouldn't want that."

"I mean it. This is official police business."

"Don't worry, I'm invisible."

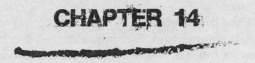

CHAPTER 14

Dani hiked up the steep driveway to the cabin, glancing cautiously around for a dog. She saw no movement, canine or otherwise, as she neared the wooden steps to the front door.

The cabin was surrounded by ponderosas and spruces. It was neatly built, with a steeply pitched roof and a narrow balcony that wrapped around the second floor. The bottom level consisted of a small enclosure beneath the deck. A dusty white pickup truck was pulled up close to the door, blocking the path.

Dani glanced upstairs to the second level, where a door flanked by two neat stacks of firewood appeared to be the main entrance.

"Hello!" she called as she tromped up the steps. "Anyone home?"

She tried to sound friendly in case Collins was the gun-toting sort. This whole area had a definite Wild West feel to it.

At the top of the steps she was surprised by the expansive view. The west side of the cabin was all windows looking out over the treetops to the wide valley. A low mesa rose up on the other side, and the sun was sinking low, casting the valley in shades of gold. Dani shielded her eyes from the glare and surveyed the property. She saw another barbed-wire fence, a rickety-looking shed, and another stack of firewood. But she didn't see Scott.

"Can I help you?"

Dani spun around. Nathan Collins stood behind her at the top of the stairs. She hadn't heard him come up, and she'd been paying attention.

The man was tall and thin and had greasy long blond hair that hung over his eyes. He wore a plaid flannel shirt, jeans, and hiking boots. Despite a full beard, he seemed young, too young to be a PhD. He looked more like a lumberjack strung out on meth.

"Dr. Collins?"

He gave a slight nod and approached her, his brown eyes wary.

"I'm Detective Daniele Harper, San Marcos PD." She expected to have to explain further, but his expression told her she didn't need to.

"You're here about James and Tessa."

"That's right. I'd like to talk to you for a few minutes?" She tried to sound low-key, but he didn't respond. "It won't take long."

He probably knew that was a lie, but he gave another nod and moved to open the door. It hadn't been locked and she hadn't heard a vehicle, so she guessed he'd been out walking around somewhere nearby. If so, had he noticed Scott?

Inside, the cabin was the same warm temperature as outside. Dani stood by the door for a moment and looked around. The place smelled faintly of burned toast. To her right was a sitting area with a sofa draped in a Mexican blanket. In the corner of the room stood a wood-burning stove.

"Tea?"

She glanced at Collins. "Uh, no. Thank you."

The small kitchen had old appliances and a drop-leaf table. He darted a look at the notebook computer on the table before stepping over to the sitting area.

"You're pretty far from home, aren't you, Detective?"

She shrugged as if the trip up had been nothing. "It was a quick flight." She took a seat on the end of the couch, and he moved a pile of files off a wooden chair and sat down.

"I heard it from a coworker," he said.

"A coworker at Trinity or . . . ?" She trailed off to see if he'd pick up the thread.

"Earlier this week when I stopped by to pick up my mail." He shook his head and looked at the floor. "Really unbelievable. I talked to James just the other day. It seems impossible that he's gone."

She watched him carefully, trying to get a read.

He played the harmless academic pretty well. He certainly wasn't physically intimidating. But something about his eyes, a sharpness, told her he was choosing his words carefully.

She tugged a notepad from her pocket. "And did you call James or—"

"He called me."

She knew this already, but she jotted it down. He hadn't mentioned Tessa calling, which was interesting.

"What was James calling about?"

"Work stuff." Collins gave a shrug. "You know, research."

"And what was he researching?" She smiled sheepishly. "I heard something about nuclear plasmids, but maybe you could put it in layman's terms?"

He looked reluctant to answer the question, and she

wished she could go back and ask something else to warm him up. But it was too late now.

He leaned back and stroked his beard. Another academic-looking pose. "Are you familiar with recombinant DNA technology?"

"Not really."

"Well . . . it's complicated, but basically James had run up against a wall and wanted to compare notes, see if he could get back on track. See, I've been doing a lot lately with YACs, or yeast artificial chromosomes. James's research has more to do with BACs, or bacterial artificial chromosomes. But there's a lot of overlap and sometimes we like to catch up and exchange ideas."

"I see." She didn't see at all, but she wanted to watch where he steered the conversation. Unfortunately, he'd stopped talking.

"And were you able to help him?"

"I don't know." Another shrug. "He said he'd call again this week, but obviously he didn't, so . . ."

"And Tessa?"

"What about her?"

"She called you, too, according to her phone records." She paused to watch him. He didn't look surprised by the idea that she'd been through both victims' phone records.

"Yes, that was personal. We were friends more than coworkers. She just wanted to touch base."

"Were you romantically involved with her?"

"No." He chuckled.

"Why is that funny?"

"Just . . . Tessa." He shook his head. "She was all about James."

Yet she'd called a man who *wasn't* James just to touch base.

"So, you knew she and James were having an affair?"

"Everyone knew." He tipped his head to the side. "Except maybe his wife. What's her name? Amy?"

"Audrey."

"Right. I never actually met her."

"And how did Tessa seem when you spoke with her recently?"

"I didn't."

"You didn't?"

"She left me a message, but I hadn't gotten back to her yet. I was planning to call her sometime over the weekend." His brow furrowed and he gazed down at the floor. "I can't believe any of this. It feels totally surreal."

"Dr. Collins, why did you decide to take a sabbatical this summer?"

His eyebrows arched. She'd wanted the question to catch him off guard, and it had.

"Excuse me?"

"You're on sabbatical right now, correct?"

"Who told you that?"

"When I stopped by the biology building—"

"Phyllis." He rolled his eyes. "That sounds like something she'd say. I think it's more accurate to say I'm on unpaid leave. You didn't know?"

"No. What happened?"

He sighed heavily. Then he stood up. "I think I will have that tea. You sure you don't want some?"

"I'm fine." But she got up and stepped into the kitchen so she could watch his body language as they continued the conversation.

"I'm on unpaid leave because—*allegedly*—I had sexual relations with a student."

"Did you?"

"No." He took a metal teapot off the stove and shook it. Water sloshed around and he put it back on the burner, then reached under the stove to light the pilot. Dani watched him, taking note of his calm demeanor and his voice. He seemed . . . annoyed. As though being falsely accused of something that could destroy his career was a minor inconvenience.

"The charges are bogus," he said.

"You think so?"

"Trinity's lawyers are all about cover-your-ass, so if a student makes the slightest complaint, they go into crisis mode. Same thing happened to James."

"James Ayers?"

"Right. That student was making it up, too. James didn't even know her. But still they put him on leave."

How was Dani just now hearing this? This was definitely something James's wife should have mentioned. Or Kreznik when he'd been interviewed by Ric.

"Do you happen to remember the woman's name?"

"The woman who accused me or James?"

"James."

He sighed and stared down at the stove. "I can't remember it offhand, but I can look it up." He glanced at his notebook computer, but didn't move to look up anything.

Dani scanned the cabin. It was small and outdated, but the view wouldn't come cheap. Did he own this place, or did someone else? She saw no sign that anyone lived here with him. Unwashed dishes had stacked up beside the sink, including a Darth Vader coffee mug. This guy had *bachelor* written all over him.

Dani cleared her throat. "So . . . do you mind if I ask how you're paying the bills while you're on unpaid leave?"

"Why?"

"Just curious."

He turned up the heat on the teakettle. "I'm not. They're piling up. I'm looking for another job, actually, but don't tell my landlord that."

Dani glanced down at her notepad, a little thrown by all the twists and turns the conversation had taken. She flipped the pages as Collins watched her expectantly.

So far everything about this discussion seemed odd, but most especially the nonchalance of it. She'd flown here from Texas to talk to this guy about his murdered friends, and he didn't seem surprised to see her or anxious about the interview.

Maybe the man had a screw loose. He was definitely smart, but he could easily have mental issues, too.

"According to our investigation, Mike Kreznik— another former Trinity colleague—called you last week as well." She flipped a page in her notebook. "Thursday evening, it looks like." She glanced up at him, and he was frowning now.

"Yeah. So?"

"So, what did he call about?"

"His message didn't say, and I haven't called him back yet."

Dani's pulse picked up. She watched him closely, trying to read his eyes, his mouth, every nuance of his expression. "Do you have any idea why Kreznik would call you?"

His brow furrowed. "I'm sorry, but . . . whose phone

records are you investigating here? I thought we were talking about James and Tessa."

"And Mike Kreznik. He's dead, too."

His jaw dropped. All the color drained from his face. "He's . . . *what*?"

Either this guy was a good actor or he'd had no idea.

"You didn't know?"

"I—wait. You're telling me *Mike* is dead?"

"Yes."

"But how?"

"Homicide."

He stared at her as the kettle began to hiss. When it reached an earsplitting whistle, he seemed to notice its existence. He moved it off the burner and switched off the stove.

"But I don't understand." He rubbed a hand over his face and beard. "Mike was just . . . I mean, I just talked to him. I just talked to *all* of them."

"I know. That's why I'm here. Do you know why Mike was calling you?"

"No. I told you, I hadn't called him back yet."

"Do you have a guess? Was it work? Personal?"

He hesitated. Only a beat, but Dani caught it.

"I don't know."

It was a lie. She couldn't say why she felt sure of it, but she did. And excitement surged through her because she'd come all this way and she was finally onto something. She could feel it in the air.

Collins darted a look at the cell phone sitting on the counter. He wanted it. He wanted to contact someone. But he didn't want to do it in front of her.

He glanced at his watch. "I'm sorry, Detective, but . . . I actually have to be somewhere. I need to go."

Dani watched him, debating how to respond. She wasn't nearly finished yet. But he wanted to connect with someone on his phone, and whoever that someone was might prove to be a lead. And if he really *did* need to go somewhere, and that wasn't just a ploy, Dani could always follow him.

"I have a few more questions," she said. "And I still need that name."

"Name?"

"Of the woman who filed the complaint against James."

"Oh. Sure. Can I call you with that?" Another glance at his watch. "And you can ask me any follow-up questions after I take care of this . . . errand."

"Sure, no problem. I'm in town overnight." She tugged a business card from her back pocket and his gaze flicked to her sidearm and badge. For the first time since she'd been here, he looked guilty of something. She just didn't know what it was yet.

"Thanks." He took the card without looking at it and tucked it into the pocket of his flannel shirt. Then he grabbed his car keys and slid the phone into his back pocket.

"I'll get out of your way," Dani said.

He hustled her out the door and down the steps, and she glanced around. The cabin and the entire hillside were bathed in yellow now as the sun neared the horizon.

"So this errand . . . are you heading into town or—"

"Just down the road." He nodded vaguely in the direction of the highway. "I'm a caretaker on someone's ranch. Brings in a little extra cash." He forced a smile, but she knew all of it was bullshit, and he couldn't wait to get on his phone.

"I'll call you tonight for that name."

"Yeah. No problem."

He headed for his pickup and she turned toward her car, which was still parked at the bottom of the hill. Before she even reached it, he rolled past her in the grimy white truck. She glanced at the license plate as he rattled over the cattle guard. Then he swung onto the road and the pickup was lost in a cloud of red dust. Dani stared after it.

"He lit out quick."

She turned around at the voice. Scott was watching her from beneath the deck. She hadn't heard his footsteps, and he definitely hadn't been there a moment ago.

"You hear any of that?" she asked.

"No."

She took out her notepad and jotted down the license plate number. She and Scott tromped down the hill toward the rental car.

"He got spooked when I mentioned Kreznik."

"When you mentioned him, or when you mentioned he's dead?"

"Both. And he definitely didn't know already. I could see it in his face." She stopped beside the car as Scott pulled the key from the pocket of his leather jacket. "You want me to take a turn driving?"

"No."

"You sure?"

A thunderous boom shook the ground. Fire shot up from the trees, followed by a billow of smoke. Dani caught a flash of movement in her peripheral vision as Scott lunged toward her and tackled her. They hit the ground together and rolled, and he was on top of her and everything went dark.

She tasted dirt. Her ears were ringing. And she couldn't breathe with the tremendous weight pressing her face-first into the ground. She tried to lift her head, tried to see.

"Head down!"

Scott's words sounded far away, which seemed impossible because he was right there on top of her, covering her with his huge body.

Suddenly the weight disappeared. Dani pushed up on her palms, blinking and coughing and spitting dust. She couldn't breathe. Scott's tackle had knocked the wind out of her, and she blinked up at him. He was crouched beside her now with his Sig in his hand, yelling something she didn't understand as a plume of smoke rose up above the treetops.

He grabbed her arm and pulled her to her feet, then dragged her behind a big tree, still yelling something as he thrust a phone in her hand.

Dani stared down at the device, her ears still ringing. She should call 911. There had been an explosion. She looked ahead at the dusty red road and understood exactly what had exploded without even having to see it. Scott was running down the road now, and she took off after him, tapping at the buttons on the phone with a trembling hand.

Scott rounded the bend and halted, and she looked past him at the wreckage engulfed in flames. Smoke poured out of the blackened carcass that now only vaguely resembled a truck. Dani gaped at the scene and felt a spurt of fear as Scott raced toward the fire. She wanted to scream at him to stay away, stay back, but she couldn't make her voice work. She stumbled to the side of the road and caught her balance against a tree.

Nathan Collins was dead. Incinerated. Three minutes ago they'd been having a conversation.

Something stung her neck. She turned to look at the tree beside her.

And then Scott was sprinting toward her at full speed, the look in his eyes ferocious. She had a split second to brace for the impact as he once again tackled her to the dirt, and they rolled over and over and smacked into something hard. Dani's head hit a rock, and pain pulsed through her skull, and she was blinking up at Scott's face looming over her. She glanced around. They were in a ditch. Her head throbbed and something was poking into her back, but despite the smoke and dirt and the pain, Scott's words penetrated the chaos.

"*He's shooting!*"

• • •

Scott registered a hundred different details, all flashing into his brain with equal intensity. The acrid smell of smoke. The orange flames. The soft, womanly feel of Dani's body underneath him. She stared up at him, her green eyes wide with shock and fear.

He had to get her out of here.

That bullet had missed her by an inch, maybe less, and she already had a welt on her neck from where the tree bark had nicked her.

He ignored the pain in his arm as he rolled off her and shifted into a crouch. Dani grabbed his wrist and tried to pull him down.

"The truck exploded. It *exploded*." She clutched his arm. "And someone's *shooting at us*?"

"That's right." He looked around, taking in every element of their position with a quick glance.

They were surrounded by brush, but it was low and much too thin. The two shots had come fast and close, barely more than a second apart. And they'd revealed a wealth of information, none of it good.

The shooter had the high ground. He was set up to the west, with the sun over his shoulder, giving him a distinct advantage if Scott had been in a position to shoot back, which he sure as shit wasn't with a short-range firearm. The high ground west of them was a mesa, maybe a hundred feet tall, that stretched along the side of a valley that was at least five hundred yards wide. That distance told Scott the shooter was both trained and well equipped.

"Fuck," he muttered, glancing around. The foliage here provided concealment but definitely not cover—at least, not the kind that could stand up to a bullet moving twenty-two hundred feet per second at the moment of impact.

Dani rolled onto her side and tried to push up.

"Head down!" Scott ordered, pushing her to the ground. He surveyed the area, throwing together a plan. It wasn't great, but there weren't a lot of options. Scott checked his Sig as Dani watched him with confusion in her eyes.

"But . . . where are they?" She looked toward the setting sun. She'd instinctively sensed what he had, that the shooter was positioned to the west where the elevation and the lighting gave him a clear advantage.

"Dani, look at me." Scott needed her full attention, but her pupils were dilated, and he could tell she was in shock. "*Daniele*."

Her gaze met his.

"Get onto your knees. Keep your head low." He helped her to her knees, using his body as a shield. As she sat up, she pulled out her Glock and checked the clip, which he took as a good sign. She was shaking off the daze and getting her head in the game.

"Behind you, about ten yards, there's some tree cover," he said. "Pine trees. Better than these bushes. Are you with me?"

She nodded.

"When I say the word, run as fast as you can for those trees. Stay low. Follow the trees all the way back to the car. Get behind it, stay behind the engine block, and wait for me."

"But—"

"Stay *low*, do you understand?"

She grabbed his arm, and he tried not to wince. "What about you?"

"I'll take a different route." He took her free hand and pressed the car key into it. "I'll meet you at the car."

"We should stay together."

"It's better if we split up so he has to choose between targets." And he was going to choose Scott.

"But you can't—"

"Just do it, God damn it! Don't argue with me for once. I'll meet you back at the car in three minutes."

Her grip on his arm tightened, and beneath the shock in her eyes he could see the fear threatening to paralyze her. They had to move *now*.

He touched the side of her face. "Are you listening to me, Daniele?"

She nodded.

"Good. Now, look at those trees."

She turned and focused on the trees.

"I'm going to take off first. You wait two full seconds, and then you race for that cover. Stay as low as you can and don't stop running. Don't look back or stop for anything, you got that?"

"Yes."

He searched her eyes for understanding. "You locked and loaded?"

She glanced down at her gun and nodded.

"Okay, let's move."

• • •

She sprinted for the tree, her heart thundering as she waited for the pain of a bullet. She reached the tree and crashed to her knees behind the thick trunk. She hunched there, making herself small as she glanced around.

Where was Scott? He'd disappeared into the bushes, gone completely invisible somehow. But then she saw a flash of his black jacket as he darted behind a tree. Suddenly the reality of what he was doing hit her like a sledgehammer.

What was wrong with her? Why hadn't she understood? He was drawing the shooter's fire.

Dani cast a frantic glance at the western tree line. Beyond it, from the safety of some ridge she couldn't even see, someone was staring through a rifle scope at this dusty stretch of road where what had once been a truck and *person* was now a flaming wreck.

She squinted through the smoke and glanced around, looking for her next destination. The closest tree was just ten feet away.

She sprinted.

Crack.

The noise reverberated through her brain as she dived to the ground. He'd missed.

He'd missed missed missed.

But what if he'd been aiming for Scott? She gripped her useless pistol and hazarded a glimpse around the tree, desperate for a sign of Scott, but she saw nothing besides smoke.

She glanced up the hillside. Beyond a row of trees she caught a glimpse of their canary-yellow car.

Crouching low, she dashed for the next tree. And the next. And the next, barely stopping behind each thick trunk for fear she might panic and loose her ability to keep going.

Crack.

She yelped at the noise as she lunged behind a flimsy cedar tree. Was he aiming at her or Scott? She couldn't tell, and she wished desperately that he hadn't convinced her to split up. She wanted him beside her, but she knew this plan was better from a tactical perspective.

In her left hand she clutched the key fob. She trained her gaze on the little yellow car, staring at it with all her might, as if staring could somehow bring it closer. Twenty feet away. Twenty-five, max. She could do it.

Her heart was pounding so fast, it felt like it might jump right out of her chest. She was gasping, desperate for air. A minute ago she hadn't been able to breathe at all, and now she couldn't seem to stop.

She murmured a prayer. And then she made a run for it.

CHAPTER 15

Dani raced for the car and ducked behind it. Thank God. She leaned her head against the wheel well for a moment as she caught her breath.

Then she crawled to the back bumper and looked around.

Scott, where are you?

She made her way to the front and opened the passenger door. Should she climb behind the wheel and start the engine? She could be ready to go the instant Scott appeared. Where was he?

Dani searched the surrounding brush, but saw no sign of him. Smoke stung her eyes. Her lungs itched from it. She coughed and looked around.

Her gaze landed on the cabin at the top of the hill, and her stomach plummeted.

Flames licked up from the deck. The smoke wasn't just coming from the truck wreckage—the *cabin* was on fire now, too.

She blinked at the house, trying to get her head around everything. Someone was nearby, someone besides that shooter on a distant ridge. Dani glanced around, clutching her Glock, searching for any sign of movement.

She made a snap decision and climbed into the car, hunching down as she slid across the console and into the driver's seat. She kept her head as low as possible while she switched her Glock to her left hand and managed to start the engine.

Where the hell was he?

She looked at the cabin and saw flames dancing behind the windows. Black smoke poured from the door, the very door she'd walked through just a few minutes ago. What was happening here?

She caught a flash of movement in her side mirror as Scott lunged for the car and yanked open the door.

"Move over," he yelled, and she was already sliding to make room for him. He glanced at her. "You okay?"

"Yeah."

"Snap that seat belt and stay low. This is going to be a rough ride."

• • •

Scott tore onto the road, spraying gravel behind him as he made a U-turn.

Dani lifted her head to peek above the dash. "What—"

"Stay down!" He pressed her head against his thigh.

He sped past the fiery truck, hardly glancing at it as he raced through the billowing black cloud. The wind had changed directions, sending smoke right along the exfil route. Visibility was for shit, so he navigated by feel, using the ruts to guide him as he waited for the turnoff. It came sooner than he expected and he slammed on the brakes and swung right. The car skidded as they burst from the cloud of smoke into the brightness.

Damn it, they were out in the open now, a long,

paved straightaway that went on for at least a mile. Scott searched for another turn.

Ping.

"Son of a bitch," he muttered, jabbing the gas. He had to get off this road.

He glanced down. Dani was tapping frantically at the navigation system, seeming to read his mind. Or maybe she'd noticed the car was taking fire. She had her head in his lap, so at least it wasn't a target.

"There's a left turn up ahead," she said.

"Dead end or no?"

He'd take it either way, but he hoped to hell it was a through street. He barely tapped the brakes as he swung into the turn. The car fishtailed.

"Looks like . . . it links back up with a highway in a little ways."

Scott scanned the surroundings. It was flat here, a road that snaked through the valley, still within range of the shooter. But some trees lined the west side, so maybe they'd get lucky.

He wished for his truck, with its V-8 engine and all-terrain tires. He'd be out of here in no time. But off-roading it wasn't an option in this sardine can, not unless he wanted a blowout. Scott floored the accelerator, and the overworked engine reached a fever pitch.

"Where's this thing lead?" he asked.

"About two miles southwest, then hooks north to the highway."

Dani started to sit up, and he pressed her head back against his thigh.

"Scott, I can't *see*!"

"That's good. Then he can't see you."

Ping.

God damn it. Scott was getting pissed now.

"Please get your head down," Dani said, and he heard the plea in her voice.

He slid lower in the seat, but there wasn't much room. Up ahead was a solid bank of trees. He glanced at the speedometer. He was pushing eighty in a car built to top out at sixty-five.

"There's a turn up ahead here. Looks like a short-cut," Dani told him.

"Left or right?"

"Right."

Up ahead on the right was tree cover, lots of it. Scott braked. The tires squealed. He smelled burning rubber as he whipped into the turn, fishtailing once again as Dani gripped his knee.

"*Scott.* Oh my God."

He glanced down at her head in his lap and couldn't help but smile. How many times had he fantasized about this? But in his fantasies she'd always been naked and into it. She hadn't been shaking and terrified, looking like she was about to hurl.

And, holy hell, he was getting hard right now. *Now,* when Dani's life was in his hands and some fuckhead with a rifle was taking shots at them. It had to be the adrenaline.

"Scott, let me sit up."

He glanced around. The road was shaded with fir trees now, and a low ridge rose up to their west. They were still within rifle range, but they weren't sitting ducks like they'd been in the middle of the valley.

She squeezed his thigh. "Scott, come on."

"Looks clear." At least for now.

Slowly, she lifted her head from his leg, and the

pinch of regret he felt told him exactly what a sick bastard he was. She brushed the hair from her eyes and glanced around.

Then she looked at him. "What the *hell* just happened?"

He heard the anger in her voice. Anger was good. It meant the shock was wearing off, and she was getting back into the game here. Which was good, timing-wise. He needed her alert and lucid because the shock was wearing off for him, too, and his shoulder was starting to hurt like a motherfucker.

"Scott?"

As he looked around for somewhere it might be safe to pull over, he heard sirens in the distance. Dani seemed to hear them, too, and she glanced around.

"Someone called it in," she said.

"Was it you?"

"No." She pulled Scott's phone from her pocket and stared down at it like it was some alien object she'd never before seen. "I was about to make the call when the shooting started." She looked up at him, and he could see the disbelief on her face.

"Someone rigged his truck with a bomb," Scott said.

"A *bomb*," she repeated, as if saying it might make it more believable. "Are you sure it wasn't, I don't know, maybe whoever was shooting at us hit the gas tank and made the truck fireball?"

"That only happens in movies."

"But . . . are you sure?"

"Trust me. I've seen my share of car bombs."

She shook her head. "Well, we have to go back."

Scott checked his speed. He pressed his hand against his shoulder and winced at the burn.

"Scott?"

"Not happening."

"But we have to report it! We have to talk to the first responders. We have to turn around."

"Not now."

"*When?*"

Never, if it were up to him. But he knew she couldn't do that. She was a cop.

"Stop the car."

He glanced at her.

"Stop the car, damn it!"

He looked around before pulling onto the shoulder and putting the car into park. The engine sputtered, and he darted a look at the dashboard.

He looked at Dani, really *looked* at her for the first time since she'd been underneath him in that ditch. She had dirt on her face and leaves in her hair. Her eyes looked wild, but they also looked alert, and he saw the outrage there. She had that look that guys got right after a firefight, right after their position had come under enemy attack and they'd somehow managed to squeak out alive.

She was starting to get it.

"We're not turning around," he said. "My objective right now is to keep you alive, and I'll be damned if we're going back into the kill zone."

"But I have to give a statement. I have to help the sheriff or whoever's responding to the scene right now." She paused and looked around, and the distant wail of sirens filled the silence. It sounded like at least two emergency vehicles, maybe three. Dani was a cop, through and through, and he knew he was asking her to go against every instinct she had.

"Help all you want, but you can do it later and from a distance." He reached over and cupped the side of her head. "Daniele, look at me."

She met his gaze.

"Are you okay?"

"Yes."

"Good. Because I need you to drive."

Alarm flared in her eyes. "What happened? Oh my God." She was leaning over him, searching him for injuries, before he could even respond. "Scott, you're *hit*! Why didn't you tell me?"

"It's just a scratch. Fuck!" He flinched as she touched his shoulder.

"Are you crazy? We have to get you to a hospital!"

She was practically on top of him now, and it was all he could do not to curse her out as he wrapped his good arm around her waist and lifted her away from him.

"Calm down, all right? It's a scratch."

"It's not a *scratch*, it's a bullet wound!"

"I've had bullet wounds before, and this is a scratch." He was pretty sure. "But I'd like to take a look at it, so if you don't mind driving . . . ?"

She sat back in her seat. "You're a lunatic, you know that? I swear to God."

"Switch places with me."

She gaped at him a moment. Then she shook her head and shifted position. He eased himself over the console and she climbed over him, giving him a nice glimpse down the T-shirt she wore under her jacket.

That he was noticing her breasts was a good sign, because that meant it really *was* a scratch even though it burned like a cattle brand.

He got into her seat and glanced at her.

"You need help with your jacket?"

"No." To prove it, he carefully pulled it off and checked his shoulder. Blood had saturated his T-shirt and dripped down his arm, but he peeled the fabric away and found just what he'd expected: a short, shallow trench where a bullet had grazed his skin.

"Oh my God, *Scott*." Her eyes widened.

"It's nothing. Let's go."

"It's not *nothing*."

"I mean it, Dani. We need to get out of here."

• • •

She drove in a haze. They'd been out of the smoke for miles, but still she felt like it was following them, gaining ground. She kept glancing in the rearview mirror expecting a roiling black cloud to catch up with them and overtake the car.

Don't lose it.

Dani gripped the wheel and tried to hold herself together as she sped down the two-lane highway headed God only knew where.

Where was she even going?

She glanced at Scott, who was dousing water over his shoulder and dabbing at his *bullet wound* with a T-shirt he'd dug out of his backpack.

Don't lose it. Don't lose it. Don't lose it.

He glanced at her. "You okay?"

"Fine." She focused on the highway. She wanted to go back. Needed to. No matter what Scott said, she needed to turn the car around this second and return to that crime scene.

"Not happening, Daniele."

She glanced at him. Had she said it out loud?

"I can see what you're thinking, and we're not going back."

"But—"

"How wide is that valley?"

She blinked at him. "The valley? I have no idea."

"Take a guess."

She stared at the road ahead, trying to picture the valley. "I don't know. Five hundred yards."

"More like six. And that first cold-bore shot came within an inch of taking your head off."

Her stomach knotted at the words, but she didn't say anything.

"Someone planted an IED and killed the witness you just interviewed. Someone set fire to the house you just visited. Someone just tried to take us *both* out with a sniper rifle. We're talking about multiple bad guys in multiple locations. Think about that."

"I am thinking about it!"

"I am, too. And I can tell you whoever is doing this is trained in long-range weaponry. And explosives. This is someone with combat experience. And the first rule of combat is, never go where the enemy expects you to be."

She stared ahead at the road, but she didn't respond. Her heart was still racing, and she was afraid if she tried to talk, she'd lose it.

"We are not going back there right now."

For a while they drove in silence. Dusk had fallen, and the landscape looked purple and shadowy. They were on a state highway headed north. A green sign told her she was two miles from a rest stop and twenty-two miles from some town she'd never heard of.

She looked at Scott. A sheen of sweat covered his face, but that was the only sign of stress as he settled back against the seat. He wasn't even breathing heavily. They'd just fled bullets and bombs and death by incineration, and he looked totally calm.

Meanwhile, *she* was about to have a heart attack. Or a panic attack. Her hands gripped the steering wheel but her palms felt slippery, and her stomach was doing a queasy somersault as though she'd just stepped off a roller coaster.

She stared ahead at the yellow lines of the highway. *Don't lose it.*

She pictured Nathan Collins with his stringy hair and his plaid shirt. She pictured his intelligent brown eyes and his look of surprise when she told him his friend was dead. She pictured his dusty white truck. And then she pictured the blazing wreckage.

Her stomach pitched and she clutched her hand to it. A sign came into view and she swerved for the exit.

"What's wrong?" Scott asked.

"I have to stop."

She had to puke. She slowed the car and swung into the rest stop. A minivan was pulled over near the concrete restrooms. She drove past it and whipped into a space, then shoved the car into park.

She flung the door open. But then . . . nothing. The nausea passed. She felt dizzy.

Scott gripped her knee. "You okay?"

"Yeah, just . . . I need to use the bathroom."

She walked briskly down the sidewalk, barely glancing at the minivan as a woman buckled a little girl into a car seat and slid shut the door. Dani went straight into the restroom, one of those indoor-outdoor places.

She could still hear the highway noise through big gaps between the wall and the ceiling. She walked up to the sink and leaned over it.

She closed her eyes and all she saw was Nathan Collins holding that teakettle. Just minutes before he'd been blown to pieces.

A sob burst from her chest. Then the tears came, hot and wet and streaming down her face. She clutched the sink and dipped her head down and squeezed her eyes shut as she tried to hold everything back.

The man was dead. She'd come inches away from being dead, too. Scott had been shot.

Just thinking about all that blood on him made the tears come back again, and she gripped the sink and tried to force them to stop. She had to pull it together. She was a *cop*. She couldn't do this.

She took a deep, ragged breath and turned on the faucet. Her palms were scraped and bloody, and she rinsed them and washed out the gravel. She splashed water on her face, then straightened and looked in the mirror.

Scott stood in the doorway, watching her.

She turned around. "Sorry."

"You all right?"

"Fine." She grabbed some paper towels and blotted her face. "I just needed a minute. How's your shoulder?"

He was wearing the jacket again, and she couldn't see the wound. She stepped toward him but he stepped back.

"I'm fine. Let's go."

The minivan had left, and the rest stop was empty as they walked back to the car. Scott approached the driver's side.

"I should drive," she told him.

He didn't reply, just opened the door and slid his huge body behind the wheel. Dani went around to the passenger side.

She was still shaking and her heart was still beating too fast and she didn't want to argue with him. She pulled the door shut and stared straight ahead through the windshield.

"It's twenty miles to Big Rock," Scott said matter-of-factly. "We can stop there and regroup."

"That's not too far from Santa Fe. It'll probably be crowded with festival people."

"Crowded is good. We can blend in. Go off radar for a while till we sort this out." He started the car. "Sound good?"

She didn't say anything.

"Dani?"

"Sounds fine."

She glanced at him. His face was shadowed, but she could see the tension in his eyes.

"Sorry." She swiped at her cheeks. "Please don't tell anyone I had a meltdown."

He looked perplexed. "Who would I tell?"

"I don't know. My brothers."

"Jesus."

Tears filled her eyes again and she looked away. What the hell was wrong with her? She was a homicide cop.

"Hey."

She shook her head.

"*Hey*." He took her hand. "Look at me."

She did.

"It's okay. It's a natural reaction to stress."

She laughed through her tears. "*Stress*? That's what you call seeing someone die and . . . and getting shot at and driving through smoke and fire?"

He just stared at her, and the look on his face made her laugh again because he was so impossibly *calm* and she felt like she was losing it. And maybe she *was* losing it, because the damn tears started pouring out again.

"I'm sorry."

He reached over and cupped the side of her face. "It's all right." He kissed her forehead. "Stop apologizing." He kissed her lips and his mouth hovered over hers. "It's okay, Daniele."

She kissed him. It was light and soft, and he kissed her back just as softly. His fingers felt rough against her cheek but his touch was gentle as he wiped her tears with his thumb. He made a low, soothing sound, and she felt her shoulders relax. The tightness in her chest started to loosen as she leaned into the kiss and really tasted him. It was slow and sweet—different from their other kisses. This one was about comfort. She knew that. She also knew she should pull away, but she only wanted to drink him in. His hand slid down to curve around her waist, and he pulled her closer, and she twisted her body to get a better angle.

Then everything turned hot. His mouth. His hands. His tongue. She combed her fingers into his hair and pulled him close, and he dragged her across the console. She shouldn't be doing this. He was injured. He might even still be bleeding, but she couldn't let go of him.

His tongue delved into her mouth and tangled with hers, and she ran her hands over his face and felt the stubble on his jaw and smelled the smoke on his skin.

And she couldn't believe they were doing this, but she didn't want to stop and neither did he. His hand slid under her jacket and around her waist, and he pulled her onto his lap.

An ear-piercing *whelp* had her jumping back. She turned and blinked at a patrol car that had pulled up behind them. Inside it were two big silhouettes.

"No loitering," came a voice over an electronic megaphone. "Please move along."

Dani slid into her seat and glanced at Scott.

He glowered at the rearview mirror. But when he glanced in her direction, his expression softened. "You okay?"

"Yeah." She straightened her clothes and looked out the window. "Come on, let's go."

CHAPTER 16

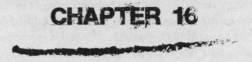

Fifteen minutes later she was shaking. Still. Scott didn't know if it was fear or pain or emotion, or maybe a combination of all three. Whatever it was, it was having a definite effect that was impossible to ignore.

What the hell was wrong with him? Minutes ago they'd nearly been killed, and he'd never been so hard for this girl. She was *bleeding*, for Christ's sake, and he wanted to pull the damn car over and pound himself into her just to convince them both that they were still alive.

It was twisted. Definitely. But that didn't make it any less real, and Scott shifted in his seat, hoping she wouldn't notice what was going on with him. He had to get himself under control because she sure as hell wasn't going to do it.

He focused on the road, going through events in his head and retracing every step from this afternoon. The more time he had to consider everything, the less he liked what it told him about their attackers. The first cold-bore shot was the toughest, and the shooter had nearly made it from more than five hundred yards out.

A bullet behaved differently coming out of a cold gun. In combat, you didn't get the benefit of practice shots to warm up yourself or your weapon. The very first shot had to be right on target. No second chances. The importance of this concept had been drilled into Scott during sniper training. Every day, he had to be on the range at 0600 with his rifle and a single bullet. Making that first cold-bore shot took skill. Precision. Training.

Scott had no doubt that whoever put Dani in his sights had all three.

Scott spotted their exit sign and veered off the highway as Dani stared out the window. He passed a couple of gas stations and fast-food joints before turning into what looked to be the bigger of the town's two visible motels. The place was two stories and mostly occupied, judging from all the cars and trucks crammed into the parking lot. Scott checked the window of the motel office, hoping to get a glimpse of whoever was working behind the desk.

The clerk was young and female, which was their first stroke of luck since not having their heads blown off.

"What are we doing?" Dani asked.

"I told you. We need to regroup."

"You mean over*night*?"

He definitely heard the alarm in her voice, and he did his best to look unfazed. "I need to clean up. And get something to eat."

She looked at him like he was crazy.

"And I need to dress this wound," he said, playing on her sympathy.

Her expression instantly turned worried. "You need an ER."

"I need a shower." He pushed the door open and glanced at her. "Don't go anywhere. I'll be back in five."

• • •

Yeah, right. Where would she go?

She watched him disappear into the motel office, still feeling dazed by everything that had happened. He had his leather jacket on again and he walked in there with his typical swagger, his lady-killer smile up and operating as he approached the clerk, who surely had bad news for him about the availability of a room.

Crowded is good. We can blend in.

Dani glanced around at all the cars and SUVs filling the parking lot, many with out-of-state plates. They definitely had overflow from the music fest here, and Dani highly doubted Scott would be able to land them a room.

Which probably meant the shower he so desperately needed was going to end up being a rinse-off in some gas station bathroom.

Which was for the better. They could get back on the road and hit the nearest emergency clinic on their way back to the crime scene, where they could give a statement to investigators.

Dani closed her eyes and squeezed the bridge of her nose.

What had just happened?

She still didn't understand it. She simply knew that she'd gone to interview someone, and minutes later he'd been killed.

She'd nearly been killed, too.

And Scott.

Bile welled up in the back of her throat, but she swallowed it down. She opened her eyes and stared through the windshield at the traffic along the sidewalk—carefree young festivalgoers returning from cheap dinners to their cheap motel rooms with cases of cheap beer tucked under their arms.

Scott stepped from the office. He held the door open for a pair of girls in halter tops, who smiled and ducked under his arm. One of them said something to him—something flirtatious, judging by the smile he gave her in response. Dani watched with resignation.

Scott returned to the car and slid behind the wheel. He backed from the space, but instead of exiting the lot, he pulled around the side of the building.

"No way did they have a room," she said.

"Two."

Two. The little word stung, but she tried not to react. "You said you wanted to go off the radar. What name did you give?"

"I didn't. I paid cash."

"Cash doesn't matter. You still have to show ID."

He cut a glance at her, as if to remind her that rules didn't apply to him. How did he get away with this crap? He must have tipped the desk clerk. Or maybe all he'd had to do was wink at her.

Scott pulled around back, out of view of the highway, and parked their little car in the shadow of a Dumpster. He grabbed his backpack and got out, popping the trunk as he did. He took out her roll-on suitcase and carried it as if it were a lunch box. Dani followed him across the lot, and he stopped in front of a gray door.

"You're here." He shoved in the keycard. "I'm on the end there. One-sixteen."

Dani stepped into the dark, musty-smelling room, grateful for the dimness so he couldn't see her face as he tossed the keycard on the dresser and dropped her suitcase onto the sagging double bed. What had she expected? That he'd check them into some fleabag motel and make wild, passionate love to her?

He was exploring the room now, examining the window latch, opening the closet, leaning his head into the bathroom.

"What in the world are you looking for?"

He ignored the question as he stepped past her. "Stay in the room. Don't drive anywhere, don't walk anywhere, not even down the street, you got that? You need to keep a low profile."

"What I *need* to do is call my lieutenant. And I should probably call the local sheriff, too, and mention that I witnessed a murder in his jurisdiction. You know, just in case he's interested."

Scott gazed down at her and had the nerve to look disapproving.

She folded her arms over her chest. "What, you disagree?"

"Do what you gotta do."

"I will." She glared up at him. "What are *you* going to do?"

"Take care of this shoulder. Clean up." He glanced at his watch. "I'll be back here in twenty minutes, then we can make a plan."

She looked up at him, and something felt off. So many fears and questions were still tumbling through her mind, and she still felt shaky from the trauma of everything. But that wasn't all it was. Something was off with Scott, too, and she couldn't put her finger on it. She looked at his injured shoulder, and he moved for the door.

"Secure the latch behind me."

She nodded, and he walked out without a backward glance.

Dani latched the door. Then she stood beside the window, parting the heavy brown curtains to watch him as he walked down the sidewalk and let himself into his room.

Dani glanced around. She took off her jacket and tossed it on the faded brown bedspread. Then she stepped into the bathroom and gazed with horror at her reflection.

Her face and neck were smeared with dirt. Leaves clung to her hair, and the front of her T-shirt was covered in mud from taking a dive into that ditch.

She leaned close to the mirror to examine a cut on her lip that she hadn't noticed before. And then there were the tear tracks down her cheeks, a glaring reminder of how she'd totally lost her shit in the middle of a crisis. She looked like an escaped mental patient.

She closed her eyes and took a deep breath. She had to shake it off. She had to pull herself together and handle this.

First, a shower. She needed to clear her head, to think. She turned the water to hot and then retrieved some necessities from her suitcase. She stripped off her clothes and stepped under the steamy spray, and by the time she finished scrubbing away the dirt, she'd had a chance to formulate what she would tell both her lieutenant and the local sheriff.

She'd had a chance to think about Scott, too. Two rooms. She tried not to let that hurt, but it did. After everything that had happened, after their kiss at the rest stop, she'd thought . . . Well, she'd thought wrong. And it was probably for the better, because everything was crazy enough right now without throwing sex into the mix.

She stepped out of the shower and dried off with a miniature towel, then slipped into the only other clothes she had—a strappy black tank top and yoga pants. Next, she picked up her phone, took a deep breath, and dialed her lieutenant.

Voice mail.

She left a message and dialed Ric. He didn't answer, either, and she sent him a text telling him to call her.

Dani stared down at her phone, thinking. She tried to imagine the crime scene right now, swarming with emergency vehicles.

Do what you gotta do.

Her stomach knotted and she tossed her phone on the bed. She threw on some flip-flops, then grabbed the keycard off the dresser and hurried from her room, casting a look up and down the sidewalk as she strode up to room 116. She rapped on the door.

A lamp glowed in the room, but she didn't hear a television or running water, only the deep *thump-thump* coming from a room upstairs where someone was having a party. She stepped over to peek through the narrow gap between the curtains and saw a sliver of a bedspread that looked identical to hers.

Two rooms.

She rushed around the side of the building, but she already knew what she was going to find even before her gaze landed on the rusted Dumpster.

"You lying son of a *bitch*."

The little yellow car was gone.

• • •

Scott pulled off the dirt road and checked the map on his phone. This was it. He cut the engine and the headlights and then got out and looked around.

It was a full moon, at least. That would help. He leaned against the hood and waited. It would take twenty minutes, fifteen minimum, for his eyes to adjust to the darkness. He would have loved a pair of night-vision goggles right about now, but all he had was what nature had given him, along with the compact tactical flashlight he kept stashed in his backpack.

So he sat there among the spruce trees and waited for his pupils to dilate, wondering what Dani was doing and how many creative ways she'd come up with to maim him since she'd discovered he'd ditched her.

Finally his eyes were ready and he set out. He moved due east toward the ridge, maneuvering his way through rocks and trees as he navigated the darkness. The intel he needed would have been a lot easier to gather in the daytime, but he figured by tomorrow this area would be crawling with law enforcement, and anyway he didn't have time to wait.

He was careful to keep his footsteps light and his tracks minimal. He had a vivid image in his head based on the Google satellite map he'd studied, and he knew his destination, he just had to find it in the dark. And, yeah, a pair of NVGs would have been nice, but he was trained to go by feel, too, and he didn't mind the inconvenience. SEALs did some of their best work in the dark—and that wasn't just a pickup line.

The incline grew steeper. He was almost there. He felt tempted to check the map again, but the glow of the screen would screw up his vision, so he kept his phone in his pocket. He stepped through some trees and was rewarded with a killer view.

The valley stretched out in front of him, a million shades of gray under the moon. Scott stepped up to the ridge and watched the flicker of flashlights six hundred yards away as emergency personnel worked the crime scene on Spruce Canyon Road.

Scott stood for a moment just watching. The fire-fighters had responded quickly and managed to douse the blaze before it spread to the surrounding woods. So they were off to a strong start, but their investigation was only beginning, and they didn't have a clue what they were up against.

Scott didn't know everything yet, but a few things were clear. They were dealing with two men, mini-mum, and at least one had a military background. It didn't take a spec ops warrior to set a cabin on fire or to detonate an IED using a cell phone. But someone had to make the IED in the first place, and that took skill.

The bomb had been brutally effective. But also care-less. As murder weapons went, bombs were generally a bad option, especially stateside. Bombs tended to kill their targets, but they also tended to reveal a shitload of information about their makers.

Even without examining the device itself, Scott could tell this guy was trained. But he was arrogant, too, which meant prone to mistakes.

Scott shifted his attention away from the activity across the valley and started exploring the ridge. He trekked along the edge of it, searching for an arrange-ment of rocks or trees or even just low bushes that would provide a decent hide. As he moved through the darkness, his thoughts kept going back to those critical moments earlier. When Scott had seen that bullet hit that tree, his heart had nearly stopped beating. And it hadn't really started again until Dani was under him in the ditch, wide-eyed and trembling and alive, thank God. And although she probably wanted to strangle him right about now, Scott didn't give a damn. His top priority was to keep her safe, and that trumped everything else.

So she was safe now. Safe from bullets and IEDs, if not from him.

He trekked through the darkness, trying to tamp down the frustration that had been tormenting him for days now. Weeks. Months. Dani was back at the motel, waiting for him. The thought of it put a knot in his gut, because he didn't know what to do about it. Despite her tough talk, Dani had a weakness for him and had since she was a teenager. Even as a stupid, self-absorbed teen himself, he would have to have been blind not to see it. And he could still see it now.

That weakness was messing up her judgment. She was too invested emotionally. Scott had known it since the day he became a suspect in her murder case. He was *still* a suspect, and even though they both knew he hadn't done anything, that didn't matter. He was on the wrong side of this case, yet he'd managed to convince her to let him come along on this trip. Then he'd convinced her to ignore law enforcement protocol by leaving that crime scene. Dani had risked her badge for him, and that told him a lot. It told him she was vulnerable, and the dead last thing he should do was take advantage of that vulnerability. It would be wrong for multiple reasons, including the simple fact that she was Drew's little sister.

If Scott had any loyalty to his best friend, any sense of the basic rules of decency, he'd forget about this thing with Dani. He'd forget how she looked and felt and tasted and he'd leave her alone.

But Scott had never been much for rules. Or decency, really.

Loyalty was different, though. And it was his iron-clad loyalty to Drew, his determination not to break an unspoken promise, that held Scott in check when every instinct was telling him to zero in on what he wanted and go after it hard.

Scott walked between two juniper trees and spied some rocks near the ledge. He halted. The hair on the back of his neck stood up. He stepped closer to study the formation, then turned and studied the moon-drenched valley spread out before him.

Here. He could feel it.

He crouched down. For a moment he remained perfectly still, just listening and absorbing and trying to get a feel for the place. He dipped his head down and looked through the rocks that created a nice V shape while providing cover. He looked across the valley at the flicker of emergency lights.

It was perfect, and he could imagine the shooter setting up right here with the sun over his shoulder and a clear line of sight to not just the cabin but the road in front of it. The location had all three elements of a good position. Vegetation provided concealment from view, rocks provided cover from potential gunfire, and the shooter had good eyes on the sector.

Scott gazed across the valley, picturing it, until a hot, murderous fury started flowing through his veins. He let it. He didn't suppress it or try to control it. He let the feeling flow because it filled him with determination for what he needed to do. This thing had gone way beyond any other case he'd ever worked, and it was personal now.

Scott took a deep breath. He scanned the area and listened closely. No distant footsteps or voices or cars, only the faint hissing of wind through the rocks.

He switched his flashlight to low mode and kept it close to the ground as he examined the area. He spotted it right away.

Arrogance.

In the form of a brass shell casing left on the ground. Scott methodically scanned the surrounding dirt and grass and discovered five more casings.

He took a latex glove from his pocket and pulled it on. He studied each casing for a moment and selected two, leaving the others for someone else to find, if they ever did.

He dropped the casings into an evidence envelope and tucked it into his pocket. Then he checked his watch.

He'd been gone two hours, and Dani was probably ready to castrate him. Which solved one of his problems.

He stood up and looked across the valley at the lights on the distant road as he thought about what he'd learned tonight. Before, he'd sensed it, but now he knew for sure.

Whoever was doing this was trained, and he was funded, and he was ruthless.

And he wanted Dani dead.

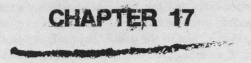

CHAPTER 17

Mia stroked her hand over her belly as her son gave another little kick. They'd decided to name him after Ric's grandfather, but secretly she'd been calling him Pele.

"Everything okay?"

She glanced at Ric, who was watching her intently from his place beside her on the sofa. "Fine. He's just active tonight."

Ric took her hand and squeezed it as he searched her face for more.

"Relax," she added.

But he didn't relax, because he was a master at reading people. And he knew damn well she wasn't giving him the full story, at least not anymore. They'd had two false alarms—two panicked, middle-of-the-night trips to the hospital—and after the last one Mia had promised herself she wouldn't mention anything until she was absolutely certain.

She snuggled closer and leaned her head on Ric's shoulder. They stared at the television, even though neither of them cared about the baseball game.

"Thanks for being home. I know you'd rather be working."

"Nope."

"Okay, I know you think you *should* be working."

Ric didn't deny it. He had been going in early and

staying out late for days. He often got restless about his murder cases, but this one was particularly stressful, especially since the fire death in the neighboring county had been linked to the double homicide at Woodlake Park. Even though Ric wasn't in charge of the investigation, Mia knew he felt responsible, and that if it hadn't been for her and the baby, he would be in New Mexico right now following up on the best new lead.

Ric's phone rattled on the coffee table and he let go of her hand to reach for it. The name HARPER flashed on the screen.

"Hey, I just texted you back. How's it going?" Ric listened for a moment and leaned forward. "*What?*" His shoulders tensed as he listened to whatever Dani was telling him. He seemed to be hanging on every word.

Maybe there had been a break in the case, and the investigation would wrap up soon. Was that too much to hope for? That her husband might be present at the birth of their child without being distracted by murder and mayhem?

"Are you all right?" A pause. "You sure?" Ric glanced at Mia, and the expression on his face told her something was very wrong. "What did Reynolds say?" Ric listened a moment, and by the way his mouth tightened, Mia could tell he didn't like his lieutenant's response, whatever it was. Ric didn't think much of Reynolds and had been much happier working for Don Harper, Dani's father.

Ric combed his hand through his hair. "This is big. I should call Rey, get his take on it."

Mia arched her brows at that. Ric's brother Rey was an FBI agent in San Antonio, and he specialized in violent crimes.

What on earth had happened in New Mexico?

Ric shook his head, and Mia knew what he was thinking, what he'd *been* thinking since yesterday afternoon when this lead had come up. He wanted to be in charge of this thing. He wanted to pursue every lead and interview every witness and personally deliver every bit of evidence to the lab. But instead his young protégée was in charge, and as much as Ric liked her, he hated not being in control.

"Okay, keep me posted. And watch your back." He hung up and stared down at his phone.

"What happened?"

"Dani interviewed that witness."

"The college professor?"

"Yeah. Five minutes later he was killed."

Mia grabbed his arm. "What? How?"

"Car bomb."

"*What?*"

Step by step, he took her through the account Dani had given him over the phone. Most of it, anyway. Mia could tell he was leaving out some details.

When he finished talking, she stared at him in shock. "A *sniper*? You can't be serious."

Ric scrubbed his hand over his face, clearly shaken, and she knew that he was totally serious. And she also knew what he was thinking. He regretted not being there, which made Mia feel sick.

"But . . . is Dani okay? Is she somewhere *safe*, for God's sake?"

"She's safe." Ric shook his head. "At least, I think she is. Scott Black is with her."

"What is he doing there? I thought he was a suspect."

"He's not." Ric was on his phone now, composing a text message to someone, probably his brother.

"But I thought—"

"Well, officially he is, but we've pretty much cleared him. It looks like he was framed."

Mia stared at Ric as he tapped out a message. Tears welled in her eyes, and she cursed her stupid hormones. She felt a surge of fear for Dani and for Scott. And for Ric, too, because he was neck-deep in this mess, whatever it was, and she couldn't do a damn thing about it.

Ric finished typing and hit SEND. Then he looked up. "I have to go in."

"I know."

"I'm sorry." He leaned over and kissed her, resting his hand on the baby. "You know I'd much rather be here with you."

"I know."

He must not have believed her, because he kissed her again, longer this time, reminding her of all the creative ways they'd found to make the nights go by when she had trouble sleeping. When she'd first gotten pregnant, she'd worried her expanding body might be a turnoff for her husband, but that hadn't happened at all. Her pregnancy seemed to be an aphrodisiac. She savored Ric's kiss, wishing she could pull him into the bedroom to continue it.

Finally he pulled away, and the obvious frustration in his eyes made her feel somewhat better.

"I'll be home soon as I can."

"I'll be waiting."

• • •

Dani wasn't in her room.

Scott stood at the door, cursing her refusal to follow simple instructions. He rapped again, harder this time, just in case she was tucked into bed and ignoring him. But the lights were out and the room was silent, and a peek through the gap in the curtains told him what he already knew.

She'd left.

He'd told her to stay in her room, and so she'd done the exact opposite, purely to piss him off. He scanned the surrounding area, but didn't spot her among the clusters of people congregating beside the pint-size swimming pool in the motel courtyard. He didn't see her in the parking lot of the convenience store, either, or at the gas station across the street. He glanced at the vending machine near the stairwell, but she wasn't there, either.

Scott gritted his teeth as he checked his phone. She hadn't texted him since the brief missive he'd received two hours ago: *WTF??*

Yeah, he could say the same to her. What the fuck was she thinking? An unknown number of extremely dangerous people wanted her dead, and she needed to keep a low profile. Instead she'd gone off somewhere, probably to buy junk food. It was totally reckless. But it was intentional, too. Scott had pissed her off, and she was lashing out.

He took a deep breath and walked away, and only his complete faith in Dani's temper kept him from worrying. Wherever she was, she was probably fine, just mad. She'd get over it.

Scott let himself into his room and dumped his bag on the bed, which looked just as saggy and uninviting as when he'd left. He needed food. Badly. But he had a few things to take care of first, such as the blistering-hot pain in his shoulder. He tossed his jacket over the chair, then took off his holster and T-shirt and went into the bathroom to check out the wound.

It had scabbed over pretty well, but it still hurt like a bitch and he needed to clean it. He soaked a washcloth with water and managed not to howl as he rubbed the scab away. He poured some hydrogen peroxide over it, then dabbed it dry and spent a few minutes sealing the wound with superglue—a handy technique he used in less-than-ideal circumstances, which described pretty much all circumstances in Afghanistan. When he was done, he dipped his head down and guzzled some water from the faucet. More than anything else right now, he could have used a cold beer. A hot woman would have been nice, too, but he wasn't going to go there.

He washed his face and thought about Dani. Where the hell was she? And how hard was it to follow one simple command?

The people partying upstairs turned up the bass, and he shot an annoyed look at the lightbulb trembling in its socket above the sink. He was dog-tired, and it was going to be a long night.

He turned off the water as someone pounded on the door with what definitely sounded like a woman-size fist. Relief poured through him, followed by some tight, suffocating emotion that made it hard for him to breathe.

Another round of thuds, and he went to answer the door.

"What the hell?" She strode right past him and turned around. "I called you three times."

"I had my ringer off."

"Where were you?" She turned around again, not waiting for an answer. She picked up the plastic bag on his bed and poked through the first-aid supplies, then tossed it down. "Huh?"

"The nearest pharmacy is forty minutes away."

She gave him a *Get real* look. Then she swooped down on his backpack on the chair and started unzipping pockets.

"You were gone two and a half hours." She rooted through all the front pockets, then unzipped the main one. She rummaged through his gear and glared up at him. "Where is it?"

"Where's what?"

She muttered something he didn't catch as she continued to search. Scott folded his arms over his chest and watched her. She'd cleaned up. She had on formfitting yoga pants and she'd swapped out the businesslike shirt for a tank top with thin little straps. No bra, he couldn't help but notice as she bent over his backpack.

"It's illegal, you know." She finished with his pack and moved on to his leather jacket.

"What's that?"

"Removing evidence from a crime scene." She searched through his empty pockets and tossed the jacket away. She looked around, then glared up at him with frustration. "So, how was it out there?"

He arched his eyebrows.

"I'm guessing pretty crowded by now? ATF show up yet?"

"No idea. I was at the pharmacy."

"Don't insult me, Scott." She pointed a finger at him. "I know you, remember? And I know you went after those slugs, so cut the bullshit."

Scott gazed down at her. She had no clue how hot she was, her cheeks all flushed with anger as she jabbed her finger at him. He couldn't stop staring at her nipples in that shirt, but she was too caught up in her rant to notice.

He had to get her out of here.

"Stealing evidence from a crime scene is serious. Cops get *fired* for that sort of thing." She threw her hands up. "But, hey, what do you care? Rules don't apply to you."

"I don't know what you're talking about."

"Bullshit! You don't want to involve me. You want to protect me from danger and treat me like some *civilian*." She stepped closer and planted her hands on her hips. "I'm a detective, in case you haven't noticed. And this is *my* case you're jeopardizing."

He sank down on the bed and started unlacing his boots. "Hey, you mind? I need to shower and get this wound cleaned."

"Yes, I mind! I mind being lied to. I mind that you're shutting me out of my own investigation and treating me like I'm stupid."

He pulled off his boots and chunked them against the wall.

She was right. He was shutting her out, but it had nothing to do with her intelligence. Or his respect for her as an investigator. His problem was that he didn't want to compromise her ethics by pulling her into something that was definitely questionable if not outright illegal.

"Well?" she demanded.

"Well, what?" He stood and folded his arms over his bare chest.

"Are you really going to stand there and pretend you don't know what I'm talking about?"

He heaved a sigh.

"I let you in on this investigation against my better judgment. And then you *ditched* me and went behind my back." She shook her head. "What the hell is wrong with you? How could you do this? I trusted you. I thought—" She stopped short. Her mouth fell open. She stared up at him for an endless moment, and something in her look made the back of Scott's neck prickle.

"What?"

Her arms dropped to her sides, and she shook her head. "Oh my God."

Now it was his turn to glare at her.

"I get it now." Her cheeks flushed and she closed her eyes for a moment. "I can't believe I didn't see it. You intentionally picked a fight because I scare you."

He just looked at her.

"This whole thing scares you."

"Right."

"No, I *am* right. This whole weird thing with us"— she waved her hand back and forth between them—"it totally freaks you out."

Scott sighed. "Are you done psychoanalyzing me? Because I'm dead on my feet here, Dani. I'm tired and I'm dirty and I'm hungry as fuck, and I'd like to clean up and go get some food before everything closes."

She stared up at him and nodded slowly. Then she turned and walked toward the door, and he felt a pang of yearning. Relief, too, but mostly yearning. He clenched his teeth and managed not to say anything as she reached the door. She secured the latch at the top. Then she stepped to the window and pulled the curtains together.

She turned around, and his heart gave a wild kick as she stepped toward him. She held his gaze as she

crossed the room, and when she stopped in front of
him and tipped her head back, the look in her eyes was
unmistakable.

"Daniele . . ."

She lifted her eyebrows. "What?"

• • •

He wanted her.

She could see it in his eyes. But she wanted him to
say it.

Daniele. He was the only one who ever called her
that. To everyone else she was always Dani, or Dani
Girl, or Danno, all those buddy names that kept her
firmly in the friend zone. But to Scott she was Daniele.
Not always, but sometimes. It was as though he saw
something no one else did, something sensual and
feminine that everyone else missed.

She watched his gaze heat as she got so close her
breasts almost touched his chest. The room was dim,
but a wedge of light from the bathroom fell over them,
and she could see every detail of his face, from his dark
layer of stubble to the muscles bunching at the side of
his jaw. She let her gaze drift down to check out his
sculpted pecs and well-defined abs. A rush of nerves
went through her and she reached out to trace her fingertip over the dark line of hair above his jeans.

He caught her hand in an iron grip. "Daniele."

"What?" Her response came out breathy and inno-
cent—not like herself at all—but her heart was racing
as she tried to project confidence she didn't feel. She
ignored the pain, as well as the clear signal that he
wanted her to back off.

Because he didn't really want that. She eased closer, brushing the tips of her breasts against him, and his grip on her wrist tightened.

"This is a bad idea." His low, dangerous voice sent a shiver through her. "Didn't your brother warn you about me?"

"No."

"*I'm* warning you."

He sounded adamant. But the way his eyes glinted down at her told her he wasn't fully convinced.

She slid her free hand around his lean waist and went up on tiptoes. Slowly, she pressed a soft, open-mouthed kiss beneath his collarbone. His breath came out in a hiss, and she kissed him again, this time sliding her tongue over his skin. He tasted salty, and his body tensed as she trailed featherlight kisses across his chest and dipped her fingers into the back of his jeans.

She looked up at him as his blue eyes blazed down at her. Her heart pounded and she waited, holding her breath.

"You're going to be sorry you did this."

She felt a surge of triumph. She pressed herself against him as she rose up again, this time to kiss his lips, and he kissed her back, sweeping his tongue into her mouth and giving her another taste of victory. He shifted his thigh, drawing a gasp from her as he pressed against the juncture of her legs. She moaned, and it was swallowed by his kiss as he took her mouth hungrily, giving in to all that pent-up need she'd seen in his eyes. He tasted so good and male and earthy. His thigh was strong and thick, and her legs parted for him. They kissed and kissed, not even coming up for air, and she loved the way he kissed her, craved it. She loved the commanding way he moved, as though nothing in the world would stop him from taking everything he wanted.

Nothing but himself.

All this time, he'd stood in his own way. She would have been willing, and he had to know that. He had to know how much she'd looked and wondered and fantasized about him all these years. Had he done the same?

She didn't know, but she wanted to think so. It sure *felt* like he had, the way he took over the kiss. He cupped her head in his hands and combed his fingers through her hair, taking her mouth exactly how he wanted. He was feeding on her, devouring her like he'd never get enough, and all the while his thigh between her legs was a magical force that had her throbbing and grinding against him.

"Christ, Daniele."

His hands slid down and gripped her hips, and before she knew what was happening, he lifted her off her feet and plopped her on the dresser beside them. She blinked at him in the dimness, and a flutter of panic went through her. Was he pushing her away *now*? But the intense look on his face told her that wasn't it at all. Then he kissed her again, and she slid her arms around his neck and pulled him down, wrapping her legs around his waist as she did.

This was unreal. She couldn't believe they were doing this *here*, in some dumpy motel room in Middle of Nowhere, New Mexico. But she didn't care about the room or the circumstances. The only thing she cared about, the only thing she *needed* in this moment, was him. She needed his mouth and his hands, and his hot, hard body pressed against her.

He burrowed his fingers into her hair and pulled her head back, and the sharp sting to her scalp felt shockingly erotic as he slid his lips over her neck. His warm palm glided inside her shirt and slid up to cup her breast. His mouth closed over her, sucking her through the thin fabric, and she arched against him, wanting more.

He stopped what he was doing and leaned back, and the simmering look in his eyes gave her a warm rush. He took the hem of her shirt between his fingers and lifted an eyebrow in question, and she melted at the notion that he was asking permission. She lifted her arms up, and he pulled the shirt over her head and flung it away.

He stared down at her for an endless moment, and she felt a tremor of nerves because this was *Scott*, and he was seeing her this way for the first time in her life. He settled his big, warm hand at her waist and lifted his eyes to hers, and the raw desire there made her breathless with anticipation. For so long she'd wanted him to touch her, and now it was happening.

He kissed his way down her body, cupping her breasts in his hands and stroking his thumbs over the sensitive tips. He squeezed her nipple and the sensation went straight to her core. She arched her spine and leaned her head back as his tongue teased her.

"So hot," he murmured against her skin, and she felt a giddy rush. She combed her fingers into his hair and dragged him closer, loving the heat of his mouth and the rasp of his stubble against the sensitive skin of her breasts as he kissed her. He gave a hard pull and she moaned and pressed herself closer.

He glanced up at her, and she widened her thighs

and pulled him in with her heels. She was offering herself to him, completely, no strings attached. Like one of those women she'd never wanted to be. But she wanted to be here. Right now. With him and no one else, and she didn't care about the fallout or the consequences, or anything but seeing this through.

He glided his lips up her body and took her mouth again as his hand settled at the small of her back and dragged her closer to the edge of the dresser, close enough to feel the hard bulge of his erection through his jeans.

"Scott," she whispered.

"Yeah." He dipped his hand inside her pants, and the warm slide of his fingers was an electric shock as he quickly found the perfect spot.

"Oh my God." She closed her eyes as he teased her, making soft, relentless circles that set her nerves on fire and made her dizzy with need. His fingers dipped lower, and she arched against his hand.

"Scott, *please.*"

"What do you want, Daniele?"

He knew exactly what she wanted, and he wanted her to say it.

She reached for his jeans and got the snap undone and the zipper down before he leaned back. Their eyes locked, for a moment everything they were doing was right there between them, and she felt a stab of fear that he was going to put the brakes on.

She leaned back on her palms and watched him, heart hammering, and he hooked his fingers into her pants and pulled her remaining clothes off in one smooth motion, and then he was back between her legs gazing down at her with pure male appreciation

in his eyes. He stroked his hand over her thigh and
her waist and her breast, and she felt the fire of his
touch in every cell of her body. She dipped her hand
inside his jeans to curl her fingers around him, and
he made a low sound deep in his chest. He kissed her
and pulled her against him until she felt the hot length
of him right where she desperately needed him to be.
She shifted her legs. His body went rigid as he entered
her, and she cried out at the sharp thrill. She moved
her hips, taking him deeper, but it still wasn't enough.
"More."

"I need a condom," he said tightly.

"No."

"Damn it, Daniele."

"I'm on the pill."

He leaned back and looked down at her, his face
taut. "You sure?"

"Yes," she gasped, and tipped her head back as he
pushed into her again. And again. The next thrust was
fierce and deep, so deep she saw stars. Before she knew
it she was shaking and coming apart in his arms.

"Oh my God, *Scott*."

She clutched him and churned her hips. It was too
much, too good, and she couldn't stop herself from
climaxing. She gripped him against her as her body
quaked and trembled. He held her through it, held her
tight against his chest, and she could hear his heart
pounding against her ear, and she knew he wasn't finished but she didn't know why he'd stopped.

He kissed the top of her head. "You all right?"

She nodded against his chest, not looking at him,
embarrassed that she'd gone off so impossibly fast. It
had been a long time for her, much too long, appar-

ently, and all she needed was a naked man and about three seconds of penetration.

But he wasn't naked, she realized, looking down at where their bodies were joined.

"Hold on to me," he said as he pulled out of her and kicked his jeans away. He gripped her waist and picked her up and walked her the few steps to the bed, then dropped her onto it. The mattress sank with the weight as he knelt between her knees and leaned over her.

"Are you—"

He cut her off with a kiss that was even hungrier than before, and his hand glided up the inside of her thigh, making her shiver.

He pulled back. "Done with you? No." He kissed her again, propping his weight on his arm as he settled between her legs. Her body was still quivering as he slid into her with a rough thrust that made her gasp.

"You like that?"

She nodded.

"Say it."

"I love it," she said, and he did it again.

His strokes were slow and deep. She glided her hands over his body and reveled at the hard muscles of his arms and shoulders.

She gazed up at him, and she felt a wave of disbelief because this was *Scott*, naked and inside her, and gazing down with those blue eyes that were smoky with need for her. For *her*. The intense way he looked at her made her feel like she was the only woman alive, and she knew now why she'd shied away from this all these years, why she'd tried to deny her feelings for him, even to herself.

He had the power to crush her.

She held on to him as he shifted her hips and started a steady rhythm. He was so hot, and so amazingly *good*—which shouldn't have surprised her at all because he was good at so many things. She inhaled the warm, musky smell of his skin as he moved over her. They fit together perfectly, and she loved the feel of his flesh against her as he moved into her again and again with the same insatiable need that she felt, too.

Dani pulled him closer, wrapping her legs around him, and he quickened the rhythm as the need grew. It was all so *much*, so much heat and friction, and yet still not nearly enough. She found herself racing him, trying to keep up with his relentless pace as he drove into her, and she felt the tension building inside her all over again, and she could feel the same tension in his arms and shoulders as she clung to him.

"Daniele."

She clutched him tighter.

"Come on, baby."

"I can't," she gasped. She couldn't do it again, not so soon, no matter how much she wanted to, and she gripped him closer, burning and shaking with the intensity of it.

He murmured something against her forehead. She knew he was waiting for her, and she wanted to get there so desperately, but she couldn't, and she was nearly sobbing from the frustration of it.

"You can. Come on."

She gripped him tighter as he reared back and gave a deep thrust.

"*Daniele.*"

Her name was a command, and it sent her flying over the edge, and she came all over again in a blinding explosion of pleasure, and this time he was right there with her, and for an endless moment there was nothing but light and heat and ecstasy.

His arms collapsed, and his weight crushed down on her, pinning her against the mattress as they gasped for air. She felt shattered. Annihilated. Every inch of their bodies felt fused together, and she didn't want him to move, even though she couldn't breathe beneath him.

He pushed up on his arms, and she knew the shocked look on his face would stay with her forever.

He rolled onto his back and gazed at the ceiling. He cast a sideways glance at her, but she couldn't read it. She had absolutely no idea what he was thinking right now. Suddenly the fused-together feeling vanished, and a yawning chasm was between them.

Nerves swept over her. What had they done? What had *she* done?

She stared at the ceiling and tried to catch her breath as reality rained down on her. She'd done exactly what she'd always told herself she wouldn't. She'd thrown herself at this man she cared about. And she didn't know if his stunned reaction was because he'd never expected her to do it, or he'd never expected himself to let it happen.

Panic washed over her. Her pulse started to race for reasons that had nothing to do with sex. She had to salvage this. She had put them on some sort of normal footing again.

He rolled over, caging her in with his arms, and she stared up into those gorgeous blue eyes, and her heart skittered. This was Scott, naked and looming over her in bed, and she didn't know what to say.

"You still hungry?" Her words surprised her. She had no idea where they'd come from.

He looked surprised for a moment, too. Then he looked suspicious, as if she'd asked him a trick question.

"I could eat." He dipped his head down and nuzzled her neck, and a shiver of relief spread through her as his mouth traveled down to her breast. He cupped it in his hand, kissing her as she squirmed under him.

"How about pizza?"

He stopped and looked up at her. "Pizza's good. If anything's open."

"I've got one in my room."

He blinked at her. "In your room."

"Yeah."

"You're serious?"

"I picked it up while you were gone."

A shadow moved over his face. Was it the reminder of how he'd ditched her and lied about it? Or how she'd failed to follow orders?

He sat up and looked down at her, and the sight of his bare chest took her breath away. Then he stood, and she was pretty sure she'd never be able to breathe again.

Dear. God.

She'd always known he was well built. But knowing it and actually *seeing* his glorious male perfection were two different things. He was all broad shoulders and sculpted muscles and narrow hips.

"Hey."

She jerked her gaze up from the most droolworthy part of him.

The side of his mouth curved into a smirk as he gazed down at her. "You sure you want pizza?"

"Yes." She sat up.

"I'll get it." He grabbed his jeans and stepped into them. He retrieved the keycard off the floor. It had been tucked into the waist of her yoga pants when she'd stormed over here in a snit. "This yours?"

"Yeah."

He slipped the card into his pocket. Then he leaned over her, pressing his palm against the headboard as he looked down at her body. He stared without hesitation until she felt a blush sweeping over her skin. Then his gaze met hers.

"You're beautiful."

Her heart squeezed. What did she say to that?

"Stay right here." He kissed her forehead. "I mean it."

CHAPTER 18

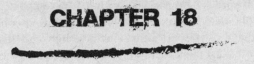

Scott returned to find that she hadn't followed directions at all. She'd turned on a lamp and was searching through his backpack again. And, worse, she'd put on clothes.

"Hey." He tossed the pizza box on the bedside table. She'd folded the covers back, he noticed, which at least gave him some hope about what they might be doing later.

She turned around and planted her hand on her hip. The sight of her in only his rumpled T-shirt made him hard all over again.

"I wasn't kidding earlier. You could really get in trouble here, Scott."

"Tell me about it." He eased up behind her and slid his hands down her thighs, then back up again. He couldn't get enough of her. He couldn't look at her and *not* want to touch her.

"Unlawfully removing evidence from a crime scene is a serious offense."

"I know you're right, and I have a confession."

She tensed. "What?"

He slid his hands up to her breasts. "It turns me on when you talk cop."

"I'm serious."

"So am I. Maybe you should arrest me."

"Don't patronize me."

He pressed his cock against her. "I'm not."

She went lax, and he slid his hands down her body. Suddenly she spun around behind him and shoved him against the wall, pinning his arm behind his back.

"I've taken down stronger men than you."

He snorted. "I doubt it."

She wrenched his arm higher.

"Ouch!"

"That hurt, tough guy?" She sounded like she was enjoying this, although not nearly as much as he was.

"Seriously, that hurts, Dani."

She loosened her hold a fraction, and the next instant he had her up off her feet. He tossed her onto the bed and then dropped on top of her, pinning her to the mattress as he caught most of his weight on his arms. She bucked beneath him, making his shirt ride up around her hips.

He grinned down at her. "This your idea of a takedown?"

She bucked and pushed, which only made his shirt move up around her waist, and he was grateful now that she'd turned on the lamp.

He lifted an eyebrow. "Nice view."

Her cheeks flushed. She went still and pretended she didn't see him gawking at her.

"I'm really not joking, Scott. I'm trying to help you here. You could get in trouble."

He heard the fear in her voice. She was actually worried about this, about *him*, and he felt an uncomfortable pinch in his chest. He was used to being the one to protect people, not the other way around.

"Don't worry about me." He dropped a kiss on her

forehead. The concern on her face got to him. But what got to him even more was the hazy look in her eyes when he spread her thighs apart with his.

"Scott . . ." she whispered.

He kissed her.

He didn't know what she wanted to tell him, but he was pretty sure he didn't want to hear it. He just wanted to touch her and taste her and hear her say his name as she clenched him inside her body. Suddenly the playfulness was gone as she fumbled with his zipper, and he pulled his shirt off her as she freed him from his jeans. He shifted her hips under him and entered her in one hard stroke, and she made a little squeak.

"Sorry."

She kissed him, twining her legs around him and pulling him close as she somehow managed to match his pace again. It was crazy. Desperate. And much too rough, and he had to force himself to slow the fuck down before he hurt her. But she pulled him even tighter, gripping him to her as he felt her begin to shake and come, and he wanted to draw it out, to keep it going, but as she clenched around him, he felt himself start to lose it. She gasped his name and scraped her nails down his back, and that was it, game over, and he came inside her in a powerful rush.

For seconds or minutes he was numb. Completely. Then he was dimly aware of the soft, feminine scent of her hair against his nose. Damn it, he was crushing her again.

He pushed up on his palms, worried until he saw the blissed-out look on her face. He eased out of her and rolled onto his back, hauling her with him.

"Hey," she murmured.

He shifted her hips, settling her right where he wanted her. She tucked her head under his chin, and he closed his eyes and waited for his heart rate to come down from the stratosphere.

She sighed. "That was fast."

"You're blaming *me*?"

"Yeah."

He was too wrecked to care. His mind was totally gone. Sex with Dani had deleted everything—fatigue, hunger, gunshot wound. The only thing with any sensation at all right now was his dick, and it was singing.

They lay together, sweaty and sticky, listening to the rhythmic *thump-thump* of someone's party upstairs.

He felt the tickle of her fingernails tracing a path down his arm, then up again, then down. It was relaxing. Something about that nagged at his brain, but he didn't have the energy to analyze it. He just wanted to lie here, holding her warm, naked body against him like he'd dreamed of doing so many times.

Her nails trailed over his shoulder. She pushed up on her palm and stared down at him, and her brows drew together with worry. "What's this gunk on your wound?"

"Superglue."

"Are you kidding me?" She sat up straighter. "What is that, some SEAL trick?"

She had perfectly round breasts with small pink nipples. He sat up to kiss them, but she tipped his chin up. "Hey. Do you need to go to the ER?"

"No." He leaned back against the headboard and arranged her in his lap so she was straddling him.

"There's one twenty-five minutes from here. It's in the next town."

"Forget it." Nothing short of nuclear Armageddon would make him leave this room right now.

The volume of the bass increased and she darted a look at the ceiling. "It's getting worse."

"So?"

"So, it's obnoxious."

"You weren't really planning to sleep tonight, were you?"

"Maybe."

He pulled her forward to kiss him. "That's not happening."

"How would you know?"

"Trust me, I know."

CHAPTER 19

Sean tromped through the woods, ducking low under a branch.

"Watch your step there," the deputy told him, shining his flashlight on a rut in the ground.

Sean stepped across it and followed the deputy through some bushes into a clearing. He halted and stared. The car in the center of the clearing was burned beyond recognition.

"Borrow your light?"

The deputy handed it over, and Sean aimed it inside the car. No human remains that he could see. It was hard to tell, given the extreme damage caused by the fire. Not even the glass windows were left—they'd evidently shattered in the heat. Sean walked around the four-door car. The plates had been removed. He took out a pair of gloves and pulled them on, although he doubted he needed to worry about marring any prints here. He managed to pull open what was left of the door and located a VIN number. He took out his phone and snapped a photo of it.

Beside him, the Clarke County sheriff's deputy shifted from foot to foot, clearly nervous. He looked about twenty and couldn't have had more than a few months on the job.

"No witnesses to the fire?"

"No, sir." The deputy cleared his throat. "Course, people burn trash around here, so it might not have attracted much notice. We wouldn't have found it at all except we had a team back here today looking for some meth heads from that trailer park over there." He nodded in the direction of Shady Creek Estates, a notorious haven for meth cooks.

"When was this raid?"

"This afternoon. And then I saw that message come across my computer. That you guys were looking for a Ford Taurus? I happened to notice the make and model, so thought I'd pass it along."

Sean swept the flashlight over the backseat. The cushions were almost completely incinerated.

"You think it's the car y'all are looking for?"

"Might be." Sean rounded the front, shining the flashlight over the soot-covered hood. Beside the driver's-side window was an exterior spotlight that could be controlled from inside the vehicle. Every patrol unit used by Sean's department, and even most of the unmarked units, were outfitted with the same type of spotlight.

Sean's pulse picked up as he stared at the light. He muttered a curse and pulled out his phone. Brooke answered on the second ring, and he smiled at the sound of her voice.

"You agreed not to bug me."

"That's not why I'm calling. This is something else." Silence.

"Work related," he added. "I'm at a crime scene and I could really use a hand."

"Let me guess. It's related to your all-important murder case? And I need to drop everything I'm doing and get there right now, this minute, and it can't wait till morning?"

"You guessed right."

• • •

Dani woke up alone.

The room was quiet, and a band of gray seeped through the gap between the curtains and the wall. She closed her eyes again and took a mental inventory. Her body felt heavy. Her limbs were cemented to the bed, and she felt sore in places she hadn't been aware of yesterday.

A door opened, and she smelled steam and soap. She heard Scott rummaging through his stuff, and then he came to stand beside the bed. The mattress dipped down as he sat beside her.

She opened her eyes. He wore jeans and boots—no shirt—and his hair was damp from the shower. She looked at the boots again, and something bothered her, but her mind was too groggy to follow the thought.

He picked up her hand. "We need to talk, Dani."

His expression was unreadable, and she felt a flurry of nerves as she sat up. She glanced around and her gaze landed on the clock: 7:13.

She pushed the covers away and got out of bed, grabbing a T-shirt off the nightstand. She slipped it over her head.

"Talk about what?" she asked, crossing the room to pick up the rest of her clothes.

He stood and watched her, and she realized why the boots bothered her. She was still half-asleep, and he was practically out the door already. He grabbed a fresh shirt from his backpack and pulled it on. "This could get complicated."

A tiny dart landed in the center of her chest.

"I don't see why. It's not like I have any expectations of you."

He looked at her. "That's a little harsh."

"Scott, come on. I know you, remember?"

His gaze narrowed. "What is it you think you know?"

"Your MO with women. Everything's short and sweet with you. Commitment isn't your thing."

He folded his arms over his chest. "Are you trying to make me feel like shit here?"

"I'm not trying to make you feel anything. That's the point." She slipped on her panties and yoga pants, as if getting dressed in front of him were no big deal. "Look, this was a onetime thing. I get it. We can go back home and pretend nothing happened."

Surprise flared in his eyes. And something else, too. *Relief.* He covered it quickly, but she knew him too well.

She needed to get out of here. She grabbed her key-card off the nightstand and crossed to the door, but he caught her arm.

"Hey."

"What?" she asked.

The sound of a car outside had him glancing at the window. He released her arm and stepped over to shift the curtains.

"God damn it."

"What?"

He glanced at her. "Did you call the feds?"

"What? No." She stepped over and peeked through the gap. Sure enough, a four-door Taurus was parked in the handicapped space near the motel office. Two men in suits were out of the car, and one was looking at his phone.

"Ric must have called them," she said. "Or Ric's brother." She turned to see Scott zipping his backpack. "What are you doing?"

"I've got a flight at ten thirty."

"A *flight*?"

"Whatever they're doing here is going to involve red tape and paperwork and bullshit." He shrugged into his jacket. "I don't have time to get involved."

"But you can't just *leave*."

"Wanna bet?"

"But you were there last night. They're going to want a statement."

"They're here to talk to you, not me. You can connect the dots for them." He shouldered his backpack, and she felt a stab of panic.

"But . . . what about the car?"

"I'm sure they'll give you a ride back to Albuquerque. That's where they're based." He walked over and looked through the curtains again before turning to face her. "They're in the office now. I need to hit it."

"I'm not going to lie for you."

"I would never expect you to. Give them an honest statement, but do it without me."

She stared up at him, fuming. Tears stung her eyes, but she forced them back.

"We're not done talking, Daniele."

She ignored that. "These are *federal* agents, Scott. You're putting me in an impossible situation here! What the hell do you expect me to do?"

"Do what you always do." He reached for the door. "Handle it."

CHAPTER 20

Brooke stepped out the doors of the Delphi Center and stood for a moment in the fresh air. The day had flown by in a blur of work, and it was already almost dark. Her windowless lab reminded her of a casino sometimes—it was much too easy to lose track of what time or even what day it was.

Friday, she reminded herself as she hurried down the steps. And she was heading into yet another weekend with nothing on her calendar besides work and maybe some laundry. She walked toward her car at the far end of the parking lot, wondering why she wasn't more depressed about her lack of weekend plans. Maybe something was wrong with her. But the simple fact was that she enjoyed her job more than she enjoyed socializing.

"Brooke Porter?"

She jumped and whirled around. Holy crap, how had she missed the muscle-bound man lurking in the parking lot? He sat against the back bumper of a pickup truck, watching her. Slowly, he stood up and walked toward her. His gait was casual, and she could tell he was trying to look nonthreatening, but her heart was hammering anyway.

"Sorry to startle you. You don't know me, but—"

"Scott Black."

He didn't respond.

"I've seen you around." She cleared her throat. "What can I do for you?"

"A favor." He stepped closer, watching her carefully. He dipped his hand into the pocket of his black leather jacket and pulled out an envelope.

She waited for him to explain.

"I've got two shell casings I need fingerprinted. It's important." There was a certain force behind the last two words.

She glanced around the parking lot but saw no one else there. Her gaze settled on him again. "Why should I help you?"

"Truthfully, you shouldn't. I'm suspended right now. It's probably better if you don't even talk to me."

She laughed at the words. And because his blue eyes looked so sincere. She'd heard he was a charmer, and she could tell why people said that. It was some kind of stealth charm that you didn't see coming.

"You're friends with Roland," she said, because she'd seen them talking together in the coffee shop. "Why don't you ask him?"

"You're the best we have."

She gave him a *Yeah, right* look. "Flattery won't work with me."

"It'd be a personal favor."

She watched him, weighing what to do. She'd already decided, but she was still trying to understand her decision. She didn't even know this guy, and she was swamped with work, and another favor was the last thing she had time for.

She sighed and held out her hand. He gave her the envelope. It felt heavier than she'd expected.

"Two casings," he said again.

"Type of ammo?"

"Three hundred Win Mag."

"When do you need the results?"

"Soon."

She sighed. "Of course."

"Check military databases."

"*If* I find prints, you mean."

He nodded. "I'll text you my number and you can call me. You probably shouldn't do it from work."

Her gaze narrowed. "You don't have *my* number."

"Yeah, I do." He backed away, hands in his pockets, looking completely harmless, as though he hadn't just ambushed her in a parking lot and blown up her plans for Saturday.

Not that she'd had anything planned besides work, but still. "I'll try to get to it, but I'm not making any promises."

"Understood."

• • •

The station house was unusually busy for a Saturday morning. Dani topped off her travel mug with coffee on her way to the conference room where Sean and Jasper waited for her, looking annoyingly well rested.

"Hey," Sean said, "heard you had an eventful trip."

"You could say that."

"You all right?"

"Never better." She took a chair and guzzled some coffee to bolster her energy. She was still feeling the effects of her ditch-diving incident as well as a grueling trip back that had included a four-hour delay in the

Albuquerque airport. When she'd finally made it home, she found the window on her door fixed—thanks to Dax—but her nerves were in an even worse condition than when she'd left. She'd tossed and turned most of the night and barely managed two hours of sleep.

"Thanks for coming in early," she told her team as Reynolds stepped into the room. The lieutenant parked himself at the head of the table, and Dani tried to gauge his mood. Not good, judging from his sour expression.

She was at the top of her boss's shit list since New Mexico. He'd threatened to not only make Sean the lead but yank her off the case completely because she'd been "consorting" with a possible suspect. Dani wasn't sure exactly what he meant by "consorting," but she couldn't argue with him. Letting Scott get involved had been a bad idea. She had no defense, and now she had to prove herself all over again.

"So," she said, looking at Sean and Jasper, "where's Ric?"

"Don't know," Sean said.

"Let's get started," Reynolds said gruffly. "Ric can catch up."

Dani opened her file and tried to collect her thoughts. She felt exhausted, both physically and mentally. But she was also inundated with responsibilities and she didn't have time for a break. She had to push through.

Do what you always do. Handle it.

Dani swallowed the bitter lump in her throat. She hadn't spoken to Scott since those glib parting words that had made her want to slap him.

She took a deep breath and plunged in. "Before Nathan Collins was murdered, I had a chance to interview him about his three former coworkers. He told us some things we didn't know." She glanced at Reynolds. He knew all this already from their phone conversation, so this rundown was mostly for Sean and Jasper. "One thing he mentioned that we definitely *should* have known was that at the time James Ayers left Trinity, he was being investigated by the administration for possibly having sexual relations with a student."

"Was Tessa the student?" Jasper asked. "I thought she was his research assistant there."

"She was. This was a different woman. I have her name, and I plan to talk to her. Another interesting point, Nathan Collins *also* was being investigated for improper relations with a student. He claimed the charges were bogus, but Trinity had put him on leave anyway."

"Ric interviewed Kreznik, who supposedly hired James down here," Sean said, "and he didn't tell us anything about that. Were the charges legit?"

"I don't know. But while I was in New Mexico, I had a chance to talk to Tessa's older sister in Santa Fe."

"Oh, yeah? How was she?" Sean asked.

"Emotional. And busy. They were having the funeral that day, so our conversation was short, but she said Tessa was fully aware of the allegations against James, and she insisted they were made-up." Dani flipped through her notes from the conversation. "The sister wasn't buying it, though. She said she never liked James Ayers and she told her sister any man who would cheat on his wife would probably hit on a student, too. She'd been trying to talk Tessa into breaking up with him, but Tessa blew off that advice. Even after the move, she continued to try to convince her sister to end the affair, but supposedly Tessa wouldn't listen."

"Baby sis was in love," Sean quipped.

"Very much so, according to this woman. Love wasn't the only reason she moved here, though. The sister also said Tessa thought it was, I quote, 'a killer opportunity' that she couldn't pass up."

"'A killer opportunity'?" Reynolds frowned. "She really said that?"

"According to the sister, those were her exact words."

"It's slang," Sean said. "I doubt it means anything."

"Whether it does or not," Dani said, "I'm not seeing how taking a pay cut to be a research assistant is much of an opportunity. I think there was more going on in that biology department than we know."

"How sure are we that the murder in New Mexico is related to the killings here?" Reynolds asked.

Dani stared at him. He stared right back, waiting for the answer that seemed beyond obvious.

"Well." She cleared her throat. "A number of things. For one, the timing. Four deaths in five days? That can't be a coincidence. All four of these people worked together on the same project at the same university, at one point. And three of them worked together here. And the three Texas victims each called Nathan Collins shortly before they were murdered."

"There're some parallels with the crimes, too," Sean added. "Especially when you look at the new forensic evidence we have." His phone rattled on the table, and he bent forward to check it. "Brooke's here. I invited her in to explain the results. Just a sec." He got up and stepped out of the room.

"Who's Brooke?" Jasper looked at Dani.

"Brooke Porter, with the Delphi Center. She's working on the house fire and the car."

"Kreznik's lake house?"

"That's right."

Sean returned, ushering Brooke into the room. The CSI wore a black hoodie and jeans that made her look about fifteen years old. Dani cast a glance at Reynolds, who continued to look unhappy as Sean made quick introductions.

"Could you explain to everyone what you were telling me on the phone?" Sean asked her.

"Sure." Brooke opened a blue file with the Delphi Center logo on it. "On our second examination of Dr. Kreznik's cabin, we discovered remnants of rags soaked in accelerant that had been tacked to the structure just beneath the hot-water heater closet. Fire investigators now tell me they believe the hot-water heater was tampered with to make the incident look like an accidental fire." She glanced at Dani. "I ran tests on the accelerant used. It's camping fuel, which is the same accelerant used with the Ford Taurus."

"Are you sure it's the same Ford Taurus?" Dani asked.

"The tire tread is a match, according to our examiner."

"So, now we have forensic evidence linking the murder scenes to the car fire," Sean said. "I'm thinking he committed the three murders and then torched his vehicle to hide any evidence before hopping a flight to Albuquerque."

"You're assuming this same perp is responsible for the murder in New Mexico," Dani said.

"There was a fire there, too." Sean shrugged. "Makes sense to me. Sounds like this guy likes to torch things."

"What else do you have on the house fire?" Reynolds asked Brooke.

"That's it in terms of the accelerant. Camping fuel.

You could try tracking it down, but it's sold all over the place, so I doubt that's much of a lead."

"The Taurus is a lead, though," Sean said. "It's dark blue and it has a spotlight mounted on the driver's side, which makes it look a lot like an unmarked police unit. I think he pulled up behind James and Tessa while they were having their little lakeside staff meeting, and he posed as a cop, which would explain how he got the drop on them."

Dani had a flashback of the rest stop near Big Rock. She'd been in Scott's lap when that patrol car had pulled up behind them and made her jump out of her skin.

"Dani?"

She looked at Sean. "Huh?"

"Did you read Brooke's report yet?"

"No, sorry." Dani looked at her. "I'm behind on my email. You're talking about the trace substance report you sent me this morning?"

"Yes. I had a chance to track down the powdery substance on the carpet of the Accord driven by James Ayers. It's lime."

"Lime?"

"Finely ground limestone. Pretty common here in central Texas, where we have a lot of quarries, so I'm not sure if that constitutes a lead for you."

"Okay, what about fingerprints?" Dani asked Brooke. "Anything recovered from the burned Taurus?"

"No."

"Any more word on that partial print?" Dani asked. "The one from the Glock nine recovered from Wood-lake Park?"

"Nothing so far."

"Try military databases," Dani said.

Brooke lifted an eyebrow and made a note in her file.

"There's something weird about the fire scene," Sean commented.

"Sounds like there's a lot weird about it," Dani said.

"I'm talking about the boathouse. Supposedly, the place is a fishing cabin, right? He keeps a fishing boat there. The neighbors said he liked to come out there frequently, at least once a week, and spend a night or two at a time."

"Yes?" Dani asked.

"Well, the boat looks like it hasn't been used in months. It's covered in dust and cobwebs, and the switch to activate the hoist is all corroded."

"Maybe he goes out in a buddy's boat," Reynolds said.

"Or," Sean said, "maybe he's not going out there to fish."

"Could be he has a mistress there," Jasper suggested.

"Kreznik wasn't married," Sean said. "But I get your point. He could have been going out there to visit a girlfriend."

"If so, she might be able to give us some insight into what was going on with him around the time he was murdered," Dani said. "We should check into it."

Her phone vibrated in her pocket, and she pulled it out to find a message from Ric: *New development. Meet me at my house.*

She glanced around. "Okay, so . . . Sean, how about you go back and interview Kreznik's coworker Oliver Junger and see if he knows anything about a girlfriend out at the lake house where Kreznik died." She looked at Brooke. The CSI didn't report to her, so she needed to be diplomatic. "And if you could keep me posted on anything new with that partial fingerprint, that would be really helpful." She turned to Jasper. "Jasper, you follow up on the VIN from the Taurus. We need to find out whether it was an actual police vehicle that the killer somehow got ahold of, or if it was a regular Taurus he made to look like a police vehicle. Either way, it could give us a lead."

"I'm on it," Jasper said.

Reynolds got up and slipped out while Dani jotted notes in her file and finished giving out marching orders.

"We all set?" She stood up and looked at everyone. "Sean and Jasper, we'll reconvene here same time tomorrow morning—"

"On Sunday?" Jasper looked alarmed.

"Yes, and no bitching. The lieutenant's authorized overtime. Meanwhile, if you come up with anything new, I want to hear about it ASAP, you got that? Day or night, don't hesitate to call me."

CHAPTER 21

Ric and Mia's house looked even more picturesque in the light of day, and Dani thought again about the sorry state of her yard as she walked up their flower-lined sidewalk.

Ric opened the door before she had a chance to knock. "Rey's on his way. You want coffee?"

"Definitely."

She followed him into the kitchen, where stacks of neatly folded baby clothes covered the breakfast table. The sink was filled with dishes, and the entire counter was covered in cookbooks, all with little yellow sticky notes poking out.

"Mia's on a mission," Ric said. "She's convinced she won't have time to cook anything after the baby comes."

"She probably won't."

"We've got nine casseroles in the freezer. I had to take out the ice tray."

Dani glanced down the hallway toward the bedrooms. "Where is she?"

"Walking."

"In this heat?"

"On a treadmill at the gym." Ric combed a hand through his hair. "I tried to get her to stay home and put her feet up, but she won't listen to me. Says she's stir-crazy."

The front door opened and Rey Santos stepped inside. Dani had never seen him in anything other than a dark suit, and today was no exception. He walked into the kitchen and raised his eyebrows at all the cookbooks, but didn't say anything.

Rey had the same simmering good looks as his brother—brown-black eyes, olive skin, and that seductive half smile that made women stupid. Yet somehow he remained stubbornly unattached.

"Rey, you remember Dani," Ric said.

"Detective." He nodded at her.

"Hi."

Rey got a mug from a cabinet and poured himself coffee as Ric grabbed a file sitting on the bar. "Let's work in here," Ric said, leading them into the living room.

Dani took a seat on an ottoman and watched Ric's brother. He had to be going into the office later. Otherwise, why the tie? Dani couldn't imagine being a federal agent. The pay would be better, but she couldn't fathom dressing up all the time.

Rey sat down on a sofa opposite Dani. "I made some calls, and there's definitely something going on, like you said."

"Like who said?" Dani looked at Ric.

"I told Rey how we were getting the runaround from Albuquerque. The agents there aren't even taking my calls anymore."

"I'm not surprised," she said. "I told you how tight-lipped they were with me. All questions, no answers."

Her two-hour meeting in her motel room in Big Rock had been frustrating on so many levels. They'd basically questioned her like a suspect in Nathan Collins's murder. Then they hadn't extended the basic professional courtesy of giving her any information in return. Also frustrating—she'd had to explain Scott's involvement, and they had clearly been unhappy that he wasn't there to be interviewed, which meant they'd have to get his statement at a later time.

"Yeah, well, I got the same treatment," Rey said. "They definitely wanted to know why I was interested, but they wouldn't tell me anything."

"Did you tell them why you were interested?" Ric asked.

"No. But they'll put it together eventually."

Dani scoffed. "Yeah, Santos and Santos, both asking about the same case. Even the feds should be able to figure that out."

"I contacted a guy I know with ATF, and he was a little more helpful," Rey said. "He confirmed they had agents on the scene *and* that they found explosive residue. He hears it was a PETN-based device."

"PETN?" Dani asked.

"A type of explosive," Rey clarified. "It's military-grade. This was a sophisticated IED, according to my source."

Dani's stomach tensed. She pictured Scott racing toward the flaming wreckage, then racing toward her when the shooting started.

"How was it detonated?" Ric asked.

"Cell phone." Rey nodded at Dani. "You're lucky you weren't close by."

Ric gave her a look, and Dani knew he still felt guilty that she'd been there at all.

Dani felt guilty, too. Maybe if she hadn't gone to interview Collins, he might not have been targeted. Her investigation could somehow have drawn attention to him and caused his death.

"Also recovered from the scene," Rey continued, "two slugs, both embedded in a tree near Spruce Canyon Road."

Dani tried to hide her surprise. "That's good news. Where are the slugs?"

"At the FBI ballistics lab. They're looking for any sort of lead that might help them run down this sniper you told them about."

"So they *believe* me." Dani hadn't been sure. Everything she'd told the agents had been met with cool skepticism, as if they thought she might be making it all up—a sworn officer of the law just spinning lies to waste everyone's time. It had been infuriating. Even more so because she hadn't had Scott there to corroborate her story.

"I can't tell you what they believe or don't believe," Rey said. "Like I mentioned, they stonewalled me, so all the information I have is secondhand. What I know about the bullets came from a sheriff's deputy up there. I can give you his name so you can follow up. I also understand they've located a spot on a ridge across from the crime scene where they've recovered some shell casings."

"Okay, what did you find out about Collins?" Ric asked.

"As for him, I can tell you he was on our radar."

"You mean being investigated?" Dani asked.

"That's right. The FBI has a file on him, but I wasn't able to access it."

Ric's brow furrowed. "What do you think that's about?"

"No idea. I tried poking around and didn't get anywhere. I got some more on Collins himself, but it's general, the kind of stuff you could get."

Ric blew out a sigh. "Tell us what you have."

"Basically, the guy was a child prodigy." Rey pulled out a notepad and flipped through it. "Graduated high school in Sunnyvale, California, at age sixteen. Went to UCLA. Got a PhD in biology by twenty-three and went to work for some biotech company in San Francisco. After a few years there he took a job with Trinity. Collins was twenty-nine. Single. Clean police record, except for a speeding ticket."

"Roswell, New Mexico," Dani said impatiently. "I have all this already from his background check. But it doesn't make sense."

"What doesn't?" Ric asked.

"Why Trinity?" She shook her head. "This guy's lighting it up career-wise, so then he takes a job in Podunk, New Mexico? And I saw his living situation. He lived in a cramped little cabin and was complaining about his bills stacking up. It didn't look like he was raking in the money or anything, so what was the motive to be in New Mexico?"

Both brothers looked at her, but neither ventured a guess.

"And that's not the only thing that doesn't make sense," Dani said. "There's some serious money involved here, and I don't get where it's coming from."

Rey's eyebrows tipped up. "How do you mean?"

"*Four* professional hits in two states? These crimes are elaborate. We're talking about a car bomb, multiple house fires. Plus, a complicated double homicide with a fall guy set up *months* in advance to take the blame."

Just the thought of Scott's involvement made Dani's stomach queasy.

"She's right," Ric said. "This operation is complex. Someone's bankrolling this thing, and we have to find out who."

"What about the cabin?" Dani asked. "Collins said he was renting there. I wonder who owns it."

"I wondered that, too." Rey took out his phone and scrolled through it. "Turns out the land is owned by a corporation, Sunland LLC. As for who's behind that, I'm looking into it now. I've got some calls out but I'm waiting to hear." Rey checked his watch. "And speaking of waiting, I need to go. I'm going to be late for my noon meeting."

Rey stood, and they walked him to the door. Dani felt more confused than ever. Why did the FBI have a file on Nathan Collins? And what did any of this have to do with her investigation in Texas? She couldn't see it. She felt like she was working a jigsaw puzzle and little pieces were starting to come together, but she had no idea what the big picture was supposed to look like.

Ric closed the door behind his brother and turned to look at her. Dani realized she hadn't even said good-bye to the man, and he'd spent the last twenty-four hours busting his ass to help them.

"You okay?" Ric asked.

"I don't know."

"You look like hell, by the way. No offense."

She couldn't get offended because she knew he was right. She was going on four days with almost no sleep. Her nerves were raw, and her emotions were much too close to the surface.

"Maybe you should go home," he said.

"What, and put my feet up?"

"You won't do any of us any good if you have a crash. I think you need a break."

She took out her keys. "Well, since you put me in charge, it's really not up to you."

"I'm serious, Dani."

"I know." She pulled open the door. "I'm going back to the station to work these new angles. Call me if you come up with anything."

He sighed, but he seemed to know it was pointless to argue. "You do the same."

• • •

It was dark by the time Dani swung into the Smoky J's parking lot and spied a number of familiar cars. Inside she found half a dozen of her coworkers around a table covered with drinks and plates.

As she approached, Sean glanced up from a platter of ribs. "Hey, we were just talking about the case. What's the latest?"

"You tell me. I guess there's been an arrest since everyone's done working?"

He smiled. "People gotta eat, Dani." He took a swig of his beer. "Why don't you pull up a chair?"

"I'm fine."

"Really." He gave her a sharp look and pushed out the chair beside him. "Take a load off."

She glanced around and noticed the cool looks aimed in her direction. It probably wasn't a good idea to alienate everyone while she was leading up her first big case, so she relented and took a seat.

"Want a beer?" Sean asked.

"No." She looked at Jasper. "What's the word on that vehicle identification number?"

He wiped his mouth with a napkin and had the decency to look guilty. "I, uh, got something back on that. The car used to be in the motor pool with San Antonio PD." He pushed his plate away. "Not anymore, though. It was in a wreck, so they put it in an auction with some other vehicles."

"When?"

"'Bout six weeks ago. Car was purchased by a guy in San Antonio, but then ten days ago it was reported stolen."

"Ten days?"

He nodded. "I requested the police report, but I haven't heard back yet."

"Why didn't you call me?" She didn't bother to hide her annoyance.

"I was waiting on the report."

"San Antonio is a lead, with or without the report. Didn't I say to call me with all leads anytime, day or night?"

"Yeah, but—"

"Anytime means *anytime*."

Sean was staring at her now, clearly annoyed.

"Sorry." Jasper checked his watch. "I'll put in another call, see what the holdup is."

"Thank you."

He left a twenty on the table and headed for the door, and Dani felt a twinge of guilt. But only a twinge.

She looked at Sean. "What?"

"I didn't say anything."

He didn't have to. His face said it all. He thought she was being a bitch, and she was, but she didn't care.

Sean sipped his beer, watching her as he rested it on the table. "What's the problem, Dani?"

"This is a murder case, not a purse snatching. Why the hell is everyone sitting around eating barbecue?"

"It's called meeting basic human needs." Sean wiped his hands on a napkin and tossed it on the table. "What's the big deal?"

"The big deal is, I could have been following up with the San Antonio thing."

"How?"

"Maybe our suspect got on a flight to Albuquerque after the murders."

"Maybe so, but how are you going to check without a name?" Sean paused and watched her. "What else is wrong? You don't look good."

Dani bit back a retort. She knew she looked like crap. She *felt* like crap. She was running on coffee and Yoo-Hoo, and the headache she'd been trying to squash all day had reached monstrous proportions.

Sean leaned closer. "Come on, Dani." He kept his voice low so that only she could hear. "Don't run yourself into the ground. That doesn't help anyone. You're supposed to be leading this thing."

"I know."

"So, stop cracking the whip on everyone and take a break for once. We'll all be better off."

She looked at him but didn't respond. She knew he was right, but she had trouble admitting it. This whole leadership thing still felt unnatural to her.

He leaned closer. "I'm saying this as your friend, Dani. You need to ratchet it down."

● ● ●

Scott found her at Smoky J's surrounded by men. He shouldn't have been surprised. She was surrounded by men more often than not because of her job. But Scott hadn't seen her since she'd come home, and the sight of her at a table with a bunch of jacked-up cops put him on edge.

He stayed by the door to watch her. She looked tired, and her hair was pulled back in a messy ponytail. He had the urge to get her alone somewhere so he could take it down and run his hands through it, but he doubted he'd get that lucky tonight.

Three seconds. Scott knew he was skilled, but he'd never managed to make a woman come inside three seconds before. And it hadn't happened just once, but over and over. He couldn't stop thinking about it. Maybe it had been a long time since she'd been with anyone. The idea cheered him up. But the inevitable afterimage of her having that kind of mind-blowing sex with anyone else quickly killed his mood.

Sean Byrne slid his beer in front of her and leaned close to tell her something. Dani picked up his bottle and took a sip, and Scott bit back a curse as he crossed the restaurant.

She glanced up. "Hey," she said, clearly surprised to see him.

"You got a minute? I need to talk to you about something." He nodded at the door.

She hesitated a moment, then got up and walked out with him, keeping plenty of distance between them. When they were out on the sidewalk, she turned to look at him. "What is it?"

"I need to show you something," he said, leading her

to his truck in the front row. He stopped beside the passenger door and opened it.

Her brow furrowed. "What?"

"Could you get in, please?"

She watched him, her eyes suspicious.

"Please?"

Maybe it was the uncharacteristic manners that did it, but she climbed inside. He closed the door, then went around to the driver's side and slid behind the wheel. For a long moment he just looked at her.

Was something going on between her and that detective? Scott didn't think so. The guy wasn't her type. But what did he know, really? It wasn't like she told him about the men in her life. And he'd never had a reason to ask before now. If he did ask, she'd probably tell him it was none of his damn business.

He wanted to ask anyway.

"How's your injury?" she asked, looking at his shoulder.

"Fine. How are *you*?"

"Fine."

"You look tired."

"That's because I am tired. What did you want to show me?"

He opened the console and took out an iPad. He tapped a few icons and opened up a picture for her. It was a driver's-license photo from the Virginia DMV.

"Rodney Doern." He handed her the tablet.

She studied the face, then looked up at Scott. He took the tablet back and clicked open another photo, a still shot from the security footage taken at the firing range.

"This is the same guy?"

"Same guy."

"Who is he?"

"Marine, Special Forces. Left the service in 2008, went to work in the private sector."

Her head jerked up. "He's the one who shot at us?"

"Yes."

She stared at him for a long moment, as if she didn't believe him. "But how can you be sure?"

"He didn't pick up his brass. His prints were on two of the shells."

"What the *hell*, Scott? You picked up his brass?"

"That's what I do."

"I *knew* it." She pounded her fist on the door. "You lied to me!"

Scott didn't respond.

"You freaking *lied* to me, over and over. You shouldn't even be involved in this."

"I *am* involved."

"Not like that. Not with evidence." She leaned closer. "What do you expect me to do with this, Scott? The chain of custody is destroyed. Any chance we might have had to connect him to the crime is blown to hell, thanks to you."

"Not true."

Her eyebrows tipped up.

"I left four shells on the ground. Plenty of evidence left, even for the feds. I called the sheriff's office and gave them an anonymous tip about where to look, too. They can recover the shells and make the same ID we did."

"*We* didn't do anything! You did this all by yourself." She turned toward the window, shaking her head. Her hand was still clenched in a tight fist resting on the door.

"After he quit the marines, Doern took a job with

Black Echo, which is a private security outfit in South Carolina. He spent almost five years OCONUS, out of the continental US. The last three years, he's been off the radar, but I wouldn't be surprised if he's been in Iraq and Syria, where the company has covert contracts with various foreign governments."

"He's a mercenary."

Scott nodded. "Lot of money in it. Death for hire is a lucrative business."

"How would you know?"

"I know people. Guys who went to the dark side. Happens all the time."

"But why?"

"Lot of reasons. People are disillusioned. Desperate. Broke. Take your pick. Some people come home and realize there's nothing here for them. Or maybe they're addicted."

Her brow furrowed. "To what?"

"Conflict. The adrenaline rush. The insanity of it."

She stared at him. Okay, too much information. She didn't need all this from him.

She gazed down at the photograph again, and Scott watched her face, trying to read her reaction.

"What do you see?"

She glanced up. "You mean—"

"Is he familiar to you?"

She stared at the picture. "I don't know."

"Really *look*, Daniele. Is this the man who broke into your house?"

Seconds ticked by as she studied the image. "Maybe."

Scott's stomach twisted. The answer didn't surprise him—he'd expected it. What he hadn't expected was the white-hot fury he felt right now.

"Daniele, look at me."

She lifted her gaze.

"If you see him anywhere, pretend you don't. Do not mess with him, you understand me? He's dangerous."

Her eyes widened. "What should I do? Maybe call the police?"

"Don't be a smart-ass. You cannot apprehend this man alone. He's highly trained and extremely lethal. I need you to promise me you won't confront him."

She blew out a sigh. "The way this case is going, I won't be lucky enough to even *see* him, much less apprehend him. He's probably not even in Texas."

Scott wasn't so sure. Whatever was going on, they seemed to be at the epicenter of it. Scott believed Doern planned to come back here. Scott also believed that when he did, he planned to put Dani in his crosshairs.

She set the tablet on the console, and Scott clamped his hand over hers.

"Promise me, Daniele."

"Fine."

"Fine what?"

"I won't confront him alone." She jerked her hand away, and in that one little movement he realized something important. He'd hurt her. Way worse than he'd thought.

His hightailing it out of that motel room hadn't been all about rushing back to run evidence, and Dani knew it.

Everything's short and sweet with you. Commitment isn't your thing.

Her words definitely bothered him, which was her intention. He'd pissed her off, so she'd taken a cheap shot. But, looking at her now, he understood that she wasn't so much angry as she was hurt, and the realization put an uncomfortable tightness in his chest.

He needed to make things right with her. But right now she was determined to blow him off.

She pushed open the door. "I need to go."

"I'll follow you home."

"Thanks, I'm good."

"I'm not asking."

"Well, I'm not going home, so I guess you're out of luck tonight, huh?" She slid from his truck.

"Where are you going?"

"Back to work. Thanks to you, I've got a new lead to follow."

• • •

It was almost midnight when Dani left the station house, but the roads were still busy with Saturday-night traffic. She battled drowsiness as she made her way home, trying to stay alert for any suspicious cars or pickups in her rearview mirror.

Rodney Doern.

She pictured the flinty look in his eyes. Had he been in her home?

He had. She knew it. For some reason she felt certain, even though she hadn't wanted to tell Scott.

A cold-blooded mercenary had been in her house.

And the very next day he'd put her in his sights and tried to kill her. The only reason she was alive right now was that Scott had been there to yank her out of her shock and formulate an escape and evasion plan. He'd done it calmly, too, as if dodging bombs and bullets were no big thing.

Had he ever thought about crossing over, like those men he knew? Something was in his voice, something . . . empathetic, when he talked about vets coming home and realizing there was nothing here for them.

Dani's heart ached at the thought. She hoped he'd never felt that way, desperate or alone or like he didn't have anything to come back for. He had a darkness about him now, and she yearned to talk to him about it. But he kept his personal life locked up tight. So often she'd wanted to coax him into sharing things with her, even painful things.

But . . . that would require intimacy, which he didn't seem to want.

How had she ever thought she'd be okay with this? How had she thought she'd ever be satisfied with an offhanded compliment after sex?

He'd looked into her eyes and told her she was beautiful. She'd felt his sincerity, and his words had filled her up. But now she wasn't full at all. She wanted more. She wanted *him*.

She shouldn't let her thoughts go there. She'd slept with him—seduced *him*—with her eyes wide-open. He'd even warned her. She had no right to feel disappointed.

It wasn't just disappointment, though. It was wounded pride. The only thing worse than throwing herself at him was clinging to him afterward and pressuring him to feel things he didn't.

Dani pulled into her driveway and checked her mirrors one last time before climbing from her truck. She glanced up and down her street for any unfamiliar vehicles, but didn't see any. Her neighbor's daughter was home from college, from the looks of it. Her little hatchback was in the driveway, and her dad's pickup was parked on the street. It had a vanity plate that said HOOKEM along with a UT bumper sticker: MY MONEY AND MY DAUGHTER GO TO UT.

Dani stopped in her driveway and stared at the license plate.

Someone's bankrolling this thing.

A shiver of excitement moved through her, and she hurried up the steps and unlocked the door. She dumped her stuff on a chair and yanked out her phone to call the station.

"SMPD."

"Jasper? You're still there?" She locked her front door but didn't turn on any lights yet so she could look out without being seen.

"That report just came in. I'm sending you an email now."

"The stolen Taurus?"

"That's right."

"Listen, there's something else I need you to do. I have a hunch I need to follow up on, but I can't do it from home. Can you look something up for me? You have a pen?"

"Hang on."

She stood beside her window, gazing out at her darkened street as she waited.

"Okay, shoot."

"I need a rundown on a red Ferrari with New Mexico tags. It's got a vanity plate: *A-M-I-S-H*."

"*Amish*? For real?"

"That's right."

"Okay, I'll see what I can find."

CHAPTER 22

Sean watched Dani hurry up the sidewalk. Today she looked just as tired as she had last night, but now she was armed with an extralarge cup of Starbucks.

"What do we got?" she asked, looking around. So far, it was just an unmarked unit and a patrol car out front.

"Audrey's neighbor called it in," Sean told her. "She came by to pick her up to go to a prayer group. When Audrey didn't answer the door, the woman let herself in."

Dani mounted the steps and paused beside the beveled-glass front door. "What do you think?"

Sean shrugged. "Hard to tell. It could be nothing. Audrey's purse isn't here. Her cell phone isn't here. Her keys aren't here. So, maybe she just forgot about the prayer group and went out to do some errands."

"You said her car is here, though?"

"Yeah, that's why the neighbor's worried. Evidently, the Jeep is in the garage. I haven't had a chance to look yet. I just got here five minutes ago. Christine took the call from Dispatch and rolled up before I did."

Dani walked into the house, and Sean followed her. He was once again assaulted by the cloying smell of funeral flowers. Almost every tabletop had an arrangement.

Dani stood in the marble foyer and looked around. Audrey lived in a fancy house. It was big, too, even though she and James hadn't had any kids. Dani paused beside a hall table and glanced at a tray filled with sympathy cards. She looked at him. "What's the neighbor's name?"

"Joanne Applegate. She said she was supposed to pick up Audrey at eleven."

"For a prayer group?"

"That's what she said. She's been calling and texting but Audrey hasn't answered, which isn't like her, supposedly."

Dani walked through a living room that reminded Sean of a Restoration Hardware catalog and into the kitchen, where almost every inch of counter space was covered with pies and Bundt cakes. None looked like they had been touched.

Christine sat at the kitchen table, chatting with the young neighbor. The woman had been nearly hysterical when Sean showed up, and after taking her statement he'd asked Christine to try to calm her down with some small talk while he had a look around.

Dani introduced herself and got the conversation rolling. While she was occupied, Sean crossed the kitchen and slipped through the laundry room.

The Ayerses had a spacious three-car garage, and Audrey's white Jeep Cherokee was parked in the center bay, just as the neighbor had said.

The floor of the garage was immaculate. No oil stains or paint spills or even dirt tracked in from someone's shoes. The far wall was lined with stacked red and green tubs, probably containing Christmas decorations. To Sean's right were three entire shelving units filled with paint cans, all arranged perfectly like they were on display at some hardware store. The wall to

Sean's left was home to an elaborate scheme of hooks and bungee cords that kept expensive camping equipment off the ground.

"Sean?"

He turned around as Dani walked up behind him. "Her Jeep is here," he reported. "It's a three-car garage, though, and that's the only vehicle."

"The Accord is still at Delphi."

"Yeah, but maybe they had a third car. Her dad's in the auto business, right?"

"Good point." Dani rested her hands on her hips. She was in her typical jeans and blazer, with her detective's shield clipped to her belt. "And it adds to the picture that maybe she just went out on her own. There are no obvious signs of foul play here. Nothing broken, no sign of a struggle."

"I checked all the locks, and no evidence of forced entry."

Dani looked at him.

"What?" he asked.

"Nothing. I feel like we shouldn't even be here. Maybe she blew off the prayer group and went to a Pilates class."

"Yeah, her friend checked there already."

Dani rolled her eyes. "You know what I mean. Audrey Ayers is an adult. She's only been 'missing' a few hours, and it looks like she took her purse, her phone, and her car keys with her, so what's the big concern?"

Sean just looked at her. They both knew what the big concern was. The woman's husband was part of an ever-expanding murder plot. Four people were dead already—that they knew of—and they still didn't understand what was going on.

"Okay, I admit this feels off," Dani said. "But I can't put my finger on why, specifically."

"So, what do you want to do? Send the neighbor on her way and take off?"

Dani tipped her head back. "I'm thinking." She glanced into the kitchen.

"There's an address book in there by the phone," Sean said. "I could make a few calls, see if Audrey's parents or siblings know where she went today."

"Good plan. At least we should be able to figure out how many cars should be here." Dani peered past him. "Damn, that garage is almost as big as my house."

"No kidding."

"This place is huge. Are you sure you checked all the doors?"

"Every one. No sign of anything wrong. And the house is clean, too. Every bed is made and the carpet's been vacuumed recently. And yet—" He started to say something and shook his head.

"And yet what? Spit it out."

"Same as you. I've got a bad feeling about this."

•   •   •

Dani returned to the station and found Ric with his files spread out in the conference room. He had several case files open in front of him and a half-eaten sandwich at his elbow.

"The widow still missing?" he asked.

"She's not officially missing yet."

He leaned back in his chair and laced his hands behind his head. He wore a dress shirt with the sleeves rolled up, which meant he'd probably been to mass earlier.

"I don't know. Everything looks okay, but Sean's following up." Dani nodded at his paperwork. "How's it coming?"

Ric pulled a piece of paper from beneath one of the folders and slid it toward her.

"Ten Most Wanted?" She looked up from the mug shot. "When did this happen?"

"Rey called this morning to give me the heads-up. The sheriff in New Mexico received a tip about where to find the shell casings from the ambush up there. The prints on the shells trace back to someone who's already on their radar."

Dani sat there watching Ric, wondering if he realized how deeply Scott was involved in all this.

She glanced down and read the description of Doern, as well as the paragraph about his being wanted for murder, armed robbery, and racketeering.

"Whose murder?" she asked.

"It's a three-year-old case. Evidently, he was involved in a bar brawl up in South Carolina, got kicked out of the place. Next day the guy he was fighting with turned up dead in an alley. Doern's DNA was found at the scene, but they never could locate him."

Dani studied the picture. It was a DMV photo like the one Scott had shown her, except this one looked more recent. His hair was longer, and a sleeve of tattoos covered his right arm.

She read the description again. Six-two, 220. He was almost the same size as Scott and could have passed for his brother.

Dani sank into a chair and stared at the eyes.

"So, the FBI's all over this." She looked up at Ric. "Why?"

"That's what I'm trying to figure out. I don't know, and neither does Rey. I wouldn't be surprised if someone shows up and tries to yank our investigation."

"Bring it on. They don't have jurisdiction."

"They'll say they do if they want in."

Anger surged through her. "That's bullshit. They don't have a clue about our case."

"Funny, that's how I feel, too."

Jasper walked into the room holding a slip of paper. "Hey, Dani. Got that plate you wanted. Comes back to a Marco Varela of Mission Hill, New Mexico."

Dani stared down at the scribbled name. "This ring any bells with you?" she asked Ric.

"None. Why?"

"It was just a fluke. I'm trying to track down the money. This guy has a Mission Hill address and drives a Ferrari."

"Not just any Ferrari," Jasper put in. "An Enzo. I checked into it, and that's a limited edition. They only made four hundred."

Ric whistled.

"The guy's from Chile," Jasper said. "Used to be a big polo star."

"Where'd you get that?" Dani asked.

"I looked him up." Jasper handed over a printout of a Wikipedia page. The photo alongside the article showed a handsome man atop a horse. "I was curious about the car and where his money came from. I thought maybe he was a movie star or something. Anyway, he's retired now and bought a big ranch out there where he breeds horses."

Dani thought of the ranch off Spruce Canyon Road with the horses and the high-dollar fence. Was that his place?

"So, does this help?" Jasper asked.

"I don't know. Maybe," she said. "I'll look into it."

Christine poked her head into the conference room as Jasper left. "Hey, Ric, sorry to interrupt, but your wife's looking for you."

Ric pulled out his phone. "What? My ringer's on."

"She's here."

Ric jumped to his feet as Mia stepped into the room. She was flushed and breathless, and Ric dashed around the table to her side.

"Is it time?"

"I wish. That's not why I'm here."

He rested his hand on her belly. "What's wrong? Are you okay? Why didn't you call me?"

"Because." She surveyed the table and reached for the bottle of water by Ric's food. "Damn, it's *hot* out there." She took a swig while Ric looked on, clearly confused. She dragged out a chair and sank into it.

"Mia, what's wrong?"

"Nothing at all." She smiled up at him. "But there's been a break in your case."

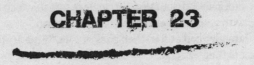

CHAPTER 23

Ric looked at her for a long moment. Then he looked at Dani.

"Sit down," Mia told him. "You're sweating bullets."

"*I'm* sweating?" He raked his hand through his hair.

"I know I'm a mess." Mia glanced down at her sweat-soaked T-shirt and leggings and then looked at Dani. "I just came from the gym. I was doing some reading while I was on the treadmill—Ric, sit *down*."

He sat.

"Anyway, I was doing some reading, and I think I know how it all fits together."

"How what fits together?" Dani asked.

"Your victims. Ayers, Lovett, Kreznik, and also Collins." She looked at Ric. "Did you know they presented at the BAA conference three years ago?"

Dani leaned forward. "The what?"

"The BAA, the Biology Association of America. I wasn't there, but someone at the lab went, and I remember flipping through the program and reading some of the seminar descriptions." Mia took another gulp of water.

"Are you okay?" Ric asked again.

"I'm *fine*, just thirsty. Anyway, I remember Dr. Kreznik being mentioned in the program. He's local, so that caught my attention. I just went back and did some research," Mia said excitedly, "and all *four* of them were part of a panel discussion on nuclear transfer technology, with a specific emphasis on enucleation."

Dani glanced at Ric, then back at Mia. "Enucleation. What is that, exactly?"

"It's an important step in somatic cell nuclear transfer. Otherwise known as SCNT."

"Sorry, babe, you've lost me," Ric said. "Back up."

Mia took a deep breath. "Okay, SCNT. The process starts with a somatic cell, or body cell. You make the cell inactive to stop the replication of DNA. Then the nuclear material and the chromosomes are harvested. That's called enucleation. Then *that* material is deposited into an oocyte, or donor egg cell, in which the genetic material has already been removed to make room."

"Wait," Dani said. "Are you talking about in vitro fertilization?" She was no scientist, but that's what it sounded like. Although maybe her mind had jumped to that because Mia was sitting in front of her nine months pregnant.

"Not IVF," Mia said. "Reproductive cloning."

Dani stared at her.

"Cloning," Ric repeated.

"You mean like . . . with sheep?" Dani asked.

"Sheep, rabbits, horses," Mia said. "It's totally taken off in the equestrian community, for example. Cloned polo ponies can fetch a hundred K or more."

Ric's eyebrows shot up. "A hundred thousand *bucks*?"

"Wait, polo horses?" Dani turned to Ric. "Maybe Marco Varela is involved."

"Who's that?" Mia looked confused.

"A retired polo player in New Mexico," Dani said.

"He lives on a ranch near Nathan Collins." She looked at Ric. "You think he might be raising cloned polo ponies?"

"Maybe," Ric said. "And maybe the dead professors were moonlighting for him. You say it's a big business?"

"Very big," Mia confirmed. "But that's not what concerns me. Rumors were floating around the scientific community that certain microbiologists and geneticists were working on a secret human cloning project."

"Humans," Dani repeated with disbelief. "Is that even possible?"

"Theoretically, yes," Mia said. "But it's highly problematic."

"How?" Ric leaned closer and looked intently at his wife. He so obviously admired her intellect, and Dani had always liked watching them interact.

"Well, regardless of where you stand on reproductive cloning technology in *general*," Mia said, "it's way too soon to apply it to humans. The vast majority of cloning attempts in mammals—at least ninety percent—fail to produce a viable offspring. Then many of the organisms that are born die very young or have severe birth defects."

"So, why would anyone do it?" Dani asked.

"My guess would be money," Mia said. "You shouldn't underestimate what people will pay, and the lengths they'll go to, to have a child that is genetically related to them. Even if it's only one parent."

"One parent?"

"Yes, the genetic material comes solely from one parent, oftentimes the mother, because the procedures tend to work better with females."

Ric shook his head.

"So you believe scientists *are* doing this?" Dani asked. Was that what Ayers and Kreznik had been up to?

"Like I said, it's all talk," Mia replied. "I heard rumors about it several years ago, but then I also heard Michelangelo never really got off the ground."

"Michelangelo?" Ric asked.

"That was the name of the project."

A chill snaked down Dani's spine. "Oh my God, the *Creation of Adam*."

Mia and Ric looked at her.

"Ayers had a print of it in his office. The fresco by Michelangelo."

"That's probably where the project name comes from," Mia said. "He had that in his office? Wow, maybe they really *were* working on it."

Ric looked at Dani but didn't say anything. She didn't say anything, either. It was hard to get her head around the very idea.

"Is it illegal?" Ric asked Mia.

"Many states have passed laws banning human cloning. And the American Medical Association has come out against it, for obvious reasons, such as the extremely high death rates. But that's not to say it isn't happening."

"Have you heard anything about this kind of research going on around here?" Dani asked.

"Where? You mean here in town at the university? That's very unlikely," Mia said. "It's not exactly a bastion of scientific research. And this sort of work is expensive. It would require big-time funding. More likely, if it's happening around here, it's in the private sector."

"So, if Ayers and Kreznik moved down here to work

on this Michelangelo thing," Dani said, "why take a job at the university? Especially a job with a pay cut."

"Maybe as a cover," Ric suggested. "Teach a few classes by day. Do some moonlighting to earn some real money by night."

"And what about Collins?" Dani looked at Mia. "Right before his death, he told me in our interview that he was working on something called YACs."

"Yeast artificial chromosomes," Mia said. "Maybe he lied. Or maybe that's what he actually *was* working on officially at Trinity. But, based on his published work, he was definitely still involved in human cloning research. And Trinity wouldn't have supported this sort of work if they knew about it. Not as a Catholic institution. The whole thing is extremely controversial. In fact, if the school got wind of this project, it's conceivable they would drum up a reason to get rid of anyone involved without drawing attention to the subject of the research, which would create a scandal."

"That might explain the sexual harassment investigations," Ric said. "Ayers and Collins were both pressured to leave."

Dani shook her head, trying to clear it.

"I know, it's a lot to take in," Mia said.

"And I'm still not sure I get it." Dani looked at Ric. "Even if we assume all of our victims are somehow involved in this Michelangelo project, who would want to kill them? And why?"

"Maybe Marco Varela," Ric suggested. "If they were helping him clone polo ponies, maybe he got pissed off when they took a job somewhere else. He would have had a lucrative business going, and then they left."

Dani's phone buzzed. It was Scott, and she'd been

dodging him all day. Maybe he had an update about the case.

"I need to take this." Dani got up and slipped from the room.

"Harper," she said briskly.

"Whoa. Your phone is working. I was beginning to wonder."

"What's up?"

"How's the case coming?"

Dani propped her shoulder against the wall and looked out at the bull pen. It was a clever strategy on Scott's part to ask about work. If he'd asked something personal, she would have jumped off the phone.

"We've got some interesting developments. Did you happen to notice the red Ferrari when we stopped at that gas station near Mission Hill?"

"The Enzo. What about it?"

Of course he'd not only noticed but knew exactly what kind it was.

"Well, on a hunch I ran the plate, and turns out the owner is some retired polo star who has a ranch out there and breeds horses now."

She stepped into an interview room for privacy and filled him in on everything Mia had just told them.

"Damn," Scott said. "Sounds like a breakthrough."

"I don't know."

"There's no way all that could be a coincidence. And if Marco Varela owns the ranch near Collins, that puts another victim just down the road from him."

"Yeah, but I'm still having a hard time with motive."

"Revenge," Scott said. "His scientists abandoned him to go work for someone else. And they took their valuable IP with them."

"You're saying he hired a hit man to kill *four* people because someone shut down his pony-making factory? That seems pretty extreme."

"Come on, Dani. People get killed over a dime bag. Or a pair of shoes. If those horses are worth a hundred K a pop? Sounds like plenty of motive to me."

"Maybe," she said, still not convinced. "Anyway, is there anything new on your end?"

"No. And that's not why I'm calling. What are you doing later?"

She didn't answer. She knew what he was asking and she didn't want to go there.

"Daniele?"

"I'm working."

"What about after?"

"What 'after'? I'm totally buried right now."

"I want to see you tonight."

A warm shiver moved through her. "I have to work, Scott."

"Call me when you get off."

"I'll try to call you tomorrow."

She hung up before he could change her mind.

$\bullet \quad \bullet \quad \bullet$

Dani swung by Schmitt's on the way home that night and found Sean seated at the bar with Jasper. This time she resisted the urge to bitch them out.

"I got your text," she told Sean. "What's the word on Audrey?"

"Still hasn't shown up." He checked his watch. "As of eight P.M., that is. I talked to several of her friends and then finally got ahold of her sister, Lesley."

"What did Lesley say?"

"She confirmed my theory that there's another car. It's a Mustang convertible, cherry red, that her parents gave her for graduating from college in four years."

"Wow, three cheers for Audrey."

Sean smiled. "I know, right? They gave Lesley one, too, but hers is white."

Dani rolled her eyes. "What did Lesley say about her sister?"

"She hasn't heard from her since yesterday, but she's not worried."

"You're kidding."

"Nope. She said her sister does this a lot."

"What, goes missing after her husband's funeral?"

Jasper chuckled, but Sean looked annoyed.

"Takes off without telling anyone where she's going and ignores her phone. She's been known to have 'episodes' when she gets stressed-out, apparently. She pulled the same thing the day before her wedding when she got cold feet. Her sister says it's no biggie, that she's probably at a luxury hotel somewhere getting a facial."

Dani scoffed. "Well, is she going to confirm this for us or just let it go?"

"She's supposed to call me when she hears from Audrey, but she didn't seem worried."

"This woman sounds like a real sweetheart."

"Yeah, she was a little chilly on the phone, like I was interrupting her Sunday."

Unbelievable. Dani thought of Dax rushing over to her house the minute he heard about her break-in. But, hey, who was Dani to judge? If there was one thing she'd learned on the job, it was that people's family dynamics often didn't make sense to outsiders.

"So, you've crossed Audrey Ayers off your list of concerns," Dani concluded.

"Bumped her to the bottom. I'll see where we are tomorrow on it. What about you? How's it coming on Rodney Doern?"

Dani glanced across the bar as Travis walked in, followed by Scott. The sight of him set off a flurry of nerves in her stomach.

"Dani?"

She looked at Sean. "What's that?"

"What's the word on Doern?"

She updated him about their suspect's being added to the FBI's Ten Most Wanted list. She'd planned to share Mia's discovery, too, but decided to save it for morning. Dani could feel Scott's gaze on her, and she wanted to leave before anyone else noticed. She couldn't let him talk her into going outside with him. They'd either end up kissing or arguing, and she wasn't up for either.

"That's it?" Sean asked. "You guys were at it all day. I thought maybe you turned up something new."

"We did, but I'll fill you in tomorrow. You guys enjoy your night off."

"What about you?" Jasper asked. "You want to have a beer with us?"

Sean nudged her elbow. "Yeah, stay and hang out. You've been hitting it hard."

She glanced at Scott, who was watching her intently from the other end of the bar. What did that look mean? It was the same as last night, only darker.

"Thanks, but not tonight," Dani said. "I need to go home and crash."

• • •

Scott pulled up to Dani's house and parked under the pecan tree overhanging the street. No lights on except for the porch, so she was probably asleep by now. Definitely a signal that he should go. Instead he cut the engine and debated whether to knock on her door.

A light in the living room went on. He watched as a shadow moved in front of the window.

Damn it, what was he doing? If she saw him out here, she'd think he was obsessed. And maybe he was. He'd gone out drinking with Travis tonight specifically to get her out of his head, but that plan had tanked the instant he'd walked into Schmitt's and spotted her at the bar.

He wanted her again. He could admit that to himself. But he felt weirdly protective, too. If he were her brother, Scott was exactly the kind of man he'd warn her to stay away from. He should do the right thing here and leave her alone.

But he couldn't stop thinking about how she'd looked in his truck last night. And he couldn't stop thinking about her in that motel room. He kept picturing her reaching for the latch on the door and then turning to face him. If he lived to be a hundred, he'd never forget the look on her face—a combination of lust and determination that had made it almost impossible to say no. Almost. He might still have had a chance, but when she'd leaned close and pressed her hot, wet mouth against his chest, he'd been completely blown away.

Everything about her blew him away, including that she'd let him inside her without a condom. Forget that she was on the pill—it was a bad idea. He hadn't had sex without a condom since he was a stupid teenager, but she didn't know that. So where did she get this ridiculous trust she placed in him? It was totally reckless, and yet she'd seemed so sure about it. Was she like that with all men, or just him?

Either scenario brought up problems he didn't want to think about. But he couldn't help it, he *was* thinking about it, and the idea of her doing the things they'd done with someone else made him crazy. The idea of her doing them with Sean Byrne made him want to kill the guy.

The living room light switched off. She was going to bed now. He should let her, but instead he walked up her sidewalk and rapped on the door. He stood under the porch light waiting for her to answer, feeling like some high school kid picking up a prom date.

Footsteps inside, and he felt her watching him through the peephole. After an endless wait, she unlocked the door and opened it.

"Hi," she said blandly.

"Hi."

She wore cutoff jean shorts and another of those tank tops with the thin little straps, and her hair was back in a loose ponytail. The blank expression on her face didn't inspire much confidence.

"Can I come in?"

She pulled the door open, and he stepped inside and glanced around. Something was different tonight, but he couldn't put his finger on it. He turned to look at her as she closed the door.

"What's up?" she asked.

"You're avoiding me."

"No I'm not."

He stared at her, daring her to argue with him.

She turned on her heel and walked into the kitchen. "You want a beer?" she asked over her shoulder.

"No."

She leaned back against her sink and folded her arms over her chest. He leaned against the counter beside her and looked her over.

"What?" she asked.

"Nothing."

"Don't you dare tell me I look tired. I know. I was on my way to bed when you showed up."

He didn't say anything. The nervous look in her eyes bothered him. She'd never acted nervous around him before, and he knew his botched attempt to handle this thing was to blame.

She sighed. "It's late, Scott. What is it you want?"

What did he want? Did she really want to know? If he told her honestly, it would freak her out.

He eased closer. Slowly, he reached up and tugged the rubber band from her hair. It fell around her shoulders, and she looked startled as he combed his fingers through it. Then he kissed her, as gently as he could so she wouldn't push him away. She tensed at first, but after a few seconds she relaxed into him.

She tasted so damn good, and when he pulled her hips against him, everything ignited. Her hands slid up around his neck, and she made a soft little moan. He lifted her off her feet and set her on the counter, positioning himself between her thighs—which was fast becoming his favorite place to be.

"Scott?"

"What?" He kissed her to cut her off because whatever it was, he didn't want to hear it. He just wanted her to keep digging her nails into his scalp and kissing him with that hot urgency, like she'd never get enough. He glided his hand under her shirt and slid his fingers over that smooth, warm skin he'd been thinking about for days. He wanted her naked.

"Scott." She pulled back, stiff-arming him even as her legs stayed wrapped around his waist. He saw some kind of battle going on in her eyes, and he prayed she wasn't going to make him leave. "We said this was a onetime thing."

"You said that, not me."

• • •

She gazed up at him, heart racing as she tried to focus on the words coming out of his mouth. Was he right? *Had* she said that? She couldn't even think right now because every cell in her body was tingling with excitement and pleading with her to just shut up and kiss him.

She didn't want to analyze it. Instead, she pulled him closer, twining her legs around him and raking her fingers through the thick softness of his hair. She didn't know what this meant or what she was doing, but she knew that she didn't want to ruin it by thinking too much—she just wanted it to happen.

Suddenly he pulled back and gazed down at her, and the look in his blue eyes was more intense than she'd ever seen. He slid his hand from under her shirt and laced his fingers through hers, then tugged her off the counter. He led her down the hallway, and her nerves did an anxious little dance as he neared her bedroom. She hadn't expected him to show up like this. She wasn't prepared. She didn't have time to think about it, though, because he dragged her onto the bed and came down on top of her, sending her breath whooshing out of her lungs.

"I've been dying to get you in here," he said against her neck.

He had? Since when? The only time he'd ever been back here was when he'd helped her haul boxes on moving day.

He was making his way down her neck now, and his hands were busy with her shirt, pushing it up around her armpits so that he could go after her breasts. His mouth closed over her nipple and gave a sharp pull, and she shot forward with a yelp.

He moved up. "Sorry," he said, crushing his mouth over hers.

But she knew he wasn't sorry at all. She yanked his T-shirt up, scraping his sides with her fingernails just to get back at him, but he didn't seem to mind as he pulled his shirt over his head and flung it away. Then he dragged hers off, too, and tossed it on the nightstand beside her, and she glanced at her alarm clock and it suddenly hit her that they were doing this in her room. In her *home*. This wasn't some sleazy motel where they could walk away and forget about everything tomorrow.

He stopped kissing her and got rid of his boots. She heard them *thunk* against the floor. Then he was back over her, sliding his hands over her body and kissing her breasts again. Suddenly he stopped and looked at her.

"What is it?"

"Nothing," she whispered, dragging him back down to kiss her. She didn't want to think about the implications. She just wanted him to kiss her and touch her and rock her world like her own personal earthquake. She wrapped her legs around him and pulled him tight against her. She felt the hard bulge of him through his jeans, and the tremors were already starting, and he wasn't even inside her yet. How did he do this to her? How was it possible?

"Scott." She reached for him, squeezing him through his jeans, and he muttered a curse against her neck. "Scott, please."

She undid the button of her shorts, and he pulled them down her legs, taking her panties, too. Then his knuckles scraped against her body as he fumbled with his zipper.

"Hurry," she said, frantically trying to help him. She was already close. So close. "*Hurry.*"

"I am."

The instant he had the zipper down, she grabbed him and guided him to her, and he pushed inside her with a hard thrust that made her vision blur.

"Oh my God." She wrapped her legs around him, squeezing him to her even as he tried to move back. "Yes."

He fought against her grip, pulling back and then pushing into her again, rougher this time.

"Yes. Yes. *Yes.*" She clamped down around him as she started shaking and coming, and again he tried to pull back, but she gripped his hips, curling her nails into his skin as she tried to hold on for that last second she so desperately needed. "No, don't—"

He reared back and crashed into her with so much force the bed frame smacked back against the wall. Lights exploded behind her eyelids as she shattered and blew apart. She held on to him, clutching him against her as his body moved over her with a relentless rhythm that pounded pleasure into her and made the bed squeak and squeal. He kept going and going. And when every last nerve in her body was on fire, he gave a powerful thrust and a groan tore from his throat as he came inside her.

His weight crushed down on her. She let her limbs go lax. For an endless moment she lay beneath him, waiting for him to roll off her so she could breathe again.

He pushed up on his elbows and stared down at her. She was surprised to see the sheen of sweat on his face.

"Holy shit, Daniele."

She laughed and smacked his side. "Get off me. I can't breathe."

He moved onto his back and pulled her against his chest, and she let her head rest against his skin. He was warm and slick, and she could hear his heart hammering against her ear.

They lay there without talking, holding each other and trying to catch their breath. He shifted to his side so she was nestled against his body. She loved it here. In her bed, in her room, with Scott's strong arms around her and the humid cloud of sweat and sex surrounding them.

He wasn't talking. Which was fine. He was still winded, and so was she.

But then the silence stretched out, and she felt a niggle of worry. She looked up and traced her fingertip over his stubble-covered jaw. He closed his eyes and murmured a curse.

She sat up and leaned over him. "How come you're half-dressed and I'm naked?"

He opened his eyes. "I'm more skilled than you are."

She eased herself on top of him and gazed down at his beautiful chest as he rested his big palms on her butt.

"You're going to kill me," he said with a sigh.

"Hey, this is *your* doing. I was on my way to bed when you got here."

He closed his eyes and smiled.

He seemed totally relaxed. Hope flickered inside her, because she hadn't seen him this way since their awkward morning in New Mexico.

She sat up and reached for her shirt, but he caught her hand.

"Don't. I like to look at you."

Her heart melted as she gazed down at him. The lamp was off and the light from the hallway cast his face in shadows, but the look in his eyes . . . If she hadn't already been half in love with him, she would have tripped right over the cliff in that moment.

He rested his hands on her hips in a possessive way that was totally new for them.

"Is this why you came over?" she asked. "You thought I'd just let you in and take you to bed?"

"No. But I was hoping."

She watched him a moment, trying to read the meaning behind his words, but she couldn't.

What did this mean? If they'd kept it to one night, they could have come home and picked up where they'd left off. But now . . .

Now he was in her bed, and she was sitting astride him, wondering where this was going. Did he think they were going to drift into some kind of friends-with-benefits thing? Because she couldn't do that. Not with him. No way. The simple fact was she'd get her heart broken.

"Come here," he whispered, sliding his hand behind her back and pulling her forward.

He kissed her, and it was hot and sweet at the same time, and she traced her fingertips over his bristly jaw. It went on and on until he eased back.

She smiled down at him as he ran his hands over her ribs and her hips. He closed his eyes and sighed, and it gave her a giddy rush to see him so content. She gazed down at his muscular chest, at his wide shoulders, at the long purple welt on the skin where the bullet had grazed him. She moved her fingertip in a circle around the wound, lightly touching the skin.

"Is it healing okay?"

"Yeah," he said, not opening his eyes.

She leaned forward and planted a kiss under the spot, then sat back. She traced her fingers over his well-formed pecs, over his abs, then up his sides. A jagged patch of raised skin marred the right side of his rib cage.

"What's this from?" She brushed her fingertip over the scar, and he stiffened.

"Shrapnel."

She settled her hands on his waist as he opened his eyes.

"What happened?"

"Long story."

She waited. His blue eyes chilled a few degrees, and his jaw hardened. He was trying to intimidate her, but she wasn't going to let him.

"This was in Afghanistan."

"The day you injured your knee?"

"Yeah."

She didn't say anything, just watched him.

He scrubbed a hand over his face and sighed. "You really want to hear this?"

"Yes."

He slid her off his lap and she felt a jab of disappointment as he rolled onto his side. He lay facing her with his weight propped on his elbow.

"We were in a convoy. Our team, plus a platoon of marines." He waited a beat, watching her. "It was end-of-the-summer fighting season. Everything was hot and dry, and this layer of dust covered everything, so it was hard to see. The Humvee in front of us hit an IED. Thing blew up and flipped over like a toy." He paused and cleared his throat. "Things were on fire, burning. People were screaming, smoke was everywhere. Couple teammates and I jumped out and tried to load casualties. Then another IED went off and killed two more guys."

She wondered about the "things" on fire. She had the sickening feeling he meant people. "These casualties were your teammates?"

"One of them, yeah."

"What about you?"

"I took some shrapnel in my side, some in my knee. It was chaos for a while, and then an MRAP raced up and got us the hell out of there."

She watched his eyes, but she couldn't read them.

He sounded so matter-of-fact, yet he was talking about people he knew being killed right in front of him.

"What was his name? Your teammate who died?"

He cleared his throat. "Dylan Scaff."

"You were close?"

He nodded.

She watched him for a long moment. His face was hard now. She reached up to touch his cheek and he caught her wrist.

For a moment she didn't move. He rolled onto his back and she lay beside him, resting her palm on his flat stomach.

"I'm sorry that happened."

"Me, too."

He was tense now, and she almost regretted bringing it up. But not quite. What happened had changed the course of his life. For years she'd been wondering about it, and now she knew.

The whole thing had some parallels to New Mexico, and she couldn't believe now that he'd reacted so calmly. But maybe the calm was on the surface.

"Do you ever talk about it with anyone?"

"What's the point?"

The bitterness in his voice made her chest hurt. She sat up and leaned on her elbow. "You lost a friend you loved and a job you loved in the same day." She tried not to shrink under his icy gaze. "Maybe it would help to talk to someone."

His jaw twitched. "Don't do that, Daniele."

"What?"

"Try to fix me. I don't need it."

Her throat tightened.

She slid out of bed and picked up her clothes, slipping them on as she avoided his gaze. She walked into the bathroom and closed the door, then turned the water on and stared down at the sink. She felt sick. Tears burned the backs of her eyes, but she wouldn't cry because she was mad, too.

She stared at the water circling down the drain. Right now, this moment, she knew him more intimately than she ever had. Yet in many ways she felt like she still didn't know him at all.

And his eyes were brutal. With only a look he could make her heart race or he could cut her to the bone. She hated that he had this kind of power over her. It wasn't fair. It made them unequal. But what she hated more was that she couldn't hide her reaction to him, so everything she felt, all her vulnerabilities, were right there in the open for him to see. She'd never had that kind of intimacy with anyone before. And it scared her.

CHAPTER 24

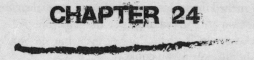

Scott stared up at the ceiling, trying to tamp down his anger. He was pissed off at her, but mostly at himself. He'd screwed this up again. He should go before he made it worse. He shouldn't have come in the first place, but he couldn't stay away. One night with her and he was hooked. Freaking addicted. Even now, after a round of wall-banging sex, he still wanted her.

He glanced at the door. She was clattering around in the kitchen now, shutting cabinets with a bit too much force. She was pissed off, too, but it was her own fault for picking at his scabs.

Yeah, keep telling yourself that and see where it gets you.

He rubbed his hand over his face.

"Fuck."

He got out of bed and zipped up.

He found her at the stove, and the sight of her standing there in only that black tank top and panties made his pulse start thrumming all over again. He leaned against the doorframe and watched her melt butter in a pan.

"Sorry. I'm being a prick."

She glanced up but didn't argue.

"You want me to leave?"

She rolled her eyes. "*No.* I want you to stop being a prick."

She jerked open a drawer and took out a fork. Then she opened the fridge and grabbed a jar of jalapeños.

"What are you making?"

"An omelet."

"I didn't know you cooked."

She shot him a look. "Is this you *not* being a prick?"

"Sorry." He watched as she cracked an egg into a bowl one-handed. She broke a second egg the same way, then whisked them together with the fork and poured the mixture over the butter. Everything crackled and sizzled, and Scott's mouth started to water.

He eased up behind her and rested his hands on her hips. He wanted to tug up her shirt, but the knife block was within easy reach, so he settled for pressing a kiss against the back of her neck.

"I don't talk about that stuff much," he said.

"I know."

He watched over her shoulder as she expertly shifted the pan to even out the eggs.

The thing was, she *did* know. She was totally familiar with the silent way he'd dealt with everything since he'd come home. He never talked about his frustrations or his temper or the black moods that sometimes came over him for days at a time. But she had a way about her, a certain stoicism that told him maybe she could handle it. She was tougher than people gave her credit for—especially her brothers. Scott knew that for a fact.

She sprinkled cheese and peppers over the eggs, then used the fork to fold everything over.

"You want something to drink with this?" she asked.

He kissed her again and turned to her refrigerator to hunt up some drinks. She slid her creation onto a plate, cut it with a spatula, then pushed the second half onto another plate and carried them to the bar.

He popped open the drinks and put them on the counter as he took the stool beside her.

"Beer with eggs," she said. "Nice."

"After-sex food."

She lifted an eyebrow as she dug into her omelet. He watched her over his bottle as he took a sip. The fact that she was feeding him instead of kicking him out was a positive sign. He'd truly thought he'd blown it for the second time in three days. And he had the urgent desire *not* to blow it with her. He didn't know what this was, exactly, but it was important. *She* was important. He'd sensed it for a while, but it hadn't truly hit him until she was underneath him in that ditch after that truck fireballed and Doern was shooting at her.

She glanced up. "What?"

"Nothing." He forked up a bite and moaned. "Damn, that's good."

"Thank you."

He took another bite and glanced around, and he suddenly realized what was different about her place. "You unpacked."

"Finally."

"When?"

"Last few nights." She shrugged. "I couldn't sleep. I was all worked up."

He stopped eating and watched her. "About what happened in New Mexico?"

"That. And the case. And us." She turned her beer bottle on the counter, but didn't look at him. "I didn't like how we left things. You made me mad."

"Yeah, I picked up on that. Your 'short and sweet' comment insulted my manhood."

The corner of her mouth curved up. "I think your manhood survived."

He nudged her knee with his. "So, you admit you said that purely to piss me off?"

"Maybe."

"If anything was short, that's on you. *I* have way more stamina."

Her cheeks flushed and she squirmed on the stool. He shifted to face her, trapping her legs between his.

"So, what's up with that anyway?"

She shot him a look. "What?"

He took her hand and held it tight when she tried to pull away. "You go off like a rocket." The first time had caught him totally off guard, and he'd been thinking about it ever since. It had happened again tonight. He'd barely had time to get her clothes off.

She definitely did *not* want to talk about this. She tugged her hand away and picked up her beer.

"I can't help it. You just . . ." She shook her head.

"What?"

"Nothing."

"No way." He took the bottle from her hand and set it on the counter. "You have to finish that. I just what?"

"Everything's just—" She looked at him, and something achingly soft was in her eyes. "—intense, you know?"

Oh, yeah. He definitely knewi

He'd been thinking about it since those first moments in that crappy motel room. He'd been with so many women—not that she wanted to hear about that right now—but Daniele was different.

He cleared his throat. "I know. It feels . . ." The closest thing he could think of was his first HALO jump—the huge rush, the sensory overload, the crash. The pure disbelief the second it was over. "Like jumping out of a plane."

Her brows arched with concerned surprise. Clearly she didn't know what to do with that comment.

"It's good. Trust me."

But she didn't. He could see it in her face. She looked wary now, like she wished she hadn't said anything, and he was fumbling the ball again.

She was so damn beautiful sitting there looking at him that way, and he felt something crack inside him. She deserved better than him. Way better. But until she figured that out, he was going to go with this, because he was an opportunist.

She stood up. "You finished?" She reached for his empty plate and carried it to the sink.

"What's wrong?"

"Nothing."

He walked over to the sink and caged her against the counter with his arms, dipping his head so that he was eye level with her. "No. You're mad again."

She shook her head and looked away. "It's hard to discuss things with you."

"What things?"

"Anything. This. Relationships." She huffed out a breath. "Forget it, okay? I don't want to talk about this."

He straightened and put his hands on his hips. "Yes you do."

"I don't."

"You do, or you wouldn't have brought up the subject. Man up and tell me what you want, Daniele."

Anger flared in her eyes. "Why don't *you* man up and tell me what you want?"

He looked at her for a long moment. Then he pulled her against him and kissed her. It wasn't soft or romantic, but it was honest. She resisted him at first, but he tipped her head back to give himself better access, and soon she was kissing him back with all the fire she usually gave him, and he slid his hands under her shirt to touch all that warm skin.

She pulled away and stared up at him, and something in her look made him stop.

"I want . . . *you*," she said. "I've always wanted you."

He saw the fear in her eyes, and his chest tightened because she was taking a risk here, baring herself like that. Her courage humbled him. It was a different kind from what he had. He had courage in combat, yeah, but emotional courage had always been in short supply.

Scott kissed her, pulling her close and fitting her hips against him. No matter how much he kissed her, he never seemed to get enough.

"Scott," she said between kisses.

"You're so pretty. . . ." He kissed her mouth, her jaw, her throat. He wanted to pick her up and take her back to bed.

"Scott, aren't you worried about everything?"

"No."

"I am." She eased back and looked at him. "This could ruin our friendship."

"I don't want to be your friend anymore, Daniele." He slid a hand up to cup her face. "It's this or nothing for us."

She gazed up at him with those soulful eyes. She

started to say something, but he kissed her. He was done with telling her things. He just wanted to show her.

• • •

He eased her back onto the bed and hovered over her. She wanted to feel his skin against hers, and she reached for his jeans.

"No." He took her wrists and moved them above her head, pinning them to the bed. He kept one hand there and the other trailed down the center of her body.

He kissed her mouth, her neck. "We do this *my* way this time." His breath was hot against her ear. "Don't rush us."

She shivered with anticipation as he worked his way down, slowly easing up her shirt and sliding kisses over her skin as he undressed her, inch by inch. When all her clothes were stripped away, he stood up and got rid of his own. He stretched out over her, giving her a stern look as he eased on top of her, a silent warning that she couldn't set the pace this time.

He kissed her, much too softly at first, and she arched against him. He moved her thighs apart and sank into her slowly, and her breath caught as he pulled back.

His way turned out to be a slow torture, with him giving her what she wanted, then pulling almost out of reach and driving her crazy. She wrapped her legs around him and tried to spur him on, but he wouldn't let her hurry him.

The desperate intensity was there, but it was in the way he looked at her now. The heat in his eyes mixed with tenderness filled her with so much emotion that had nowhere to go. She pulled him closer with her legs and tried to move her arms, but his hand clamped tighter around her wrists.

"Daniele."

"What?"

"Relax."

She tipped her head back and closed her eyes, letting the sensation wash over her like warm water. He rocked into her slowly, deeply, and gradually the tension built.

And he was right. It was this or nothing. They could never go back to how things were before, not now that they knew about *this*. It was a seismic shift in their relationship, and the realization filled her with fear and joy, both at the same.

She tried to relax like he'd told her to. She stopped thinking and simply let herself go, moaning softly as the energy between them swelled and grew, lifting her higher and higher. Finally he released her hands, and she gripped his hips as she surged against him again and again.

"Scott—" she gasped.

"Oh, yeah."

"*Scott.*"

It kept going and going, higher and higher. Finally, the wave crested and crashed, taking them both down with it as he drove himself into her.

She lay there, dazed. He rolled away, pulling her with him and settling her against his side. She rested her hand on his chest. Everything receded, every sensation, every sound, with the exception of her thundering heart.

She was utterly spent. Exhausted. As though days and weeks of stress and trauma were catching up to her. She was dimly aware of Scott's fingers combing through her hair, but she couldn't muster a response, not even to stroke her hand over his chest.

"You good?"

She would have laughed if she'd had the energy. Instead she whimpered. "So . . . tired," she whispered.

He pulled her closer and kissed the top of her head. "Go to sleep."

CHAPTER 25

Dani woke up by herself. Groggily, she stretched out her hand to confirm it, then lay there, letting the information sink in. There was other information, too. Running water. Thudding cabinets. The tantalizing smell of coffee.

She heard footsteps in the hallway and turned to face the door as Scott stepped into her bedroom. He was fully dressed right down to his damn boots.

"Morning." He set a mug of coffee on the nightstand and gazed down at her.

"Morning." She sat up, pulling the sheet against her.

"I have to go." He tucked his hands in the front pockets of his jeans and looked uneasy.

"Okay."

"Curtis called. They've reviewed my situation, and the director wants to meet with me at eight."

She rubbed her eyes and tried to get her brain to process. Curtis. His boss at the Delphi Center. "Will your suspension be lifted?"

"I'm hoping." He raked his hand through his hair, and she saw something in his expression she'd never seen before. He was nervous. And clearly he was itching to leave.

She glanced at the clock. Damn it, how had she slept past seven? She swung her legs out of bed and tried not to feel self-conscious as she crossed the room and grabbed the bathrobe from the hook in her closet.

"All right, well—"

"I'll call you later."

She knotted her robe and glanced at the clock again. "I'm going to be busy today. I'm already late, actually."

He pulled her close and kissed her mouth, then eased back and gazed down at her. "I'm not blowing you off. I'll call you, Daniele."

She followed him through the house to the front door. He was clearly in a hurry to get to his meeting.

But she had a feeling there was more to it.

After he left, she stared at her door for a long time. Then she went back into the bedroom and looked around. She wasn't sure what she expected to see. He hadn't left anything behind, not even a dent in the pillow.

She picked up the coffee and sipped it.

Black with lots of sugar. Did he know or was that just a guess?

She huffed out a sigh, disgusted with herself. She was overanalyzing this already, and it had just happened. She stalked into the bathroom and turned on the shower. This was ridiculous. She needed to toughen up and stop being such a girl about everything.

A sharp rap on her door made her heart lurch. She rushed to answer it.

Then she saw who it was. She took a deep breath and opened the door for her brother. He was dressed for work in a suit and tie.

"Hi."

"Hi." Drew stepped inside. "I passed Scott at the stop sign. What—" He halted midsentence as his gaze moved over her, taking in her disheveled hair and bathrobe. "You've got to be kidding me."

Dani sighed and closed the door.

"*Fuck*, Dani." He gaped at her. "How stupid are you?"

"Hey, screw you! Get out of my house!"

"Have you paid any attention the last fifteen years?" Drew rested his hands on his hips and glared at her, looking remarkably like their father.

"It's none of your business."

"Bullshit! You're my sister." His face flushed. "He goes through women like chewing gum."

"Yeah, so do you."

"He's got PTSD. Are you blind?"

"No." She folded her arms over her chest.

"What are you signing up for? You think you can rescue him or some shit? You think you can settle him down?"

"I'm not talking about this with you. Why are you here, anyway?"

He glowered at her. Then he took out his phone and checked something, shaking his head the whole time.

"I'm here to give you a heads-up," he said tightly. "The feds are all over your case. The US attorney called Rachel this morning. Thought you *might* want to know your investigation's about to get taken over."

"They can't do that," she snapped.

"Oh, yeah? Watch them."

For a moment they said nothing, just stared at each other. Then Drew reached for the door.

"Thanks for telling me," she said as he stepped out.

He turned to look at her, shaking his head. "He's not going to give you what you want, Dani. I can promise you that."

"You don't know what I want."

His face tightened. He turned and stalked down the sidewalk.

She watched him get into his BMW and pull away, and she had a knot in her stomach because she had a sinking feeling that he was right.

• • •

Dani muddled through her whole morning distracted, and after lunch she decided to get out of the office. She grabbed an unmarked unit and headed out to track down some leads.

Cell phone records from more than two years ago had revealed calls from Ayers and Kreznik to Marco Varela, proving the connection between the dead biologists and the retired polo player who was now breeding horses. Ric was checking into the financials to see if any of the victims had received payments from Varela. And Rey Santos had already come back with the interesting tidbit that Varela was the head of Sunland LLC, which made him the owner of the property Collins had been renting.

Yet another connection to one of the victims.

Dani still didn't feel good, though. She had a better picture of the puzzle now, but many of the pieces still didn't fit, and some pieces were missing entirely.

She wanted to talk to Audrey Ayers. Maybe she could shed some light on her husband's relationship with Varela. But the widow was still MIA, a circumstance that made Dani more than a little antsy.

Actually, it was giving her an ulcer. She downed

the last of her Yoo-Hoo as she rounded a bend in the highway and pulled over in front of 222 Mockingbird Road.

For a moment she stared at the burned cabin. Behind the charred debris, Dove Lake glistened in the afternoon sun.

She tucked her phone into her pocket and glanced up and down the street as she slid from her car. She approached the cabin from the side, taking care not to step on any wood or nails. Not much remained inside the house—a sink and a toilet, a few soot-covered appliances in the kitchen. Dani skirted around the main structure and picked her way downhill to the boathouse.

Kreznik's fishing boat was a Boston Whaler, about ten feet long. A brown tarp covered it, and Sean was right—it looked as though the cover hadn't been removed in months, maybe even years. Dani threw the switch for the boat hoist, but nothing happened. Either the electricity was out or the mechanism was broken.

Just off the dock, she spotted a man motoring past in a small skiff. Dani waved her arms and flagged him down. "Excuse me, sir?" she yelled.

He glanced around warily, then chugged over to Kreznik's dock. The man had a silver buzz cut and wore a fishing jacket.

Dani flashed her badge and introduced herself. "I'm investigating this fire. Do you live around here?"

"Two houses down." He nodded at another small cabin on the hillside.

"What can you tell me about Mike Kreznik?"

The man rubbed his hand over his chin, looking thoughtful. "He was here an awful lot. Weekdays, weekends, didn't seem to have a regular schedule. Usually only stayed for a night or so."

"Do you know if he liked to fish?"

"That I don't."

"Did you ever see him take his boat out?"

The man glanced at the Boston Whaler for a moment. "Can't say as I did. Nice boat, though."

"Yes."

Dani's phone buzzed, and she pulled it from her pocket to see Sean's number. "Excuse me, I have to answer this. Thanks for your help."

"Sure thing. You have any more questions, you know where to find me."

He motored away, and Dani answered the call.

"Hey, I'm at Kreznik's cabin. And you're right, there's something odd here. I don't think he uses this place for fishing."

"Yeah, I just heard back from the county clerk's office. Turns out, the cabin isn't actually his."

"Whose is it?"

"Property's owned by a Zachary Greene. I chatted up the clerk and found out he's got a couple more properties there on the lake."

Dani turned to look at the burned-out house. "How many?"

"Three. And he also owns a ranch out there, too, off White Hill Road by the old quarry."

"Any chance it's a horse ranch?"

"No idea."

"Text me the other addresses."

"What are you going to do?"

"I don't know yet."

"Are you alone? Don't do anything impulsive."

She felt a spurt of annoyance. "I won't. Just text me the info."

She hung up with Sean and took another look at the lake. Then she trudged uphill to her car. She'd forgotten to crack the windows, and already it felt like an oven as she slid behind the wheel. A text landed on her phone, but this one was from Scott.

Call me.

Her heart skittered. She called him back as she started the car.

"Hey, guess what? I'm back to work."

The relief in his voice made her smile. And that he'd called to tell her. She loved that he wanted to share his news with her.

"Good for you. What happened?"

"Rachel talked to the director, told him about Doern and how the case was taking a new direction."

Dani already knew Scott was on a first-name basis with the DA, so she wasn't sure why it bugged her to hear him talk about her.

"That's great. So, you're back at Delphi now?"

"Yeah. Where are you?"

"Not far from you, actually. I'm at Dove Lake, checking out Kreznik's fishing cabin."

"Anything interesting?"

"Turns out it isn't his and he doesn't use it for fishing."

She told him about Zachary Greene's owning the property, along with several more cabins and a ranch nearby.

"I don't like it," Scott said.

"Don't like what?"

"Any of it. Who is this guy?"

Another message landed on her phone. Sean had sent three addresses, and one was on Mockingbird Road. Dani made a U-turn and headed for the house.

"I'm not sure yet," she said.

"Let me run him down for you."

Dani sighed. "I suppose it wouldn't help for me to mention that you aren't an investigator on this case?"

"Nope. I'll run him down and call you back."

He hung up, and Dani dropped her phone into the cup holder. Scott's involvement still bothered her. But he wouldn't let go. And she had to admit, he'd been instrumental in cracking the case. The prints on the shell casings provided indisputable proof of Doern's involvement in the attack in New Mexico. The feds wouldn't have found those casings if Scott hadn't drawn their attention to them. And now Doern was the subject of a nationwide manhunt, thanks mostly to Scott. Where would the investigation be if he hadn't been so damn stubborn about being involved?

The road curved. She slowed to look at a mailbox and found the address she was looking for. She pulled over. The small house was on stilts and had a view of the lake. Dani noticed the car parked beside it.

A cherry-red Mustang convertible.

"No way," she muttered. She stared at the plate for a moment, then texted the digits to Sean. Her heart was racing, and she felt certain she was looking at Audrey Ayers's Mustang.

Sean came right back. *WTF?*

She called him. "That's the tag on Audrey's Mustang, right?"

"Right. Where the hell are you?"

"Zachary Greene's cabin."

Dani was out of the car now, circling the house, but everything was dark. She peeked through one of the dusty front windows and saw a small living room with mismatched furniture. This place didn't look like Audrey Ayers at all, yet her car was right there in the driveway.

"I'm on my way out there, Dani. Don't do anything without me."

"Like what?"

"Like go nosing around that cabin by yourself."

"I already did and there's no one here."

"Damn it, Dani. Would you wait for me?"

"I want to talk to Zachary Greene. Maybe Ric should come, too, since he knows all the background."

"You mean you didn't hear?"

"Hear what?"

"Ric's at the hospital. Mia's having the baby."

"*What?* He didn't call me!"

"He didn't call anyone. The man ran out of here like his hair was on fire. And don't try to change the subject. Don't go anywhere until I catch up to you, you got me?"

• • •

Dani tapped the steering wheel as she waited on the shoulder of the two-lane highway. She glanced at her watch. Then she looked at Zachary Greene's gate again and contemplated going in solo.

At last Sean pulled up beside her and rolled down his window. "I'm surprised you waited."

"So am I."

"Your car or mine?"

"Yours," Dani said, getting out.

He was in his personal vehicle today, a black pickup that would be less conspicuous than Dani's unmarked police unit. She climbed into the truck and scowled at the collection of fast-food wrappers on his floorboards.

"Jeez, Sean."

"Hey, I've been busy."

He turned into the private driveway and pulled up to a wrought-iron gate. There was a keypad with a call button, and Sean turned to Dani. "You know how you want to play this?"

"Just keep it vague."

"Why don't you talk."

"Why?"

"You're female. Less intimidating."

Dani rolled her eyes as he pressed the call button. A few seconds ticked by and then a woman's voice come over the intercom.

"Yes, please?"

Dani couldn't place the accent. Something Eastern European. She leaned across Sean to talk into the speaker.

"Yes, I'm Detective Daniele Harper here to see Zac Greene," she said, taking a chance on the nickname.

For a moment, nothing. Then: "And what is this regarding?"

"Police business."

Another long pause. "He is in a meeting at the stable."

Dani glanced at Sean.

"One moment," the voice said. There was a long buzz and the gate slid open.

Sean raised his window and rolled through. "Easier than I thought."

They made their way through a tunnel of huge oak trees. Horses stood in the shade, watching them lazily and flicking their tails.

Dani glanced at Sean. "Ric told you our theory?"

"That our vics were cloning polo ponies for that rancher in New Mexico. And a rival down here lured them away, so the guy decided to off them and eliminate the competition."

"What do you think?"

"I *thought* it sounded far-fetched. But seeing all these horses here . . . I don't know. Could be something to it."

The driveway curved, and a hacienda-style house came into view—white adobe with an orange-tile roof. A driveway circled around a large water fountain where a shiny black Mercedes was parked beside a black Porsche.

"The woman on the intercom said the stable," Dani said. "Let's try there first, maybe catch him off guard."

Sean passed the house. The tree-lined road dipped down to a wide clearing with a forest-green stable. Behind it was an enormous barn, also forest green. Between the two buildings was a paddock where a blond woman in riding attire was mounting a horse.

Sean pulled up and slid to a stop beside a black Range Rover and golf cart.

"He likes black vehicles," Sean said as he turned off the engine. "We blend right in."

Dani stared at the golf cart, which had a silver *Z* monogrammed across the front. "Z Ranch."

"What's that?"

"This is Z Ranch." She glanced at Sean. "That rich doctor lives here. You remember, his wife wrapped her Mercedes around a tree a week ago?"

"Huh." Sean glanced around. "That explains the money. You go talk to Greene. I'm going to have a quiet look around."

"Are you looking for Audrey?"

"I don't know. Maybe." He pulled his phone from the pocket of his jacket. "Set your phone to vibrate. I'll ping you if anything comes up, you do the same."

They got out. Dani headed straight for the stable, hoping to distract Greene before he noticed an unattended guest wandering around his property.

She paused inside the building for a moment to let her eyes adjust. The place smelled of manure and hay, and rock music played in a tack room to her right. Inside one of the stalls a woman with a long blond ponytail stood with her back to Dani, brushing down a chestnut-colored horse. She glanced over her shoulder as Dani walked past, but didn't say anything.

After passing half a dozen stalls Dani reached an open door. She stepped through it and nearly bumped into the chest of a tall, dark-haired man.

"Hi," she said, startled. "I'm Detective Daniele Harper." She took out her badge. "Are you Zachary Greene?"

"I am."

She could tell by his expression someone had called to give him the heads-up. Had he been leaving or coming out to meet her? She stood her ground and gazed up at him. He wore jeans and a black long-sleeved shirt that stretched taut over his chest.

"Detective." He cleared his throat. "Please come in."

He stepped back and ushered her into a small but nicely appointed office with a mahogany desk and matching credenza. Dani glanced at the Oriental rug on the floor, which struck her as strangely formal with all the dirt and hay everywhere else.

"Sit down." His tone immediately irked her.

"I'll stand, thanks."

He arched his eyebrows and sank into a black leather chair behind the desk. "How may I help you?"

She tucked her thumbs into her front pockets and looked him over for a moment. He was late forties. Attractive. Jet-black hair without a touch of gray at the temples, and a conspicuous lack of crow's-feet around his eyes. If he wasn't a plastic surgeon, he obviously knew one.

Dani glanced around the office, noting the trophies on the credenza, the crystal bowl, the framed photos. Several pictures showed Greene atop a horse and holding a polo mallet. Another photo showed him standing beside a horse with Marco Varela.

They were connected. She was staring at proof. Were they friends or business associates or both?

"So," Dani said, gathering her thoughts. "You have a nice ranch here. What is it, five hundred acres?" It was a wild guess.

"Eleven hundred." He smiled, treating her to a flash of perfectly whitened teeth.

"I see you have a lot of horses. What kind are they?"

"Criollos. And quarter horses."

Dani didn't know horses, but they sounded expensive. "And do you breed them?"

"I buy them."

"Why, if you don't mind my asking?"

Greene gave a casual shrug. "It's a hobby. Some people collect cars. Jewelry. I like animals." He tipped his head to the side. "Is there a purpose to these questions, Detective . . . ?"

"Harper."

"Right." He glanced at his Rolex and gave her a pointed look.

"Sorry, just curious." Now it was her turn to smile. "I'll get to the point. I'm looking into the death of James Ayers and Tessa Lovett."

"The professor."

"And his assistant, yes. Did you know him?"

Greene steepled his hands in front of him. "The shooting by the lake. I read about it in the paper."

Way to dodge the question.

"Did you know him?"

"No."

"Are you sure?"

"Yes. Why?"

"Because James's widow is staying in your lake house at the moment."

Surprise flickered across his face, but he quickly covered it.

"Audrey. Yes. She's a patient."

"A patient?"

"That's right."

"Excuse me," a woman said, stepping into the doorway. It was the blonde who'd been grooming the horse, and Dani saw now that she was extremely pregnant.

"Dr. Z, your wife is looking for you," she said in a soft voice with an Eastern European accent.

"Thank you, Tatiana." He stood up. "Detective Harper, excuse me for a moment."

Greene walked out. The blonde looked Dani up and down and then followed the doctor.

Dani stared after them. She glanced around the office again, and her stomach plummeted as it all fell into place.

"Shit," she muttered. She rushed out the door, but Greene and the woman were gone. Dani jogged past the stalls as her phone vibrated in her pocket.

An engine roared to life. Dani broke into a run as a blur of black whisked past the door. Dani raced outside in time to see the Range Rover peeling away with a spray of gravel.

"Shit!"

"Dani!"

She turned around to see Sean sprinting for his truck.

"Come on!" he yelled.

She ran around to the passenger side and jumped in. He gunned it backward before she even had the door shut, then made a lightning-fast three-point turn.

"He's fleeing the scene!" Sean floored the pedal and raced after the Rover.

"He's not headed for the gate. Where's he going?"

"Hell if I know. What did you tell him?"

"Nothing."

"You spooked him. What happened?"

"I don't know. I asked him about Audrey." Dani yanked out her phone to call backup, but she had a call coming in. "I can't talk right now," she barked at Scott.

"Don't hang up. I just ran Greene. He's an OB. A fertility specialist."

"I know, and he's getting away. I can't talk! I have to call it in—"

The windshield exploded.

Dani screamed and ducked, dropping the phone.

"Shit, watch out!" Sean swerved.

Pop!

They sped over a bump, catching air. Sean cast a frantic look at her. "Get down! Someone's shooting!"

Dani snatched her phone off the floor and hung up on Scott. She jabbed the button for 911 as Sean ducked low and tried to steer.

Pop!

They careened off the road. Dani braced her hands against the dash as she heard a loud *crack* and a shriek of metal.

CHAPTER 26

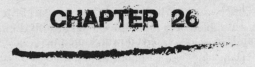

"Daniele? *Daniele?*"

Scott sailed across two lanes and pulled a one-handed U-turn in the center lane while gripping his phone. Horns blared. He swerved into traffic and stomped on the gas.

"Daniele, are you there?"

Scott's gut clenched. There was nothing, only silence so loud it made his ears ring.

• • •

"Dani."

Everything was dark. Quiet.

"Dani, come on."

She lifted her head and pain pulsed behind her eyes.

"*Dani.*"

She turned toward the sound. Sean. He was a shadowy form behind the steering wheel, and everything came back to her.

They'd crashed into a tree.

They were surrounded by leaves and branches now, and the front of the truck was tilted down. They'd plunged into a ditch or a ravine or—

"You're bleeding," she said, moving toward him. Blood saturated his shoulder.

"My leg's pinned," he said tightly.

She reached for her seat belt, but it wasn't fastened. She scrambled over the console and tried his door, but it was completely smashed in and wouldn't move.

"Damn it!"

"Dani, listen to me. We're wedged between two trees."

She looked around, trying to make sense out of their dim surroundings. Foliage blocked the view out of every window. But maybe that provided camouflage from the shooter.

Dani stripped off her jacket. "Can you sit forward?"

"Yeah, but—ouch!"

"Sorry." She carefully wrapped the fabric around Sean's arm. Sweat streamed down his face, and he'd gone pale.

"I think my leg's broken." He winced as she wrapped his upper arm where the blood was rushing out. He was lucky it wasn't a chest wound, but there was so much *blood*.

"Dani, I got this." He pressed his hand against the makeshift bandage. "But you have to get your door open and go get help."

She turned and tried her door. It wouldn't budge. Cursing, she tried it again. "It's not pinned, but—"

"Try again."

She heard the raw pain in his voice. Damn it, she needed to get them both out of here.

Where was the shooter?

Was it Zac Greene? A physician? Dani's head was spinning. Her stomach felt queasy. But even amid her confusion, she somehow knew exactly who was on the other end of that gun.

"Hang on." She repositioned herself so she could use her legs. She tried the door latch again and gave a mighty push with both feet. Branches scraped against metal as she thrust the door open.

"Thank *God*." She turned around, and Sean's head was tipped back against the seat. His eyes were squeezed shut, and blood had already soaked through the jacket tied around his arm.

"Go get help."

"I will."

"Don't come back until you find it. We don't both need to be out here."

She shimmied through the door opening and looked around. It wasn't a ditch but a ravine. A deep one. They'd plunged almost to the bottom and been stopped by two trees.

She turned onto her stomach and slid out feetfirst, trying to hold the door open with her shoulders so it wouldn't shut on her. Her toes touched the ground. As she got her footing, she was at eye level with the floor of the truck. She noticed her phone on the floor and snatched it up and stuffed it into the back pocket of her jeans.

Crack.

She glanced up at the top of the ravine, expecting at any moment to see Rodney Doern staring down the barrel at her.

She glanced at Sean. He was clutching his wound as blood seeped through his fingers.

"Those shots are way high," she said. "He's trying to intimidate us. He's probably set up on a ridge a couple hundred yards away and trying to flush us out because he can't see us."

"How would you know?" Sean's face scrunched up with pain.

"I've been in his sights before. I feel like I know him."

Sean pulled his Glock from his holster. "I'm good here. I'll call nine-one-one while you find a better place to hide and wait for backup."

"But—"

"*Go*, Dani. Get some help back here." He rested his gun on his thigh. "If he comes looking for me, I'll take him out."

She stared at Sean, debating whether to leave him. He was pale and losing blood, and she needed to get a rescue team out here right now. Maybe she could draw the shooter's attention away with a distraction, like Scott had done back on Spruce Canyon Road.

"Come on, Dani. You need to move."

"Make the call."

"I am."

The door slammed shut as she dropped into a crouch beside the wreck. She took out her gun, then looked around to get her bearings as she jogged along the bed of rocks. She wanted to stay low and out of sight. The shooter was still out there, probably watching from the safety of a higher vantage point.

Her phone vibrated in her pocket. Scott.

"Dani! What the hell happened?"

"We took a hit and drove into a ditch."

"*Where* are you?"

"Zachary Greene's ranch. We're out past the stable. Sean's been shot and he's pinned inside the truck."

"I'm on my way."

"Call nine-one-one. He needs a rescue team and—" *Crack.*

• • •

Scott's heart missed a beat.

"Daniele?"

"I'm here. He's—"

"Get to cover *now*! That's cover, not concealment. You know the difference? Find something hard that a bullet can't penetrate—"

"I know, I know."

"I'm ten minutes out."

"I'm hanging up now. Call the sheriff and the FBI. Just get us some help here."

• • •

Scott spotted the turnoff and screeched to a halt. He swung onto the road and gunned the engine. It was just ahead. Had to be. Less than a mile ahead on the right . . .

"Almost there, Daniele," he said, wishing she could hear him. He glanced at the map on his phone. Damn it, he should be there by now.

He spied the gate and skidded to a stop. He glanced up and down the road. No police cars, no emergency vehicles, not even a hint of a siren, although he'd called every law enforcement agency in three counties. Where the hell was everyone?

Scott threw his truck into reverse and rocketed backward at an angle, aligning his grille with the *Z* in the center of the gate.

He shifted gears and stomped the gas.

• • •

Dani clawed her way up the embankment, grabbing at tree roots and struggling to hang on to her pistol. He hadn't fired a shot in eight minutes. The silence unnerved her. Was he stalking closer? Or had he fled the scene?

Boom.

She hunched forward at the sound. An IED? She had no idea. She grabbed a sapling and hauled herself to the top of the ravine. Panting, she glanced around. She was in a thicket surrounding a long green pasture. Directly to her right was a corral with a trio of chestnut-colored horses, all with identical white stars on their foreheads. The horses were spooked by all the commotion. They were moving and whinnying and kicking up dust.

To Dani's left was a low adobe building with satellite dishes lined up along the tile roof. Was it a house? An office? Across the pasture, maybe a hundred yards away, was another large barn.

The black Range Rover parked there made Dani's blood turn cold. Zac Greene was inside that building.

Her phone vibrated in her pocket, and she jerked it out with a rush of relief.

"Where are you?" Scott demanded.

"At the ranch still. Did you call nine-one-one?"

"Yes. *Where* at the ranch? I just busted through the gate."

She whirled around. He was here already?

"Past the house and the stable. There's an adobe building with satellite dishes. It's across a pasture from a big green barn."

"Take cover," he ordered. "I'm coming."

He hung up. She stared at her phone for a moment and heard . . . thunder?

Not thunder, but a low rumbling.

"Helicopter," she muttered, feeling a surge of hope. Maybe a medical chopper? SMPD didn't have a police helicopter, and neither did the sheriff's office. Maybe someone had called the feds.

The rotor-blade noise grew louder. The wind whipped up leaves and dust around her and she tipped her head back to the sky. Through a gap in the trees she saw the helicopter hovering over the empty pasture.

But it wasn't a police chopper. It was black and shiny and on the side was a silver *Z*.

Crack.

CHAPTER 27

Dani ducked behind a tree, panting.

She reached a trembling hand to her cheek, and her fingers came away red.

"He didn't get me," she said, staring at her fingers with disbelief.

He *hadn't*, had he?

But she was bleeding. She'd probably been hit by tree bark, but it had been a close call. Way, way too close.

She flattened back against the tree and tried to make herself small.

"Daniele!"

She turned and Scott was there, pulling her down into a crouch.

"You're hit."

"I'm fine."

He surrounded her with his big body. "Daniele, you're bleeding."

"It's just a scratch," she said as he combed his hand through her hair, searching for injuries. "Really, I'm okay. We need to get Sean. He's in the ravine, and he's badly wounded." She peered around Scott at the barn. "Zac Greene is in that barn. He's going to escape."

"Like hell he is." Scott looked at the barn and then at her. "Do *not* move. I'll be back."

"What? Where are you going? There's a *sniper* walking around here!"

The grass flattened as the helicopter swooped down like a big black wasp. A black-clad man with a machine gun sprinted across the pasture and leaped onto one of the skids.

"It's Doern," she yelled above the noise. He wore a green flak jacket and had traded his rifle for an M4. Dani gripped her Glock in her hand, but she was out of range.

"He's going to lay down cover fire," Scott yelled back. "Stay behind this tree and keep low, do you hear me? Do *not* let him see you."

"Wait!" She grabbed his arm. "God damn it, don't you *dare* leave me here. This is *my* investigation!"

He stopped and stared at her, his blue eyes more intense than she'd ever before seen them, and she could see the war going on in his head. He wanted to leave her here and assume all the risk alone.

"Don't sideline me, Scott. I'll never forgive you."

He squeezed his eyes shut. "God *damn* it." He looked at her. "Okay, listen. We're out of pistol range here. We have to get closer. You move north, staying behind these trees as much as you can until you reach the house. Get behind the corner and fire off a few rounds to distract them. I'll circle around to the barn, then come at them from the east."

"Okay." She released his arm.

"*Solid* cover, Dani. And you don't need to hit them, just distract them. Aim for something big, like the helo."

"Got it." She started to move but he yanked her back.

"Be careful." He kissed her hard on the mouth.

"You be careful, too."

• • •

Dani sprinted for the low adobe building, keeping her eye on Doern on the skid of the chopper. She reached a black pickup parked near the building and ducked for cover behind it. Then she sprinted for the building and crouched low beside a window. Where was Scott? And what about Zachary Greene? She looked at the Range Rover beside the barn again and then glanced through the window beside her.

Her breath caught. Audrey Ayers was inside, laid out on a metal table. Dani's mind flicked to Tessa Lovett in the autopsy room.

"Holy hell," she murmured, cupping her hand against the glass for a better look. It was some sort of exam room. Audrey was alone, and she wasn't moving, and, given the thunderous noise all around them, that wasn't a good sign. She was either dead or unconscious.

Dani peeked around the corner. A flash of movement caught her eye as Greene ran across the pasture. Dani fired off two rounds at the chopper. Doern swung his weapon in her direction, and she ducked for cover as he hosed down the building with a barrage of gunfire.

Where was Scott? She got low and peeked around the corner again. Greene was almost to the helicopter when he suddenly went down.

Scott.

Dani felt a rush of relief, but it disappeared when Greene scrambled to his feet again and staggered to the chopper. He stepped onto the skid and managed to heave himself aboard.

Scott had hit him, but Greene was wearing a damn

ballistic vest. Dani watched in despair as the helicopter eased off the ground with Doern still on the skid. His attention was on the barn now, no doubt searching for Scott.

The rotor noise changed pitch and the helicopter lifted up and up. Dani's stomach clenched. They were getting away. They'd murdered four people across two states, and they'd shot both Scott and Sean. And they were going to *get away with it*.

• • •

Scott wanted the head shot, but he needed to get closer.

He sprinted for a tree, diving behind it as Doern tried to spray him with bullets. This was it. One more chance, and then it was over.

He eased around the tree and lined up his sights.

A flicker of movement caught his eye. Dani stepped out from behind the building and aimed her pistol at the tail rotor.

Scott's heart clenched as she took the shot.

• • •

Dani watched in shock as the helo dipped down, then lurched up again and careened crazily to the side. She'd made the shot!

Greene tumbled from the open door and did a ten-foot free fall to the ground as Doern clung to the skid. Then the helicopter rolled to the side and then everything happened in slow motion.

The rotor caught on the roof of the barn.

A tremendous *snap* split the air.

Doern leaped away from the chopper just before it crashed to the ground.

Then everything exploded.

• • •

Scott stumbled to his feet, choking and coughing.

"Dani!"

He raced across the field, straining to see through the dense smoke. Where was she? His lungs burned as he sprinted through the cloud. He reached the adobe building, but she wasn't there.

Movement in the corner of his eye. Scott pivoted with his gun, dropping to his knees just in time to miss a spurt of bullets from the M4. Scott lunged behind the pickup and managed to get a shot off, but it went wide.

Two rounds left.

Scott clutched his weapon, looking around for Dani. Where the hell was she?

A spray of bullets whizzed past him. He ducked low and returned fire.

• • •

Dani stumbled through the smoke, trying to stay low. Where was Doern? And Greene? The heat burned her cheeks as she neared the flaming wreckage.

A flash of movement caught her attention and she turned to see Greene hobbling toward the Range Rover.

"Freeze! Police!"

He glanced over his shoulder and broke into a lopsided run, obviously injured. He had a vest on, so she

aimed for his leg and pulled the trigger. He crumpled
to the ground and clutched his ankle.

Dani raced over, pulling out a pair of handcuffs as
she looked around for Doern and Scott. Where were
they?

Greene writhed on the ground, clutching his ankle
and cursing. She shoved him onto his stomach and
pinned her knee against his spine as she wrenched his
arms behind him and slapped on the cuffs.

Her ears were ringing. Her lungs burned. Her pris-
oner cursed beneath her as she looked around frantically. Where on earth was Scott?

• • •

Scott crouched behind the truck, waiting for his moment. Doern was on the other side. One round left,
and his enemy was wearing Kevlar. The only good shot
was a head shot.

Scott glanced at the side mirror, using it for guid-
ance as he eased around the back bumper.

A noise behind him. Scott whirled around just as a
rifle stock smashed into his jaw. Scott's head snapped
back and pain blinded him. He fell onto his side and
squeezed off a shot.

Doern staggered backward, wounded in the shoulder. He didn't even drop his gun.

Scott surged to his feet and tackled him. He tried to
rip the gun from Doern's hands, but he had the weapon
in a firm grip despite the bleeding wound. Scott's Sig
was empty, so he tossed it away and used both hands to
try to wrench the M4 from Doern's grasp. Something

had to be wrong with the weapon or Doern would have shot Scott instead of clubbing him with it. Was it jammed?

With a sudden burst of power, Doern heaved Scott onto his back and pressed the gun barrel flat against his throat.

Scott struggled beneath him, trying to push off the massive weight. Doern's face was red and his sweat dripped into Scott's eyes as he tried to crush Scott's throat with the rifle.

Scott punched him in the eye. And punched him again. The second blow tipped him sideways, and Scott used the momentum to heave him off his chest, then crash down on top of him. Scott seized the rifle and delivered a muzzle strike, but Doern rolled sideways. Scott flung the M4 away and lunged after him, tackling him to the ground, then landing a blow against the back of his head. Fire tore up his arm.

A knife. Doern's secondary weapon was a Ka-Bar.

In Scott's instant of shock, Doern rolled on top of him and crushed him beneath his weight. Scott threw his arm up to block the next slash. He grabbed Doern's wrist with both hands. The blade hovered between them, wide and black and sharp enough to slice through airplane skin like butter. The tip of the blade trembled as Scott gripped Doern's wrist, desperately trying to gain leverage.

Where was Dani? Had she taken a bullet?

White-hot fury filled him as he fought against Doern's grip and his weight and the laws of physics. The man was sweating. Bleeding. His face was purple, but his eyes showed cool determination as he struggled to sink the blade into Scott's throat.

In the distance, Dani's voice. The sound of her calling him made Scott's heart squeeze.

With a mighty groan, Scott pushed up and heaved Doern off him. He rolled him onto his back and wrenched the knife away. It was slick with sweat, and Scott almost dropped it before he got a grip on the hilt and threw a swipe at Doern's neck.

His head dropped back with a gurgling noise.

Scott stared at him, chest heaving. He climbed to his feet. Sweat stung his eyes as he gazed down at the man who'd almost buried a knife in his throat.

Scott's ears rang. His heart jackhammered in his chest. He stepped back, numb with shock.

Then his brain lurched into gear and he glanced around. "Daniele!"

And there she was. Standing in the haze of smoke. Her eyes were wide, and the horrified look on her face would haunt him forever.

He tossed the bloody knife away and rushed toward her. Her shirt was torn and she held her Glock at her side.

"Are you okay? You're bleeding, Daniele."

She blinked up at him.

"Where's Greene?"

"He's—" She turned around. "Cuffed. Over there."

"You *handcuffed* him?"

In the distance, sirens. Dani turned toward the sound as a *whump-whump* filled the air and a white helicopter appeared above the trees.

"It's the feds," Scott told her.

Dani tucked her gun away. "You called them?"

"Yeah."

Smoke and dust began to swirl around them, and

Scott took her hand and pulled her toward the building as the helo's downdrafts flattened the grass and spooked the horses.

Dani looked spooked, too, and her eyes were wide and glassy. She'd just watched him slit a man's throat. Scott felt sick for her. She stared up at him and her face was smudged, and she looked like she had after the truck blew up in New Mexico.

Doern had almost killed her, *twice*, and Scott would kill the man all over again if he had to.

Scott cupped Dani's face in his hands. "Are you really all right?"

She nodded.

"Hey!"

They turned around to see an agent in a dark suit jogging toward them.

"That's Rey Santos," Dani said. "Ric's brother."

The man stopped in front of them and peeled off his shades as he looked around. "Is that him?" He nodded at the lifeless body in the dirt, the man who'd recently topped the FBI's Ten Most Wanted list.

"Rodney Doern," Dani told him. "And Zachary Greene, the man who hired him, is over there."

Santos gazed across the pasture at the man flailing around on the grass with his hands cuffed behind him.

"What did you do to him?" The agent looked at Dani with disbelief.

"What's it look like? I arrested him."

CHAPTER 28

Dani pushed through the door and spied her lieutenant across the sea of chairs in the hospital waiting room. He was talking to the DA.

"How is Sean?" Reynolds demanded.

"Just went into surgery," Dani said.

Rey Santos broke away from a group of agents and joined the conversation. "The gunshot wound?"

"That was a through-and-through bullet," Dani said. "The doctor tells me the leg is the more serious injury. His tibia is broken in three different places, and he's going to need pins."

"Catch me up," Rachel said. "I understand you arrested a *doctor*? What happened to the horse breeder in New Mexico?"

"Marco Varela," Dani said. "We were on the right track with that, but we took a wrong turn when we started looking at Varela as the mastermind. We thought Varela hired the hits on the scientists to eliminate competition and protect his horse-cloning operation. But we were off."

"Dr. Zachary Greene hired the hits," Rey said. "One of our agents has tracked down payments he made to Doern that corroborate it. He's lawyered up already, but before he did, we at least got him to identify the pilot who was killed in the chopper. It's John Wells, who we've been looking at as an accomplice of Rodney Doern. They worked at Black Echo together."

"Wait," Rachel said. "So, you're telling me this Dr. Greene was running a cloning operation, too? Right here in our backyard?"

"Yes, but not horses," Dani said. "Greene's a fertility specialist. He's attempting to clone people."

Rachel stood there, speechless for once, as Dani gave her the nutshell version of Mia's explanation of the process and the dangers involved.

"He's become famous in his field," Rey said. "And he's made a fortune. But Immigration and Customs Enforcement has been building a file on him for a year."

"Why?" Rachel asked.

"His patients flagged our attention. He's been bringing in all these young Eastern European women to work on his ranch, saying they were grooms and riding instructors. ICE started to think he was running some kind of sex-trafficking operation with all these women."

"But he's using them as human guinea pigs," Dani said. "He's using them as breeders."

"Breeders?"

"He's trying to get his cloning business off the ground and he needs women he can experiment on."

Rachel shuddered. "Unbelievable."

"Believe it," Rey said. "He basically lured the scientists in with money, harvested their IP, and then decided to get rid of them so they couldn't share their expertise with anyone else."

"The irony is sick." Dani shook her head. "A famous baby doctor hiring hit men to kill people?"

"So, will he be facing federal charges, or do we get a crack at him?" Rachel wanted to know.

"Talk to ICE," Rey said. "But as for the murder-for-hire plot, that's all you."

"Not just one murder. *Four*," Dani said.

"And attempted murder of two police officers," Reynolds added.

"This man sounds like a piece of work," Rachel said. The prosecutor had a feral look in her eyes, and Dani knew she couldn't wait to get her hands on the case.

"Detective Harper?"

She turned around to see one of the nurses she'd spoken with earlier. "The patient you were asking about is taking visitors now."

Dani left the group and followed the nurse back to an exam room. A young blond woman passed Dani in the hall, and she did a double take. She hadn't realized that Audrey Ayers and her sister Lesley were identical twins.

The nurse opened the door to the dim room. Audrey looked to be sleeping, but she opened her eyes as Dani stepped inside.

"Hi."

"They said you wanted to talk to me." Audrey's voice sounded meek. Defeated.

Dani pulled up a chair beside the bed. Audrey wore a hospital gown and looked frail under a thin blue blanket. When paramedics found her in Greene's exam room, she'd been under heavy sedation.

Dani glanced at Audrey's wristband. "Will you be staying overnight or—"

"I've been discharged. My sister went to get some clothes for me to wear out of here."

Dani cleared her throat. She didn't know where to begin, so she plunged right in. "I read the statement you gave Special Agent Santos. I have some follow-up questions."

Audrey sighed and looked away.

"Audrey, when I first interviewed you after your husband's murder . . . did you have any idea your doctor was involved?"

Another sigh.

Which answered Dani's question.

"I guess I suspected." Audrey wiped a tear from her cheek. "But I didn't really *know*, you know?"

Dani just looked at her, seething with frustration. Why hadn't Audrey voiced her suspicions in the beginning? Nathan Collins might be alive right now. And Scott might not have been shot. Same for Sean, who was in surgery at this very moment getting pins put in his leg.

Audrey looked at Dani with dull eyes. Only hours ago she'd had a miscarriage. She was grieving, and Dani didn't have the heart to pile on.

"Did you know about the grooms? That they were part of his big experiment?"

"I didn't know. I thought it was just a few of us, and I thought they were women with fertility problems, like me. I mean, I'd seen a couple of them at the clinic, but I didn't realize they worked on his ranch until I was out there yesterday."

"But you suspected all along that Greene might be behind your husband's murder?"

Audrey nodded. "Dr. Z has this God complex. Like he's smarter than everyone. It's always given me the creeps. And when James was murdered, I thought . . . maybe he was involved. Then I heard about Mike Kreznik, too, and I just *knew*."

"And you still wanted to be his patient?"

She looked at Dani for a long moment. "You don't understand." Audrey shifted her gaze to the window. "So much in my life . . . my marriage, my family . . . It's all been a big disappointment."

Dani watched her, trying to put herself in Audrey's place so she could understand. But she truly couldn't. This woman had known who was behind the murder of four people, yet she'd said nothing.

Dani looked down at her hands, still scraped and bruised from everything that had happened that day. She thought of Sean upstairs, under the knife. She thought of Scott on the ground with Doern, fighting for his life. An ice-cold anger filled her.

Selfish, selfish, selfish. She had nothing more to say to this woman.

"I should go." Dani stood up.

"I know you don't understand me. Nobody does. You don't know what it's like to want a baby so badly you'll do *anything*, overlook *anything*, just for a chance to have a child."

Dani paused in the doorway. "Overlook anything . . . including murder? You're right, I don't understand that." Frustration welled up inside her. If only this woman had been honest from the beginning, much of this would never have happened.

Audrey obviously wanted Dani's sympathy, but she had none. She turned and left. She pushed through the double doors into the waiting room and nearly bumped into Scott, stepping off the elevator.

"Hey." He caught her arm. "I was looking for you."

At the sight of him, Dani's bitterness evaporated and all she felt was relief. She glanced at his bandage. "How's your arm?"

"It's a scratch. Could have fixed it myself." He gazed down at her for a long moment, and she was transfixed by the heated look in his eyes. "Come here."

"What?"

He pulled her around the corner to a drinking fountain and leaned her against the wall. He kissed her with a fierceness that caught her off guard. His mouth moved over hers, and she started feeling those warm shivers that only happened when they were alone. But they were in a public place.

She pulled back.

"I can't get it out of my head, Dani." He wrapped his arms around her.

"What?"

"When I couldn't find you in all that smoke, I thought . . ." He rested his head against hers. "I don't want to tell you what I thought."

She pulled back to look at him, and in all her life she'd never seen so much worry in his eyes.

He stroked his thumb over the scrape on her cheek. "You scared the hell out of me."

She kissed him. Because she didn't know what to say, and it always seemed to be the best way to communicate with him. His mouth was hot and hungry and possessive, and she wanted more than anything to go home with him right this minute.

She eased back and caught a glimpse of Rachel watching them from across the waiting room.

Drew stood beside her.

"Shit," Dani muttered.

"What?"

"My brother's watching us."

Scott just held her. He didn't seem to care who was watching. "Want me to talk to him?"

"He looks like he wants to strangle you."

As if on cue, Drew walked over, a flinty look in his eyes. Despite the late hour, he hadn't been home yet. He was in the same suit he'd had on that morning when they'd had their fight at Dani's house.

Dani tried to step away, but Scott caught her hand and held her in place, lacing his fingers through hers.

He turned to face her brother. "Drew."

"Scott."

For a long moment they said nothing, just stared at each other.

"I heard about what happened," Drew said. "We got word there was an officer down." He cleared his throat. "Thank you for getting my sister out of there in one piece."

"Um, hello? I'm standing right here."

"She got herself out," Scott said.

"Yeah, well . . . thanks anyway." Drew looked at Dani. "Can I talk to you in private?"

Scott released her hand, and she followed Drew to the nurses' station.

Folding his arms over his chest, he stared at her. "What?"

"You're all cut up. Are you really okay?"

"It's just a scratch," she said, borrowing Scott's words.

"No, I mean with him."

She sighed. "Yes, Drew."

He searched her eyes, and she could see the genuine worry there. "I have to tell you, I'm not happy about this."

"You'll get over it."

"You could get hurt, Dani. This could turn into a real mess."

"Yeah, well, it'll be my hurt. And my mess."

His gaze narrowed. "Are you in love with him?"

"Yes."

The word flew out of her mouth without her even thinking about it.

Drew sighed. "I knew it."

She went up on tiptoes and kissed his cheek. "Stop worrying."

"I can't. You're my sister."

"Try."

He sighed and walked away, rejoining Rachel and the feds. Dani turned back to Scott. He had his shoulder propped casually against the wall, but the look on his face was serious.

"You all right?" he asked when she came back.

She kissed him, long and deep—way too much for a public place, but she couldn't help herself.

She pulled away and looked up into those blue eyes she loved so much. "I am now."

CHAPTER 29

Jorge looked just like Ric. He had dark hair and big, beautiful eyes and a tiny dimple at the base of his chin. Mia snuggled him against her breast and kissed his head.

A quiet sigh had her glancing up at Ric in the chair beside her bed. "What?"

He rested his hand on her knee. "You. Him." He leaned closer, and the love-struck look in his eyes filled her with happiness.

"He's perfect, isn't he?" She gazed down at the tiny hand flexing against her breast.

Ten little fingers, ten little toes. Ric had counted them over and over. He'd interrogated the OB. And the pediatrician. And every orderly who stepped into the room to check on them. He'd watched with rapt attention as the floor nurse demonstrated how to clean the baby's umbilical cord and change his diaper and swaddle him.

Ric squeezed Mia's hand now and gazed down at his one-day-old son. "You make me happy. Both of you."

Tears filled her eyes again. She knew it was the hormones, but she couldn't seem to stop weeping.

A soft knock sounded at the door, and she glanced up to see Dani.

"Hi," she said nervously. "Rey said you were taking visitors? I can come back if—"

"Come right in," Mia said.

Dani took a tentative step into the room as Ric stood up.

"Congratulations to both of you. He's beautiful."

Ric smiled proudly. "Eight pounds, ten ounces."

"Wow." Dani stepped closer. "Impressive." She glanced at Mia. "Hope I'm not interrupting."

"You're not," Ric said. "Fact, I was just about to make a coffee run. You want anything, babe?"

"I'm fine."

Ric slipped out, and Dani took the chair he'd been sitting in. She put a little blue gift bag on the table beside a balloon bouquet.

"How are you feeling?"

"Tired." Mia smiled. "And emotional."

Dani nodded.

"But happy emotional, you know?"

Dani nodded again, but Mia could tell she didn't really understand. Maybe she would someday.

"How's Sean?" Mia asked, changing the subject.

"Doing better. I was just up there visiting, and he said they're sending him home Friday."

"That's good news."

"He's in for a lot of rehab."

"He's lucky to be alive." Mia unlatched the baby and shifted him to the other side, then rearranged her nightgown. "Sorry." She cast a look at Dani.

"Don't be sorry."

"Ric told me the helicopter pilot is the other one they were looking for? The accomplice?"

"That's right." Dani cleared her throat. "He and Doern were together at a private security firm called Black Echo. They left there several years ago and started freelancing together."

Mia shuddered. "It's so unreal that all this happened."

"Thanks for your help figuring it out."

"Sure." She glanced up. "So, what's this I hear about you and Scott Black?"

Dani smiled but it didn't reach her eyes. "I don't know. What did you hear?"

"That you two got together somehow in the middle of all of this?"

"You could say that." Dani reached out to stroke her finger over the blue-and-pink-striped baby blanket.

Mia could tell Dani didn't want to talk about it. Maybe it hadn't settled out yet.

"I don't know. It feels strange. I care about him so much that I'm scared, Mia."

"Of what?"

"I'm not sure. That I'll screw it up. Does that make any sense?"

"Yeah, it does." Mia gazed down at Jorge's soft little cheek. "It makes total sense." She looked at Dani. "How does Scott seem about everything?"

"I don't know."

"Have you talked about it?"

"He's not really a talker."

"Well. Give it time."

Jorge stopped nursing. Mia gazed down at him and stroked his forehead.

"He's so beautiful," Dani whispered.

"I know."

"Is he asleep?"

"Yeah."

Mia got up and straightened his blanket. "You want to hold him?"

"What, now?"

"Sure."

"I'd hate to wake him. I'll hold him next time."

Mia smiled and settled him into the bassinet.

Ric walked in with a superlarge cup of coffee. "He sleeping?"

"Yeah."

"I should go," Dani said. "You guys get some rest."

She hugged them good-bye and slipped out. As the door whisked shut, Ric looked at her.

"How is she?"

Confused. Terrified. In love. "She's good, I think," Mia said, lying back on the bed. "How are you?"

"Tired." He stretched out beside her. Then he pulled her into his arms and kissed her forehead. "Tired and happy."

• • •

For the first time in her life, Dani woke up in Scott's house.

She was alone again. The dark blue sheets smelled like him. She closed her eyes and soaked up the delicious scent as she listened to him rattling around in the kitchen. Six straight nights they'd spent together, and not once had she beaten him out of bed in the morning. He was a chronic early riser. She guessed it had to do with all those years in the military.

Dani got up and ducked into the bathroom. She found an extra toothbrush in the linen closet along with a clean towel. She turned on the shower and brushed her teeth. As she stared at the mirror, she itched to open the medicine cabinet, but she held back.

She didn't want to learn about him through snooping. She wanted him to open up to her, even though that would be a much slower process. Dani had never been patient, but with Scott she was determined to try.

She stepped into the shower and stood under the spray, letting the hot water sluice over her. It was Saturday, and she had the whole day ahead of her. She planned to stop into work briefly to take care of some paperwork, and then she wanted to swing by Mia's. And maybe visit her parents. And hopefully spend the evening with Scott, even though they hadn't talked about it.

She reached for the shampoo and her hand froze. On the shelf beside the big black bottle were two slender white ones. They cost fifteen bucks apiece and smelled like strawberries, and Dani stared at them until her stomach hurt. Who had put those there? Scott? Or some woman he'd had over?

She finished showering and climbed out.

She dressed in her clothes from yesterday and brushed her hair. She went into the kitchen and spotted Scott through the window, walking in from the garage, where he had a weight bench. He wore shorts but no shoes. His chest was slick with sweat and he had a towel draped around his neck.

Dani's heart lodged in her throat. She loved him. It was so plain, so clear, in the bright light of morning.

All this time she'd told herself she didn't need anyone, that she was okay being aloof and alone, and it was a lie. She wanted someone to hold her at night. She wanted someone to come home to each day, someone to tease her and listen to her and share after-sex food with at three in the morning. And not just someone. She wanted *Scott*.

She was in love with him. Her chest ached with it, and even if she was setting herself up for disappointment, she couldn't make the feeling go away.

He stepped through the door. "Morning," he said, toweling off his face and looking her over.

Her heart was racing, and she discovered she couldn't speak.

"There's coffee." He grabbed a bottle of water from the fridge.

"Thanks." She filled a mug and found some sugar in a canister beside the coffeepot.

"Travis called." He guzzled water. "We caught a big case last night. I have to go in this morning." He pulled the towel from around his neck and tossed it on the counter. Then he stepped over to her and wrapped his arms around her. "You working today?"

"Maybe a little."

"Mmm." He kissed the top of her head. "You smell good."

"Thanks. Whose shampoo is that?"

"What, the white stuff? You can use it."

"I did." She tipped her head back to look at him. "Who left it there?"

He gave her a crooked smile. "No one. I got it for you."

"You did?"

"Yeah, it's the kind you like."

She stared at him.

"What's the big deal?"

"Nothing." She pulled back and glanced down at her feet. "I'm just . . ." She looked up.

He was watching her expectantly. "You're just . . . ?"

"I thought some woman left it in your shower." She

rubbed her eyes. "Sorry. Picturing you with other people makes me crazy."

"Well, don't." He stepped closer, resting his hands on his hips as he stared down at her.

Her heart was thrumming now, and she couldn't read his expression. Was he annoyed? Feeling stifled? It was hard to know because he didn't talk about his feelings.

She took a deep breath, and her chest felt tight. She had to face up to her insecurities. Not just about other women, but about everything.

"Scott . . . what are we doing here?"

"I don't know. Maybe we should talk about it."

She looked at his eyes and had a flashback to the motel room right after she'd kissed him and made him an offer he couldn't refuse.

You're going to be sorry you did this.

But she wasn't sorry. The last several weeks had been the craziest, scariest, and *happiest* of her life, and she wasn't sorry, no matter what happened.

"You remember back at the motel in Big Rock?" A troubled look came into his eyes. "You said how commitment wasn't my thing. You remember that?"

A strange calm came over her and she nodded.

"That bothered me. A lot." He gazed down at her. "You were right that I haven't had a lot of long-term relationships. None, really. But it's not because I can't commit. I just never met the right person."

He eased closer. Dani's heart was pounding. It was thudding so loud she felt sure he could hear it.

"When something matters to me, I stick with it. I stay the course." He took her hand and squeezed it. "*You* matter to me." He lifted her hand and kissed her knuckles. "I love you, Daniele. And I want to be in your life if you'll let me."

Her throat felt tight. Tears blurred her vision, and he dipped his head down, watching her reaction.

"Hey. What'd I say?"

"Nothing." She laughed through her tears.

He pulled her into his arms and kissed her. It was deep and long, and she felt flooded by so many emotions she couldn't keep the tears from spilling over.

Then everything went from sweet to hot, and his hands were under her shirt and pulling her against him.

"Let's not work today," she said. "Let's stay here and do this."

"I have to go in." He kissed her, stroking his hands over her back. "And so do you. We can wait for tonight."

"I can't wait."

"Sure you can."

"I don't want to."

He kissed her again, and when he finally pulled away and gazed down at her, the tenderness in his eyes made her chest hurt.

"Daniele . . ." He searched her face. "What about you?"

God, she hadn't said it. In her storm of emotions, she'd forgotten to say it back.

She went up on tiptoes and kissed him. "I love you, too."

He pulled her against him. "Then we've got all the time in the world."

Don't want to leave the thrilling world of
New York Times bestselling author
Laura Griffin's Tracers?

Keep reading for a sneak peek at the next book
in this award-winning series.

Coming Fall 2017 from Pocket Books!

It was like any other Wednesday night. Until it wasn't.

Samantha Bonner had just finished sweeping up. She'd emptied the dustpan, sanitized the sink, and wiped down the pastry case. The burnt smell of coffee beans hung thick in the air, overpowering the vinegar solution she'd run through the machines. But it was quiet. She stood for a moment and let the silence surround her, glad to be free of the acoustic guitar music that had been looping through her head all day.

Sam grabbed her purse and locked up. Crossing the rain-slicked parking lot to her car, she darted a look into all the dark corners. It was a safe neighborhood, but you never knew.

She turned out of the lot, relieved to be heading home after pulling a double shift. Raindrops pitter-pattered on her windshield as she made her way through downtown. She switched the wipers to low, and her phone lit up with an incoming call. Amy.

Sam stared down at the phone for a quick moment. Then she put the call on speaker.

"Sam? Can you talk?"

"What's up?"

Amy sounded undone. More than usual.

"It's Jared. He wants to move back in."

"He called you?" Sam asked.

"He came by to drop off Aiden. I didn't let him in or anything."

Sam didn't respond as she came to a stoplight. In most areas of her life, Amy wasn't a pushover. But her two-year-old boy missed his daddy, and his daddy knew it. He used the kid as leverage.

"I know what you're thinking," Amy said. "And I just want to talk through it, figure out what I'm going to tell him. Can you come over for a bit? I can make us some coffee."

The mere thought of coffee made her want to retch.

"Sure," she said anyway. Amy was sniffling now, and Sam didn't have the heart to say no.

"Or we could talk on the phone," Amy said. "You're probably busy. Tonight's your night off, isn't it?"

"No, I closed up tonight."

Sam slowed for a bend in the road. Stately oak trees and manicured lawns soon gave way to weeds and chain-link fences. Then came the railroad tracks. White-collar to blue in less than a mile. The people in Sam's neighborhood commuted to work at all hours and didn't stop for lattes on the way.

"I'll be over in a little," Sam said, turning onto her street. "Give me twenty minutes."

"Are you sure?" Another sniffle.

"I'm sure."

She pulled into her driveway and rolled to a stop in the glow of her back-porch light.

"Thanks, Sam. I mean it. I just need to hash this out. I mean, what if he's legit this time? I owe it to Aiden to at least think about it."

Sam kept her skepticism to herself. For now. She slid from her car and noticed the white bike propped against her back deck as she walked up the driveway.

"Sam? You there?"

"I'm here."

She mounted the steps to the deck and reached for the door. A blur of movement caught her attention an instant before pain exploded at the base of her skull.

Sam dropped to her knees and pitched forward. A big arm wrapped around her neck, hauling her backward. The smell of tobacco registered in her brain, filling her with bone-deep fear as the arm clamped around her windpipe.

"Sam?" Amy's voice was far away.

Pain roared through Sam's skull. She struggled to move, to breathe. A glove-covered hand tipped her head back, exposing her neck.

No.

Sam clawed at the arm, trying desperately to buck, to kick, to scream for help. *No, no, no!* From the corner of her eye she spied her phone on the ground. She tried to call out but the cries died in her throat.

"Sam, are you there?"

Fear became panic as she saw the glint of a blade.

"Samantha?"

• • •

Brooke Porter beat the detectives, which surprised her. But then again, she'd made good time. When the message had come in coded 911, she'd dropped what she was doing and rushed straight over.

She parked beside a police unit and grabbed her

evidence kit from the trunk as she surveyed the location. It was a small bungalow, like every other house on the block. In contrast to its neighbors, though, this particular home had a fresh coat of paint and looked to be in decent repair. Potted chrysanthemums lined the front stoop, where a uniformed officer stood taking shelter from the cold drizzle.

Brooke darted up the path and ducked under the overhang. The officer was big. Huge. Brooke had met him before, but for the life of her, she couldn't remember his name.

"Jasper Miller," he provided, handing her a clipboard. "Your photographer just got here."

So he knew she was with the Delphi Center. The San Marcos Police Department typically called Brooke's lab in to help with their big cases.

Brooke scribbled her name into the scene log. "You the first responder?"

"Yes, ma'am." He nodded at the driveway. "Victim's around back. Looks like she was coming home from someplace, and he surprised her at the door."

Brooke eyed the little white Kia parked in the driveway. She wanted to see things for herself and draw her own conclusions.

"Medical examiner's people got here about five minutes ago," Jasper added.

"And the detectives?"

"On their way."

She handed back the clipboard. "Thanks."

Brooke picked her way across the stepping-stones in the grass, trying not to mar anything useful. At the top of the driveway, several uniforms stood under a blue Delphi Center tent that had been erected beside the back porch.

Brooke's stomach tightened with nerves as she lifted the crime-scene tape and walked up the drive. She noted the chain-link fence, the thick shrubbery, the trash cans tucked against the side of the house. Plenty of places for someone to hide.

A camera flashed as she reached the tent. The Delphi Center photographer had already set up her lights and had started documenting the scene. Brooke unloaded some supplies from her kit. She zipped into coveralls and pulled booties over her shoes, then tugged on thick purple gloves as the uniforms looked on silently.

Beat cops thought she was an oddity. She showed up at death scenes with her tweezers and her flashlights and her big orange goggles. She plucked bits of evidence from obscure places and then scuttled back to the lab to do her thing . . . whatever that was.

The detectives got her. Well, maybe not totally. But they'd at least learned to appreciate what she could do for them. Which ones had been assigned to this case? And where the hell were they?

Brooke pulled her long dark hair into a ponytail. She picked up her evidence kit and sucked in a deep breath to brace herself before turning around to take her first look.

Blood was everywhere.

"Holy God," she murmured.

A woman lay crumpled at the back door, her neck slashed open. Her hair, her clothes, even the wooden decking beneath her was saturated. Dark rivulets had dripped down the stairs and were now coagulating in little pools on the lower slats.

"Watch your step."

She glanced up as the ME's assistant crouched beside the body. He was reading a thermometer and making notes on a pad.

"It's slippery," he added.

Brooke walked up the wooden stairs and eased around him, taking care not to step in any puddles. Maddie Callahan stood beside the door, photographing a scarlet arc against the white siding.

Arterial spray.

She lowered her camera and glanced at Brooke. "The detectives here?"

"Not yet."

The breeze shifted, and Brooke got a whiff of blood, strong and metallic. She glanced at the gaping wound again, and stepped back to grab the wooden railing.

Maddie looked at her. "You okay?"

"Yeah."

Brooke should be immune to this stuff by now. But that *neck*.

She steadied herself and looked around. A set of blood-spattered car keys lay near the victim's hand. Brooke glanced at the woman's face, partially visible beneath blond, blood-matted hair. Brooke didn't see a weapon near the body. And any trails the killer might have left as he fled the scene had likely been obscured by rain at this point. The back door stood ajar. Had he fled through the house?

She turned to the ME's assistant. "Was this door open like this?"

He glanced up, looking annoyed. "We haven't been in the house."

Brooke turned to the victim again. Her head lolled weirdly to the side, and flies were already hovering, despite the cool temperature. Brooke stepped past the ME's assistant and slipped into the house.

She found herself in a dark utility room that smelled of fabric softener. The room was small and clean, without so much as a scrap of laundry on the floor. She switched on her flashlight and swept it around. No footprints.

She stepped into the kitchen, maneuvering around an open pantry door.

"Was this open, too?" she asked Maddie, who had also come into the house.

"Yes. And I haven't shot the kitchen yet, so don't move anything."

Brooke stood still, giving herself a few moments to absorb the scene. She always tried to put herself in the perpetrator's shoes. Had he been in here? If so, what had he touched?

The kitchen was dim, except for a light above the sink. Using the end of her flashlight, Brooke flipped a switch beside the door, and an overhead fixture came on.

No dirty dishes on the counter or food sitting out. Eighties-era appliances. A drying rack beside the sink contained a glass, a plate, and a fork. On the counter, next to a microwave, was a loose key and a stack of mail. She stepped over to read the name on the top envelope. Samantha Bonner.

Brooke zeroed in on the key. It was bronze. Shiny.

In the breakfast nook, a small wooden table was pushed up against a window. A brown bottle of root beer sat on the table unopened. Just below room temperature, judging from the condensation.

Brooke returned her attention to the pantry. Soup, soup, and more soup, all Campbell's brand, and she felt like she was looking at an Andy Warhol painting. Tomato, chicken noodle, vegetable. The shelf above the soup was stocked with paper goods. The bottom shelf was filled with healthy cereals and gluten-free crackers and a package of those pink and white animal cookies with the colored sprinkles.

"Brooke?"

"Yeah?" She leaned her head out to look at Maddie.

"Just finished shooting the door if you want it."

"I definitely want it," she said, moving back into the utility room. She put on her orange goggles and switched her flashlight to ultraviolet, looking at the floor for any fluids that might not be visible to the naked eye. Nothing.

She examined the knob a moment, and then selected a powder from her kit. Outside on the deck, the ME's assistant was busy covering the victim's hands with paper bags in preparation for her transport to the morgue.

Brooke glanced back at the kitchen, her attention drawn to the key again. It looked like a house key, and she wanted to know if it fit this door. But she couldn't move anything until Maddie finished her photos.

Brooke opened the jar of powder and tapped some into a plastic tray. Using her softest brush, she loaded the bristles and then gently dusted the knob. She worked slowly, methodically. When she finished dusting, she cast her light over the fluorescent powder and was pleased to see a pristine thumbprint on the side of the knob.

"Maddie, can you get this for me?"

"Sure."

Maddie stepped over and photographed the knob from several angles. When she finished, she moved into the kitchen with her camera.

Brooke took out a strip of clear polyethylene tape and lifted the thumbprint off the curved surface, taking care not to smudge it. She picked out a black card for contrast and gently placed the tape against the card.

One lift done, probably a hundred to go. She closed her eyes a moment and inhaled deeply. When she got laser-focused, she sometimes forgot to breathe.

Brooke heard the detectives before she saw them—two low male voices at the front of the house exchanging clipped police jargon.

Sean Byrne and Ric Santos. She'd know them anywhere.

Brooke labeled the card and tucked it into her evidence kit. So, Sean and Ric on this one. They were experienced and observant. Sean noticed everything she did, even if he seemed to be interviewing witnesses or talking to other cops. He observed where she spent her time and how, and if she lingered in a particular spot, he always asked about it later.

Brooke noticed him, too. With his athletic build and sly smile, it was hard not to. But mostly she noticed his attitude. He had an easygoing confidence she found attractive. Nothing ever seemed to rattle him.

Of course, being a cop, he also had an ego.

The voices grew louder as the detectives stepped into the kitchen. Brooke didn't look up, but she felt a jolt of awareness as Sean's gaze landed on her.

• • •

Sean watched Brooke for a moment and then turned to Jasper.

"You say the neighbor found her?"

"That's right," the officer said. "Lady let her dog out, and he started barking like crazy, so she went outside to see what was going on and spotted the victim in a pool of blood there on the porch. Name's Samantha Bonner. She works at a coffee shop."

Sean raked his hand through his damp hair, scattering drops of water on the floor. "Married? Kids?"

Jasper shook his head. "Neighbor says she lives alone."

Sean unzipped his SMPD windbreaker and glanced at Brooke again. She was on her knees by the back door, lifting fingerprints. Just beyond her was the victim, and the ME's people were already unfurling the body bag.

Damn.

Sean was accustomed to seeing Brooke surrounded by blood and gore, but this was bad. He studied the victim, noting the position of the body, the clothing.

Brooke closed her evidence kit and got to her feet as Sean stepped over.

"Hey."

"Hi," she said, looking him up and down. "Where were you guys?"

"Got stuck behind an accident near the tracks. Tow

truck's blocking the road, so we had to hoof it." He ran his hand through his hair again.

"Don't drip water all over my crime scene."

Sean smiled. "Yours?"

"That's right."

For a moment they just looked at each other, and Sean tried to read her expression. She seemed grimmer than usual.

"Detective? Can we bag her?"

Brooke shot a blistering look at the ME's assistant, clearly not liking his glib tone.

Sean stepped into the utility room to take a look at the back porch. The whole area was a bloodbath.

"Jesus," Ric said, coming up beside him. "You get all this, Maddie?"

"Yes, I'm finished with the porch," the photographer called from the kitchen.

The ME's guy looked at Sean again. "Detective?"

"Yeah, go ahead."

Sean turned around. Brooke was watching the scene now, clutching her evidence kit so tightly her knuckles were white. He motioned for her to follow him into the living room.

Brooke was short and slender, with pale skin, and a plump pink mouth he'd always wondered about. As she looked up at him, he noticed the worry line between her brows.

"What's wrong?"

Her eyebrows shot up. "You mean besides the fact that this woman was practically decapitated on her doorstep?"

"Yes."

She took a deep breath and glanced around. "This crime scene bugs me."

"Why?"

"Look at it. See for yourself."

Without another word, she stepped around him and went back into the kitchen to crouch beside the pantry door.

Sean pulled some latex gloves from his pocket and tugged them on as he surveyed the kitchen. It was clean and uncluttered, except for the stack of mail on the counter beside a key. He studied the key for a moment, but resisted the urge to pick it up.

He opened the fridge. Yogurt, salad kit, pomegranate juice. On the lower shelf was a six-pack of root beer with a bottle missing from the carton. That was the bottle that sat on the breakfast table, and Maddie was snapping a picture of it now.

Sean glanced through the open back door as the ME's people started loading the body bag onto a gurney. The victim's clothes had been intact, and she'd shown no obvious sign of sexual assault. At first glance, it looked like the killer had grabbed her from behind and slit her throat. Given the lack of blood inside the house, Sean figured the attacker had fled down the driveway to the street or maybe hopped the back fence.

Ric stepped into the kitchen. "Her purse is on the back porch. Wallet's inside, but no cell phone."

"You check the car?" Sean asked.

"Not yet. Let's finish walking through the house first."

"Don't move anything," Maddie said. "I haven't been back there yet."

Sean led the way. It was a simple layout, with rooms off a central hallway. The bathroom smelled like ammonia. Sean switched on the light.

"House is squeaky-clean," Ric observed.

"Yep."

The pedestal sink gleamed. Sean opened the medicine cabinet. Toothpaste, cough drops, tampons. Ric eased back the shower curtain to reveal a shiny tub with several bottles of hair products lined up on the side.

They moved on to the bedroom, where they found a neatly made queen bed with a light blue comforter. No decorative pillows, just two standard pink pillowcases that matched the sheets.

"Not a lot of pillows," Sean said.

"What's that?"

"Pillows. Most women put a lot on the bed, don't they?"

"I don't know," Ric said. "My wife does."

Sean studied the room. It smelled like vanilla. On the dresser were several plastic trays of makeup and one of those bottles of liquid air freshener with the sticks poking up. Sean spied a sticky note attached to the mirror and leaned closer to read the feminine handwriting: *One day, one breath.*

Was it a poem? A song lyric? Maybe Samantha's own words?

The closet door was ajar, and Sean nudged it open. Six pairs of jeans, all on hangers. A couple dozen T-shirts, also hanging.

Ric whistled. "Damn. You know anyone who arranges their T-shirts by color?"

"Nope."

Sean looked around the bedroom again. "Pretty basic," he said. "Not a lot here."

He walked back through the house, noting a conspicuous absence of anything that would indicate a male presence. No razors on the bathroom sink or man-size shoes kicking around. No beer in the fridge. The living room was simply furnished, with a sofa, a coffee table, and a smallish flat-screen TV.

"Looks to me like she lives alone," Ric said, turning to Jasper. "You say she works at a restaurant?"

"Coffee shop, according to the neighbor lady." Jasper took out a spiral pad and consulted his notes. "That one over on Elm Street."

"I've never been in there." Ric looked at Sean. "You?"

"Nope."

Sean glanced around the living room, which was devoid of clutter. Maybe the victim didn't have a lot of money for extras, but even so, most women tended to decorate their homes more than this. Sean hadn't spotted a single framed photo in the entire place.

The strobe of a camera flash drew his attention into the kitchen again. Brooke was right. This scene seemed odd. Sean had worked a lot of homicides over the years, and most boiled down to money, drugs, or sex. Sean had seen no sign of sexual assault. No drugs or drug paraphernalia or even alcohol. No hint of illegal activity. No evidence of a boyfriend.

A remote control sat on the coffee table. Sean had watched Brooke in action enough to know it would be one of the first items she collected to dust for prints.

"I don't see any blood trails or signs of struggle inside," Ric said. "Doesn't feel like the assailant was in the house."

"I'm not getting a read on motive."

"I know." Ric shook his head. "Doesn't look like a rape or a robbery. No cash or drugs around."

"We need her phone," Sean said. "I want to search her car and the surrounding area."

"I'll go check the car," Ric said.

He exited through the front door, and Sean returned to the kitchen. Brooke wasn't there. Maddie knelt in the pantry with her camera, and Sean noticed the pantry door was missing.

"What happened to the door?"

She glanced at him. "Brooke took it."

"Took it where?"

"Back to the lab."

Sean stared at her. "You mean she's gone?"

"She needed to test something. She said it was urgent."

"Yo, Sean, come here," Ric called from outside.

Sean walked out the front, glancing at his watch. Why had she left already? This scene would take hours to process and they were just getting started.

Ric was in the driveway near the Kia. Another Delphi CSI in gray coveralls was crouching beside the car.

Ric glanced up at Sean. "Jackpot."